A Pride of Poppies

Modern GLBTQI fiction
of the Great War

An anthology from

Manifold Press

Published by Manifold Press

E-book ISBN: 978-1-908312-30-3
Paperback ISBN: 978-1-908312-84-6

Proof–reading: F.M. Parkinson

Editor: Julie Bozza

For further details of Manifold Press titles both in print and forthcoming: manifoldpress.co.uk

Table of Contents

Introduction

Julie Bozza

Working on this anthology has been a source of pride and great pleasure. It feels as if it was blessed from the start – which perhaps isn't surprising for a project that has been a real labour of love.

Fiona Pickles, Editor-in-Chief of Manifold Press, has been unstintingly enthusiastic since the idea was first given breath. All our colleagues at the Press have been supportive throughout, as have our friends in the wider community of readers, writers, bloggers and publishers.

F.M. Parkinson served diligently as proof-reader, to the immense satisfaction of the authors.

And the authors! What an energetic and talented team they've made. Their professionalism – and their patience with me as editor – is all the more appreciated when I reflect that they have donated their time and creative efforts to this project with no recompense. There were no advances and there will be no royalties. All the proceeds that would otherwise be shared between authors and publisher are instead going to charity.

Our first choice of charity was The Royal British Legion, home of the Poppy Appeal – and we were delighted when the Legion confirmed it was happy to receive our support. What an honour it is to contribute to the Legion's excellent work supporting the whole Armed Forces community.

And of course we could not contribute anything but good wishes without you, dear Reader. Thank you so much for buying this book. You are supporting a worthy cause! Virtue is its own reward, of course – but we trust that you'll also find a tangible reward in this collection of entertaining and thought-provoking stories.

No Man's Land

Julie Bozza

It was a cold day in November, and as Drew lay naked on the examination table in Dr Marsh's office, he was all too aware that even the season was conspiring against him. That part of himself that never quite measured up was doomed by the chill in the air, by its own outraged modesty, by Drew's sense of injury, his sense of harm done if not to his inadequate body then to his soul.

Dr Marsh poked and prodded and quantified; performed a palpation on Drew's lower body to try to discern what lay inside; and generally considered every aspect of Drew with an oddly remote yet intense interest. This review had been scheduled for a week after Drew's birthday every year since he was a child. Familiarity, in this instance, definitely bred contempt.

Finally Dr Marsh stepped back, and nodded towards Drew's clothes to indicate that the physical examination was complete. Drew got up, and started dressing, while the doctor settled at his desk and began writing yet another report to add to Drew's voluminous file.

As soon as Drew was in pants, socks, trousers and vest, he broke the silence. "I turned twenty-one a week ago," he said – and he added, hating the slight tremble in his voice that betrayed him: "I'm a man now."

Dr Marsh tilted his head in an acknowledgement that somehow failed to endorse this last claim. His fountain pen didn't even hesitate in its smooth black scrawl across the yellow page.

"I'm not coming back," Drew blurted, as he finished dressing. "I'm not going through this ever again."

Ah. Dr Marsh paused, and after a moment lifted his head.

"I'm twenty-one now, and it's my decision."

"Well, strictly speaking, yes, but –"

"No. There's been no change now for three or four years. Has there?"

A moment passed before the doctor replied, "Perhaps nothing *significant* – or more to the point, little that's been obvious to the untrained eye –"

"No. This is *me* now. This is what I am, for better or worse. I just want to be left alone to make my own way in the world."

Dr Marsh took a breath and then let it sigh out. "Andrew," he said with an exaggerated patience, "would you please sit down? There is something we need to discuss. We can come back to this matter afterwards, if you still feel the same way."

"You're not going to change my mind," Drew insisted – though once he'd tied his shoelaces he sat, or rather perched, on one of the straight-backed chairs. "I want to celebrate a birthday without dreading what's going to happen a week later."

"I'm aware that these consultations are hardly *enjoyable*. That is not the point."

Drew stared at the doctor a bit wild-eyed, trying not to get side-tracked despite this provocation. Drew very much felt like arguing that the doctor must have got *some* kind of enjoyment out of it all, no matter how unpleasant it was for Drew, as it certainly hadn't been the patient's idea to persist year in and year out.

"Andrew. You will allow me to be concerned for your well-being."

"That's rich, coming from someone who never took my wishes into account –"

The doctor sighed again, though it was a sharper sound. "Certain decisions were made by your parents, various specialists and myself, years before you were old enough to understand anything at all of the situation. We had your best interests at heart."

Drew snorted. "My father only cared about his own interests. I hardly even remember him! He was gone as soon as he realised I'd never be what he wanted."

"It is true he very much wanted a son, and perhaps we should have tried harder to convince him that it would have been fairer to raise you as a girl."

Drew stared at the man, flabbergasted. The doctor had never been quite so explicit about that long-ago choice before. Drew knew well enough that his father had demanded a son, and his mother was determined to provide one by making the most of an ambiguous situation – but Drew had no problem with that. It was the right decision, even if made for the wrong reasons.

The doctor, of course, didn't understand. "Perhaps you are coming to see the wisdom of turning, and endeavouring to take the alternative path? Now

4

that your mother has passed." He cleared his throat. "I must confess that I foresaw this day."

"What? No! I'm perfectly happy the way I am."

Dr Marsh looked at him flatly. "Happy?" he echoed.

"Yes."

"Well, then." The doctor put the fountain pen aside. "What is this about?"

"What's it about?" Drew spluttered. "Isn't it obvious? I don't want to be your project any more. Your experiment. Your subject. I just want to live my own life now."

The doctor laid a hand on the file as if taking an oath. "You understand that this isn't only about understanding your situation, but also helping other children born with the same characteristics … ?"

"You've got enough now. You've got all the information you need right there –" Drew jabbed a finger towards the file – "and nothing's going to change now, anyway."

"I need to monitor –"

"No, you don't."

Dr Marsh let his professional demeanour slip; he sagged and gave Drew a weary look, before reaching for a sealed, addressed envelope which he held in both hands for a long silent moment. It obviously contained a letter or report of some kind, though perhaps only a brief one. "Let's put that aside for now, Andrew. There is something more urgent to consider."

"Yes?"

"You will, of course, be exempt from military service on medical grounds. I have prepared a letter for the authorities that explains – discreetly – that there is an entirely reasonable justification for you not to enlist." Dr Marsh cleared his throat again. "I trust, however, that you will choose to perform some kind of civilian work in support of the war effort."

Drew was so furious that he couldn't move, so horrified he couldn't speak. Despite all he'd been through, Drew had never felt so reduced.

The doctor finally wound to a halt, finishing with, "The country needs us all, in whatever capacity we can best serve."

Drew let a moment's silence grow. Dr Marsh finally looked at him, apparently expecting Drew to be grateful. He was surprised when Drew simply stood and picked up his coat from the back of the chair.

"I'm a man," Drew said, hating the stiffness in his voice. "Of course I'll enlist. I was only waiting for –"

"Andrew, *please* will you sit down and discuss –"

"No, thank you." Drew shrugged on the coat while heading for the door. "Goodbye, Dr Marsh."

Behind him there was only a sigh, and then the sound of the door closing.

There was only one bridge across the river, so Drew had to return home along the High Street. On some days he took a circuitous route, but he rarely had the luxury of time to spare – and on that day he was too angry to be anything other than direct.

Which meant, of course, that he was soon confronted by the recruiting posters plastered on walls and taped up in shop windows. 'WHICH?' demanded one poster. 'Have you a REASON or only an EXCUSE for not enlisting NOW!' Another asked, 'YOUNG MAN! Are you between 19 and 35? If you are YOUR DUTY is clear. ENLIST TODAY. God save the King!'

Drew hurried by the posters with his head down, knowing that he couldn't delay any longer. Any day now, some well-meaning woman would hand him a white feather, and Drew would die of the shame. He had wanted to finish his thesis, to ... well, to settle his affairs, he supposed. He only had one chapter and the conclusion left to write, though, along with the usual tidying up, and perhaps he could manage that while training. He understood that months could go by between enlisting and actually being sent overseas.

"Hey, Drew! Pretty boy!"

Drew growled under his breath and maintained his forward momentum. He hated that epithet with a passion. He always kept his hair in a neat back-and-sides, always dressed in quiet, ordinary clothes. He'd never wanted to be pretty. He'd rather not even be handsome, although that's what Henry insisted Drew was.

"Aw, which little cockerel's got his hackles up, then?"

"Shut your mouth, Lansdowne!" he burst out, slowing slightly and looking up – to see Ted Lansdowne smug and smart in a soldier's uniform. Drew stalled, and tried not to gape. They were across the road from each other, and there were other people hanging around Lansdowne, fawning on him, but Drew could hardly see anything beyond his lifelong nemesis.

"Yeah, I'm looking mighty fine, ain't I?"

Drew stuttered for a moment, and then found his voice. "I'm going to look finer still in my officer's uniform!"

This retort met with whistles, hoots and catcalls – and appreciative laughter from Lansdowne. "Be glad to see it, *sir*," he replied, with surprising sincerity. "I'll be glad enough to see it."

Lansdowne turned away, and Drew was freed to stride off home – a bit shaky at first, but soon he was bursting in through his front door, closing it firmly behind him, and at last he was safe.

Drew took off his coat, and walked through into the kitchen, where Henry was carefully rolling out the pastry crust for a vegetable pie. Henry looked up with an expression caught somewhere between happiness for seeing Drew and worry about Drew's appointment with the doctor. "How did it go?" he asked. "Did you tell him?"

Drew stood there for a moment, wishing he could think of some way forward that wasn't quite so blunt. He couldn't. "I'm sorry," Drew announced, "but I'm going to enlist."

Henry's hands stilled, and he looked at Drew in dismay. "No … No, Drew, we decided. You'll think about this once your thesis is complete."

"I'm twenty-one, Henry. I'm a man now. I've put this off too long already."

"No …" Henry said again. And then he sank onto the nearest kitchen chair, resting his hands still covered in flour on the table top. "No, Drew …"

"I'll finish the thesis while I'm training or on leave. I'm sure there'll be time before I get posted." Drew sighed. "Not that it matters very much. A hundred pages on a few esoteric points of Danelaw? Who'll even notice?"

"I will!"

Drew favoured him with a wan smile. "As my former tutor, you have a vested interest."

"You know very well the effect that Danelaw had on the development of the common law – effects that we still feel today. You can't dismiss it as irrelevant. We took the word *law* from the Norse language!"

Drew's smile turned slightly warmer. "Preaching to the converted, Henry."

"Well, then?"

He sighed, and sat down on the nearest chair. "It doesn't seem at all important compared to what's happening in France and Belgium right this very minute. Does it?"

Henry remained silent.

"And it's hardly much of a legacy for me to leave. So I had better go and do something useful."

"*No*, Drew."

Drew sat forward, and spoke a little more gently. "I know this will be difficult for you. Letting me go. When I see the parents and the wives left at home, worrying … grieving … sometimes I even fancy they carry the heavier burden."

Henry shifted across to the chair closest to Drew, and reached his hands to take Drew's – but when Drew baulked a little despite his best intentions, Henry instead reached for a tea towel and wiped off the flour and dough. Drew made amends by taking both of Henry's hands in his instead, and cradling them. These hands had experienced so much more of life. They were rougher than his own, and not as pale or slender. They were a man's hands, as well as a scholar's, and they had been to war. Drew wanted only that his own hands have the same chances, the same challenges. That he himself –

"They won't treat you well," Henry said in a low voice.

Drew huffed. "I'm not expecting it to be a picnic."

"No, I mean …" Henry glanced significantly downwards. "They won't be kind, Drew."

"For God's sake!" Drew cried, pulling away and standing up. "Not you as well!"

"What do you –" Henry sat back. "Do you mean Dr Marsh … ?"

"He wanted to give me a letter saying I'm exempt from serving on medical grounds."

"Oh, thank God," Henry fervently responded.

"What? No! I refused, of course. I can serve as well as any man."

Henry dropped his head for a moment, as if really praying. Then he looked up to say very directly, "Don't you understand? Even at the recruitment centre, you'll be examined – naked – with no privacy at all. You'll have the humiliation of being rejected – while surrounded by your peers."

"But if I explain – if I – Well, with a little discretion –"

"If they actually let you through, you won't find army life any easier. There'll be no such thing as being discreet, not for you nor anyone. You won't be able to keep anything a secret. Your own allies will shame you, hound you. Your own people!"

Drew stared at him, breath harsh in shock, and yet still a part of him wondered how much of this was an exaggeration. Of course Henry wanted to protect him.

"My God, Drew – what if you're captured? What then? No matter how bad it's been, it will be ten times worse as a prisoner of war. And you won't have any friends with you to help shield you."

Drew said hoarsely, "There may be other men out there like you."

Henry flushed, and looked for a moment as if he were swallowing bitter words. Perhaps he was jealous at the thought – not that Drew had meant anything untoward. "There may be," Henry eventually allowed. "But I couldn't keep you safe, even if I was at your side each and every day. You can't rely on anyone else managing what I could not."

That was unpalatable food for thought. Drew sat down again, though they didn't reach for each other.

"Drew. I've told you a little of my experiences, in Natal and the Transvaal. Only a little, and that was unpleasant enough. The truth is infinitely more distressing. There is precious little nobility to be found in war. Twice as many men died of disease than were killed in battle. Three times as many were injured – some horrifically. There are some injuries and illnesses you may wish you hadn't survived."

"There is suffering," Drew agreed, "but to serve a higher purpose."

"A higher purpose," Henry scoffed, softly yet painfully. "It can be the hardest thing of all to maintain such faith."

"I am sure that in the thick of it, you would not be able to see the forest for the trees ..."

"Such monstrous trees, Drew! There is little nobility, and precious little chivalry. The things a soldier or officer is required to see and do, each and every day – these things may destroy your very soul." Henry groaned. "Wherever we could, we blasted their crops, we burnt their houses. There was one place, a neat little home anyone would be proud to call their own, but we must destroy it like all the rest. A woman ran up to us, crying out that her babe was still inside, asleep in his cradle. We hardly understood her at first. The fire had taken hold. I hesitated, even once I'd understood. May God forgive me, I hesitated. And then before we could stop her she ran into that inferno and brought out the baby. I can hardly even imagine how she managed to walk out. She died of her burns, in agony, two days later. We told her that the baby was safe, that she'd saved him – but he was already dead when she carried him out. Suffocated by the smoke. And that is not the most horrific tale I could tell you, either."

"It is horrific," Drew quietly agreed. But he looked at the man askance. "*Your* soul wasn't destroyed."

Henry shook his head, his expression bleak. "Oh, part of it was obliterated. As if my soul's right arm was blasted out of existence." Henry reached a hand to grasp at Drew's. "But then I came home, and met you … and you helped to heal the wound."

"Well, then," said Drew. "I'm glad of that, for you'll be able to do the same when I have need."

Henry was again bowed by the thought. After a moment he withdrew his hands, and stood, and went back to his pie-making.

Drew sighed. A long moment passed. "I'm sorry, Henry, but I'm not sure I'm all that hungry."

"We can't let good food go to waste," Henry brusquely replied. And then they continued there in silence, each alone with his own thoughts, while the pie was baked, and eventually served, and about a third of it was eaten. Henry carefully wrapped the rest in a cloth, and stored it in the larder.

Neither of them found it easy to sleep that night. They lay awake, with Drew curled up as usual and Henry curled around him. *'I've got you,'* Henry had murmured reassuringly the very first time he'd wrapped Drew up in his arms and snugly fitted himself to echo Drew's shape perfectly. *'I've got you.'*

That night they lay awake in the darkness, and there was little comfort to be had even in this most familiar embrace. "Do you know what the worst thing was?" Henry eventually asked.

"No," Drew quietly replied.

Henry was silent for a while, until Drew almost decided that Henry wasn't going to tell him. But then Henry tentatively said, "For the others there, the ones they loved were safely back at home. Their women were at home, and would never see the horror of it. They were fighting to protect their women. But for me … the ones I loved were right there, suffering and killing and dying and being wasted by disease. For a man who loves men – for a man like me, or like you, Drew – that makes it infinitely more hellish."

After a while, Drew whispered, "Did you lose … a particular friend, then?"

"No." Henry sighed. "Yes. They were all *potentially* particular friends. Do you see what I'm trying to say? In theory, at least. It was heart-wrenching. No, it was worse than that. I hardly have the words." A moment slipped by, finally bringing them a little peace. "But then I came home," Henry continued in tones that were almost reverential, "and I met you, Drew, and I taught you, I learned from you … I loved you … and you healed me."

"I'm glad," he said, the words inadequate yet heartfelt.

A silence lengthened, and Drew at last began to feel sleep slipping down upon him.

"I'll enlist for you," Henry blurted, his embrace tightening around Drew. "I'm not too old. If you promise me you'll stay here, I'll go instead."

Drew wriggled around as much as he could within Henry's arms, and pressed a kiss to his lover's temple. "No, Henry. No, of course you mustn't do that."

"I'll go to war for you, and then I'll come home again – and you'll heal me."

"You've done your duty, Henry, and so much besides. No one could ask for more. It's my turn now, if it's anyone's."

"Then I'll enlist as a regular soldier, and you can choose me as your batman. I'll be able to take care of you. Protect you."

"No …" Drew sighed, and doubted for the first time. If it truly meant that much to Henry … If Henry was really prepared to go that far to make his point … Drew settled again, tucking in as close to Henry as he could, and wrapping his own arms around Henry's where they wrapped around him.

The silence lingered as the night grew old. Neither of them slept.

"What will you do?" Henry asked at last, his voice hoarse with anticipated sorrow. "Drew, tell me. What will you do?"

Julie Bozza

Julie Bozza is an English-Australian hybrid who is fuelled by espresso, calmed by knitting, unreasonably excited by photography, and madly in love with John Keats.

juliebozza.com
twitter.com/juliebozza
goodreads.com/juliebozza

I Remember

Wendy C. Fries

Time goes tick-tock forward, even for boys.

Though Christopher Timlock stopped for ever being any bit a boy at nineteen years, eleven months: the day his one true love went to war without him.

It wasn't supposed to be that way, because where went one, the other always followed. James and Christopher, Chrissie and Jamie, inseparable since they were both fifteen.

Chrissie was passionate, full of the fire of *possibility*; he was keen on what was out there, over, *beyond*. James was one of rare but bright smiles, his dreams grounded yet strong. He wanted a simple life, a steady one.

Then in the winter of 1914 their friends began joining the London Regiment and Chrissie said, "Should we?" and Jamie said yes.

The British Army said no.

Not to James, but to Christopher. Though Chrissie told them he wasn't born deaf, not in *both* ears, it turned out that this distinction was *no* distinction, not to the British Army.

And so this time where went one, the other couldn't follow.

Which wasn't one bit of all right with Jamie. "You'll forget me," he whispered the night before he left. "I know you will."

Chrissie laughed because Chrissie forgot little. Not the day they met at the pub, not the night they kissed back behind it, not the morning they woke for the first time side by side in a sweetly narrow bed.

"You'll forget me," said the man, certain of the thing he was saying. "London is so big, I'll be gone so long, and you are so beautiful."

Tucked away tight in James's rented room above the pub, Chrissie had busied his sweetheart's mouth awhile, then the only things they whispered the rest of that night were the poetic promises humans always make when they know tomorrow will separate them for a good long while.

In the morning James Gant went away, part of the 7th (City of London) Battalion, and just like that, Christopher Timlock discovered that though time may go tick-tock forward, making men of boys, once the man you love is gone, time turns treacle-slow though nowhere near so sweet.

Don't forget.

Every day the first week James was gone Chrissie looked at the note he'd found tucked inside his boot.

He counted the letters on that note, traced them with fingers, tasted the ink, imagined James's hand resting on the paper, then tasted that, too.

Two words, two words, two words saying what was allowed, but, if you were the man to whom those words were written, they also said what was true.

Don't forget me, Chrissie. I love you, Chrissie. I miss you already. I need you. I dream of you, want you, pray for you, fight for you, hope, plan, yearn. And I'll come back and, and, and ...

... and I hope you'll remember.

Oh yes, Chrissie looked at that note every day that first week James was gone, then he tucked the slip of paper away safe and tight, and went about proving he remembered by pretending he'd nearly forgotten.

He did this in little notes he scribbled during slow times at the pub. Tiny, silly notes that said the simple things allowed between two men, but if you knew where to look, those notes also said what was true.

I almost forgot ... began the first one, *about that time we walked from King's Cross to Ilford, and how I had to carry you for half a mile after you stepped on those bees.*

That was the first letter Christopher sent, saying what was allowed.

The truth neither would forget was how, in the carrying, the nearness of one to the other had set their hearts to triple time. Chrissie feeling James's heart pounding against his shoulder blade; James feeling Christopher's heart thrumming beneath the arms crossed over his friend's chest.

I nearly forgot ... Christopher wrote in another note a week later, *about that night at the pub, when it was just us behind the bar and those building workers from Manchester came in, fifty men wasn't it?*

That was the allowed. The truth was how, after Chrissie and James spent hours serving fast-fast-fast behind that narrow bar, reaching round one another, sliding behind one another again and again, Chrissie had felt that James was hard.

I almost forgot … Christopher wrote the week after that, *about the snowstorm night when I had to kip at the Violin & Bow.*

In James's rented room above the pub they'd made love for the first time, quiet as mice, affectionate as kittens, putting hands over one another's mouth to mute moans and laughter. In the early morning Christopher had sneaked down to curl up innocently on one of the pub's booth benches, and when Mrs Turner came in she'd tut-tutted and made him tea and toast.

Week after week Christopher sent notes to a man far away, proving that he wouldn't forget by pretending he almost had.

It wasn't until nearly the fourth month that Chrissie got his first reply. That reply had nothing to do with James's present, instead it also harked back to their shared past.

I almost forgot … James wrote, *about that dotty old man we found near St Pancras railway station year before last. Wearing just a dressing gown and slippers.*

They'd laughed at the old gent's confused mumblings, but helped him find his way home to a tiny flat back behind the railway lines. A man even older than he had opened the door to their knock then burst into tears, hugging James and Christopher both. "Thank you," he'd said. "Thank you for bringing him back."

As that front door closed, Chrissie and Jamie looked at each other, sure they'd heard one old man's whisper to the other, "Come along, sweetie, come along, my love."

That night and the one after, James had called Christopher 'sweetie' and he'd called him 'my love', but Chrissie made him stop. "You'll say it when you shouldn't and that'll be the end of that."

James's short notes arrived sporadically, always following the precedent set by Christopher.

I almost forgot … James wrote four months later, *about the day Mark got married.*

Mark's girl was from America and hadn't known a single soul in London, and so just about everyone at the wedding had been one of Mark's boyhood friends. It had been a drunken joke by night's end that the boys had had to dance all those wedding waltzes with each other, but Christopher had refused to dance even one with James.

I almost forgot … James wrote a few months later, *about how pretty Edith*

Turner is. Mrs Turner showed me so many of her pictures, the day before I left.

Oh my, yes, talk of women was allowed wasn't it, though written clear between James's words was the remembered truth.

Soon after Chrissie turned eighteen he told himself he was in love with his boss's daughter. The thing is, he sort of was. In love with the idea that he *could* be in love, that he could smile at Edie and not be afraid what others would see; that she could smile back and others would happily tease. There was a world of 'could' with Edith, a world of things allowed.

Yet by some great good fortune, it was Edith who wouldn't allow it. She didn't care about Chrissie or James, nor any boy-man who came through the pub's old wooden doors. As a matter of fact it was she who'd left London first, eventually joining the Women's Army Auxiliary Corps near the war's end. The irony was, Edith Turner would be one of those who never came back.

I forget again and again ... Chrissie wrote back the very hour he'd got James's note, *that you aren't here. Every day I talk to you still, as if you're right beside me. The pub gets crowded with all the visitors coming through and the old boys ask after you from their corner table, Mr Agra, Mr Ted, Mr William. On the weekends they buy you pints you're not here to drink, so I drink them sometimes, and I pretend* ...

Christopher pressed the backs of his fingers softly against his mouth.

... I pretend your mouth has been where my mouth is.

Chrissie badly erased this truth, so that it could be read if a man really had a mind, and below it wrote the allowed.

... I pretend we're toasting your return, as we'll do when the war is over. Mr Ted says it'll be soon, he says modern fighting can't last for long.

Ah, but even young men know this truth: wars last as long as one man wants what another man has, that the only thing which changes is how many die and how fast they do it. Or how many live but for a while wish they hadn't.

In the summer and autumn of 1915 James Gant's battalion saw action in Belgium and France. Near the winter of that same year Jamie came home a decorated veteran, missing two fingers on his right hand, the sight in his right eye, with tender-healing burns covering his body from heart to hip.

After Jamie came back, time did what time will. It went tick-tock forward as it always does and so trains continued to rattle pub windows, men and women hummed the streets busy, and a young soldier moved slowly behind a bar, drawing pints as he used to do, and for a time that soldier tried not to see the young man doing the same beside him, so that that young man could pretend not to see him.

Yet James knew that Christopher saw. That first week, the second, and on into the third Jamie saw Chrissie learning where to stand so that Jamie could see him, how to bend and reach so that Jamie didn't have to, and near that fourth week Jamie saw Chrissie lock the pub up tight, check all the doors, then check them twice, and Jamie watched Chrissie go up the night-dark stairs without him, and he knew that it was up to him whether he would pretend not to see, or whether he would follow.

After a while Jamie followed.

On that climb up creaky stairs he whispered a soft speech, one where he told his true love that it was all right, just fine to go forward toward a normal life, an *allowed* life, but then James opened his bedroom door and found Christopher naked in his narrow bed and all those words went away, a distant rattle and hum at the back of his head.

Instead of saying anything, Jamie crawled bare into that too-small bed and he learned that Christopher had remembered, just as he'd begged.

"I remember," Chrissie said, threading the fingers of Jamie's wounded hand through his own hair, then keening in quiet pleasure when James tugged hard-soft, like he used to.

"I remember," Chrissie said, wriggling close to kiss Jamie's eyes, the one that saw and the one that didn't, kissing again and again, until James started laughing and finally remembered to kiss back with a fast flutter of lashes.

"I remember," said Chrissie, placing James on his back and looking not at a fretwork of scars but at a remembered constellation of freckles he used to trace with his tongue on hot summer nights. And though it was winter-cold Chrissie did that now, licking at freckle ghosts, gentle-soft breath huffing warm across tender burns that themselves still remembered how to rise up in gooseflesh.

The rest of that night, and the night after that, and then for a thousand after those they showed one another they remembered, and gave each other new things to never forget.

And time went tick-tock forward.

Mrs Turner passed away, left the pub to Jamie. Fifteen years turned to twenty and then into twenty-five. Time brought with it a new war, and fresh young soldiers afraid of forgetting, and through it all James and Christopher did what they were allowed, and always found ways to show one another what was true.

During the day they touched each other carefully but frequently, glanced swiftly but with grins, and then in the darkness of nights noisy with train rattles and men and women humming in the streets busy below, James called Christopher 'sweetie' and Chrissie called Jamie 'love' and time went sweetly forward, and it took them gently with it.

Wendy C. Fries

Wendy C. Fries is the author of *Sherlock Holmes and John Watson: The Day They Met*, and has written hundreds of features on high tech, personal finance, and health and wellness. She's fascinated with London, theatre, scriptwriting, and lattés.

wendycfries.com

War Life

Z. McAspurren

She worked in the factory, making bombs like the rest of them. There was nothing especially special about her: maybe her hands moved a little faster than the ladies round about her, but there was nothing particularly compelling any other way. She made little conversation as she worked, and there was always a grim, set attitude in her face that made her seem older than her years. She was what could be called sturdy, of average height, and her hair wasn't any particular outstanding shade. All in all, she was a perfect example of the average woman, dedicated to helping in the war effort, and making sure that their brave boys over there would find their way home. Nothing especially special, but then all women who contributed were special in their own way.

The other ladies in the factory, they thought she had a sweetheart fighting over in France, that's why she was always so quiet when working. They gave her reassuring smiles. It'll be over by Christmas, they were already saying that again this year, and her sweetheart would be home to her before she knew it. He'd be back so soon that she'd want him out of her hair again just as quick. She just smiled, and nodded at their kindness. Her brother was fighting in France, so she supposed he could be considered a sweetheart of sorts, but there was no one who held that kind of meaning for her, at least not in the way that these women implied. Still, she worked in the factory, thinking of nothing much beyond her work, and on her rare days off, she helped to look after the neighbourhood children whose mothers were working. There was always something to do, so she never really had time to focus on the fact that she couldn't relate to that feeling of missing someone. Well, not in the way her fellow workers described, at any rate.

Before the war, she had been swept up in the Suffrage movement. She believed so passionately in the cause, in a way that she had never really felt for anything before. Everything about it had made her feel as if she were finally in the right place, the place where she belonged, a place where it didn't really matter that she didn't much feel like worrying about whom she would click with, or whether or not the butcher's boy liked her. There were more important things to consider, more important things in the world and she believed so deeply that yes, women should have the right to have a say in how these things were dealt with as they were affected by them as well. She did, occasionally while working, idly wonder if they had won the right to vote prior to the war, would Britain have entered at all? Then she would see the newsreels at the cinema, and read the papers, and the thoughts would be banished from her head as quickly as they entered them. The war might be dragging on, and they were losing far too many good people, but it was for a just cause. A cause that meant something. Just like the Suffrage had for her.

She had kept everything from the protest days. The mementoes were kept in the bottom drawer of the chest of drawers in her bedroom at home. Once a week, she would open it up and carefully examine each item, making sure that nothing had got to them and that they were still in great condition. Her hands would lightly touch the flyers that they had handed out, smooth over newspaper clippings that told of the brave deeds their women had been involved in, or the way in which the prison life had treated them. Pamphlets on what to do if arrested were tucked neatly in among the items as well. She was a vegetarian now, it had seemed the safer option. She admired them, those women who had been brave enough to speak out in such radical ways. Though she had been swept up in the movement, she hadn't got in as deep as some. There had been her brother and mother at home to consider, and when her father passed away, she was needed to go and find work so that they would be able to afford to live.

Her mother only seemed to live for each message her brother sent home now. It had been a few weeks since the last, and she forced herself not to think of the worst, but be prepared for it at the same time. The last was written in his own hand, and that was a godsend. His clumsy way of writing his words, as if each one took him effort. Their mother had always told him to put more effort into his lessons, and he never had listened. Still, it was clumsy but neat, and he mentioned how nice the men he fought beside were, and how fed up they were with all the lice. Their mother had sent him out new socks, and a pocket Bible. The reverend had said that faith in the Lord would help, and they had heard stories of the Bibles stopping bullets. Even during these hard times, her mother set great store by what she heard at church, going every Sunday as if there were nothing wrong. She supposed it was her mother's own form of comfort. She went with her; the silence of the church gave her time to think.

She thought about her work, mostly. About how the idea of being needed to do her bit for her country was deeply fulfilling, and gave her a warmth she hadn't had since the Suffrage. She would think about the Suffrage, and those brave women that she admired and aspired to be like. What were they doing now, she wondered? She knew that the movement had – mostly – gone to rest for the sake of the war, but she had no idea just how many women had been involved. Could she be working alongside some of the ladies who had stood in protest outside Parliament as some of the members invaded the halls? Her mind occasionally slipped to her brother, and how he'd lied about his age to sign up and now it was too late to try to recall him from the Front. She wondered if he were still alive, but there had been no slip with the two black bands, so he had to be. What would happen to their mother, she wondered, if news came of his dying in action or of some wound that had festered and caught an infection?

She had considered being a nurse once, having enjoyed the little science she had been taught at school. Her brother had been taught more than her, and she devoured his notes. It had only been a pipe dream – they would never have had the money to send her off for training, even if her father had lived longer than he had. He wouldn't have thought much of the idea, anyway, preferring her to find work in service somewhere, doing something useful with her hands. She thought being a nurse would have been very useful, but she would never say so aloud. Not to her father. He would have been proud of her brother for signing up so early. He always believed in serving King and country, no matter what was asked of them. She wondered if seeing the constantly rising death toll would have changed his mind. How many innocent families had been destroyed on both sides of the war, because King and country demanded service? But that was treason, so would never pass her lips. It stayed secure, tucked away until it could not just be thought any more, and then she would let it out, for a few moments, before closing it away again.

Before the war, everyone had thought – maybe expected – her and Patrick down the street to get married within a few years. They were close, people said, and they would make a good, sensible couple. She liked Patrick, and he liked her, but they were close because they *weren't* close. They each had thoughts and feelings that didn't seem to fit with others their age, and they were only safe with each other. If Patrick's thoughts had got out, he would have been hanged, she knew that much. She didn't understand why, even though she did her best to pay attention, and attend the lessons she had been taught. Patrick had just been Patrick to her, and she didn't see what was wrong with the way he thought and felt. He had died in the early weeks of the war, and she had mourned him. Not like a woman who has lost her love, but as someone who had lost a dear friend.

It was when her mind went to Patrick that she knew the women in the factory were wrong. She didn't have a sweetheart at the Front, she had never had a sweetheart in her life. She wouldn't know what to do with one if she had. She had had a friend, a dear one, and he had kept a place in her heart. She had her brother, whom she cared for, and hoped to see him return home in one piece. If that was asking for too much, then she would very much like just to see him return home alive. Patrick had followed him to the Front, and she knew the death hurt her brother more than it had hurt her, even if they had to pretend differently to the outside world. She reckoned that everyone had to pretend about something, especially in these harder times, so she didn't mind just nodding when people assumed Patrick meant more to her than he had.

Sunday was never the day of rest it was meant to be. There weren't really any sort of rest days if you were old enough. There was always something needing done: families needed visiting, widows needed consoling, socks needed darning, the list went on and on. So she made sure to keep herself busy, keep herself useful. She would help with the washing on a Sunday, if she were home, and try to help keep the house in the proud way her mother always liked it. Just because times were hard was no excuse to make it seem as though they didn't have standards. Oh, they might not have as much to eat as they once did, even with all the work she did, but their front step was clean enough to eat what little dinner they had off it.

When she was working, she knew who she was. She was someone who was helping the war effort, and even though it was only a small part, she was making a difference. That's what they said in the newspapers, even if sometimes she wondered if that's all they were doing: just saying it. Her work in the factory was hard, but it was, well, maybe fulfilling wasn't exactly the word, but she went home at night with sore limbs and a sore back and the knowledge that she had done something. Something that she was meant to do, and she had got it right. Her father always said she was a clumsy girl, and that things went wrong when she was meant to do them, so to see herself get it right, it was something that provided a little bit of needed pride for herself.

She wondered, sometimes, if she'd fit in more if she weren't where she was. If, like Alice, she found her own Wonderland, would it make more sense to her than her own life? It wasn't that her life was bad, or even dull. She did enjoy it – though it was repetitive in a way that made her wish for a little change. Saying this to people her own age got sly winks and nudges, and low mutters about 'new experiences' that always came with a leer and a sense of something that didn't sit right with her, not the way it sat with them. The girls her age spoke of their sweethearts out at the Front, fighting and winning medals, who were sure to come home heroes and then they'd be married in big lavish ceremonies. She didn't think she wanted to be married much. She'd prefer returning to the cause, to the Suffrage.

But right now, that couldn't be. So she worked in the factory, as many hours as she could, and did her bit to help the war effort. She knew where she stood when she was working, so she continued to work. Occasionally she thought back to the passion the Suffrage brought out in her, and occasionally she thought of her brother fighting in France, but mostly she just worked.

When she worked, she knew who she was.

War was hell.

That was probably the most fitting statement that could ever enter his mind at any point, though he knew better than to say anything to the trench chaplain about his thoughts. Not just regarding the war, though considering that the old Irish bastard – the chaplain's own words – had got to the point of cursing whoever's damned idea coming to the trenches was, he didn't think he'd be in too much trouble. Still, praise the Lord and all that He creates, that's how he was raised. He believed in it too, he thought so anyway, even when the mud surrounding him made him doubt. He kept his grandmother's rosary beads in his trouser pocket, and a Bible strapped over his heart as he'd promised his mum.

Didn't stop him cursing each and every day he had to stay in the rat-filled, lice-ridden trench. There was just something about the whole situation that made him so weary of everything that he often wondered where the bullet was with his name on it, and why hadn't it found its way to him yet? He tried not to entertain those thoughts often, but after Patrick died, they came more frequently than they ever had done.

Patrick was supposed to marry his sister, the perfect marriage of childhood friends. He knew his sister had no interest in Patrick, and he was absolutely positive it wasn't his sister whom Patrick was interested in. Since they had come to war, he and Patrick had never had anything more than the brief squeezing of a hand reassuringly here, a fleeting smile there, a hug when the world of the trench seemed too overbearing – but each stolen moment had been real. Short, fleeting, but beautiful moments in the hell they were living.

Patrick had been everything he himself wanted to be. Patrick was tall and strong, while he was middle-sized and probably a bit scrawny. Patrick was easily charming, with a smile that made everyone want to know him. And yet, only he himself knew Patrick properly. There were so many who could claim to be Patrick's close friend, but it was nothing compared to their bond. He wished they had kissed during those awful months, even just once, even if it had meant that they would have been shot for their actions. Life, he was realising quickly, was far too short to worry about what other people expected or thought. He had wanted to kiss Patrick, and Patrick had wanted to kiss him, just as they had done back home. But it wouldn't have been right.

Right. He had grown to hate that word. They were fighting here, far away from home with no promise of returning, because it was the right thing to do. Was it right that Patrick had died because of some Boche taking pot-shots at their section of the trench? Was it right that he had to see Patrick in pain, writhing with agony, the doctors unable to do anything except call for the pastor? Was it right that every day good men died on the orders of people who didn't even set foot on the front lines themselves? Sometimes, late at night when he was on watch, he would wonder if there was anyone across no man's land having the same thoughts. They were told that across that mess of barbed wire and unexploded mines lay the enemy, and that nothing would make the enemy happier than to see them all dead. Were the enemy being told the same thing? Was there someone on the other side who was thinking similar thoughts to him, and feeling similar feelings? Not that he could ask these questions, he was fairly certain it would be considered treason.

Patrick would have understood why he was having these thoughts. Patrick always told him that he spent too much time bothering himself with deep thoughts, trying to understand a world that didn't make sense to begin with. Patrick never bothered himself with deep thoughts, or if he did, it wasn't something he let anyone know about. That didn't bother him, he knew all of Patrick's thoughts – the other man had no mind-to-mouth filter at the best of times. That was one of the things he missed most: there was never a dull moment when talking with Patrick. He missed Patrick more than words could describe, not that he could show it, not properly anyway. He wondered how Patrick's mother took the news of her son's death. Was she allowed to have a service for him? Dying on the front lines was honourable – so the generals said, but then again, he didn't see them bunking down with the soldiers in the mud.

War was hell, and it was even more hellish knowing that while each day could be his last, if he made it through, that was just one more day he was separated from Patrick. It made his heart hurt more than he had thought possible. If this was what it meant to have loved and lost, then personally he thought that it probably was better than to have never loved at all even though the ache was something that never went away. He had watched him die, had been there to close his eyes when the infection from his wound finally managed to do away with him. Patrick had been so full of life, that seeing what happened ... the body that lay on the bed hadn't been Patrick, it had been a shell. A mockery of who Patrick was. The image of the lifeless shell ... it still burnt into the backs of his eyelids late at night, when he was trying to sleep.

The world of the trenches was almost colourless. After a while, all you saw were browns and greys, and the occasional, disheartening splash of red. Even that darkened to a brick brown after a while, and even when it wasn't there, you could still feel the red from your friends coating your fingers, seeping through them like the hot, sticky mess it always was. Patrick had given his life some colour. He could see the blue of the sky, the green in his eyes, the tinge of pink in his cheeks when he was pleased. Patrick had been just as colourful in the trenches as he had ever been out of them and the shell that was left behind had been robbed of all the colour that he was. Patrick was his everything, and now he was nothing without him. He thought of composing poetry, odes to how wonderful Patrick had been, how special he was to him, but they would just get lost in the piles upon piles that others in the trenches wrote. Everyone had a sweetheart, it seemed, everyone had thoughts and feelings and needed to let them out. He had read the humour magazine some of the troops had put together. It was nice, he realised, to see that even without Patrick, there were still people in the world who wanted to laugh, and remember that things could be good.

Not that he could see them being good any time soon. No, all he was doing now was waiting. Wondering with each bullet fired if that would be the one with his name on it, if that would be his ticket out of this hell. Could he be invalided home? It would be a mark of honour, in some way, he supposed. But then an old saying from bygone history lessons dredged up in his mind – come back with your shield, or on it. Would it matter to his mother, to his sister, if he came home wounded? Would they prefer for him to die in the 'glories' of battle, winning the war for their safety? Would his neighbours see him as a hero, or a coward – someone who let an injury take him home instead of fighting through the pain? What did they think of Patrick, he wondered, what did they think of him? What did he think of himself?

He had never got into this war to win a medal or trophy. To be praised and hailed as a hero. He had got in because … because he had read the papers, and listened to the news, and it seemed like the right thing to do. Go and fight the Boche, help to keep the world free. Down here in the trench, it didn't seem like much freedom was being won. Again he wondered if they were being told the same thing on the other side. To them, was he one of the bad guys, the ones to be beaten in a haze of glory? Maybe the stories had always been wrong, maybe neither side was in the right. Not that he could say that out loud, that would be treason, and punishment was a cigarette and a wall to stand against; not the type of news he wanted sent home to his mother in event of his death in this hellish war. Let the letter, if it needed to be sent, be a comfort to her. Let it tell of him doing something brave, of him fighting for their freedom. He might not have got in to be praised, but for his mother's sake, let it happen.

For his sister's sake, let this hellish war bring her the freedom she had been so enamoured with. He had never got involved in what it was that she devoted herself to, but he knew it had brought her a happiness that he hadn't seen in her before. Maybe she had found something to give a meaning to her life that he hadn't managed to find himself yet. He wondered if he would ever find the happiness in life, the completeness that his sister had found in her search for freedom. Mostly, though, he just wondered when he would get out of this trench, and away from the war. Be it carried by wood or by his own strength, he wanted to find his way home. To visit the places he and Patrick had played together as boys, the places they had always gone together when they were older than boys but not yet men. To visit the tree under which Patrick had first kissed him.

He didn't want to die without seeing that sight again.

Z. McAspurren

Z. McAspurren is an aspiring writer from Scotland, with a larger Disney DVD collection than she'd like to admit. She holds a BA in Social Sciences, focusing on history and criminology, and continues to study the world's history informally in her free time.

zmcaspurren.wordpress.com
insanelittledreamer.blogspot.co.uk

Lena and the Swan
or, The Lesbian Lothario

Julie Bozza

for Don

Lena flew along the lane on her bicycle, knowing just what strength was needed to maintain her speed, just how fast she could take that next turn. The air was bracingly fresh in her face, tugging strands of her hair loose as it always did no matter how carefully she pinned it up in the grey light of early morning. She wore trousers, close-fitting and cropped short around her calves so she didn't have to worry about them catching in the chain. There were still eyes in the village that looked askance at this despite her boots and socks demurely covering her ankles. Lena grinned to remember old Mr Bailey staring at her with a thrill of disapproval only yesterday – as if he hadn't had months to get used to her doing this work and dressing accordingly. As if he hadn't known her and her family's tendency towards contrariness all the days of his life.

The woods on her left veered towards the road as she sped along, thickened, loomed and then leapt across it with overarching branches. Lena coasted through the tunnel of green shade, and then followed the road around the curve, steering with little more than a perfectly-judged lean to the left. Then she stood on the pedals to power down the last straight and back into the sunshine, before taking a sharp turn down a side road and at last arriving at Amy's gate.

Lena slid off the bicycle and propped it against the fence, then hefted the satchel out of the bicycle's basket. As she walked along the path up to the front door, Lena reached into the satchel for the letter, and held it up between two fingers as she knocked. A smile full of promise came naturally to her lips as she heard footfalls coming down the hall, glimpsed movement through the window with its lace curtains. Lena had been happy to find a letter addressed to Mrs R. Martin in the sack of mail that morning, and the handwriting and return address meant it wasn't from Amy's husband, who was off fighting the Kaiser. It had been a few days since Lena had seen Amy, and that was far too long …

"Hello, stranger," said Amy with a sweet though rather distracted smile. Instead of reaching to take the letter, she stepped back a little – and that was invitation, or at least consent. Lena stepped over the threshold. "Why is it that laundry seems never-ending?" Amy asked over her shoulder as she led Lena through to the kitchen. Amy cast a whimsical gesture in the direction of the wash-house in the back garden, but Lena wasn't really paying attention. Instead, Lena glanced around looking for the children, but thought they must be at school; Amy wouldn't have let her in otherwise. "You'd think that at some point all the clothes would be clean. But no, you turn around and there's always more to be done." As Amy spoke, she topped the kettle up with water from the bucket, and set it on the hottest part of the range, apparently assuming that Lena would stay for a cup of tea.

Lena was leaning against the table, simply enjoying the sight of her. Amy's womanly figure wasn't quite so plump as it had been before the war, but it still curved deliciously. Her red hair used to be long and always kept under some semblance of control in a bun at her nape. It had been almost a year since Amy had cut it short, and now curls bobbed about her pretty face. Other than being about the same height, they were complete opposites, Lena and Amy: Lena was a slim tough tomboy with a mess of straight dark hair, and she knew there was nothing more than pleasant about her.

"Hhhmmm?" prompted Amy, apparently wanting a response.

Ah yes, the laundry. "The only way you could make sure that all the clothes were clean …" said Lena, stalking slowly towards her, "would be to do the laundry naked."

"Oh!" Amy laughed, and she blushed a little with her hand to her mouth.

Lena dropped to her knees, and pressed her face to Amy's thighs, feeling the slight warmth of flesh even though the layers of cotton, while her hands slipped under the hem of Amy's skirt and shaped themselves to her knees and then slid up and under her slip and further up …

"Oh!" said Amy again. She always sounded surprised, as if Lena didn't do this every time she was invited in, as if Amy wasn't the prettiest thing in the county, as if a woman wouldn't ever find herself doing the laundry one moment and being seduced the next, and in bright daylight, too.

Carefully Lena snared fingers in Amy's knickers, and drew them slowly down, listening to Amy's breath which was already panting in anticipation. When Lena's hands slid up again, she bunched up the skirt as she went and she followed, kneeling up taller, until at last she could apply her tongue where it would do the most good.

"Oh ..." moaned Amy, grasping at the back of a chair for support, arching delightfully and pushing forward. "Oh, Lena, Lena, you're spoiling me, you're ruining me ..."

Lena paused, and looked up with a quizzical brow.

Amy laughed breathlessly – and though a shade of doubt crossed her lovely face, she smiled, and shook it off. "Please don't stop."

Lena grinned, and continued her work.

"You're absolutely wicked," said Emily, slipping down further on the sofa and propping both bare feet on the shabby old pouffe. Her long dark hair cascaded over the back of the sofa and disappeared from view. Lena's fingers twitched; she always wanted to plait it, as she'd used to do when they were girls. And then she wanted to mess it up again ...

"While the men are away, Lena will play."

Emily was unimpressed, of course, but her smile remained fond and her gaze remained languid. "I suppose I shouldn't be thinking 'Poor Amy', though, should I?"

"It's not as if she even resists," Lena replied, "let alone fights me off. And it would take a saint to resist her. She's so adorable! She always was."

Emily took a long drag on the hand-rolled cigarette and passed it back. "You've had quite a morning, then."

"I have," Lena agreed, glancing a grin Emily's way. "Eva Rowan had a couple of letters, too."

Emily laughed as if she shouldn't be surprised any more. "Delivered personally, I take it."

"Of course! It's all part of the service." Lena huffed on the very last scrap of the cigarette, pinching it between finger and thumb until the embers finally drew too close to bear. She stubbed out the little that remained – and then when Emily lifted an arm towards her, Lena went happily enough to cosy up beside her. She curled in further, and pushed her feet in their socks – the boots having already been abandoned – up next to Emily's, before running the arch of a foot up the long curve of Emily's calf. Lena sighed. "What sort of letter will it take …" she mused, "for you to finally accept delivery?"

"Oh darling," came the brisk response, "we've been friends for *ever*. As good as *sisters*. Doesn't that disqualify me?"

"No." Lena looked up from Emily's shoulder, let her gaze roam over that face – still so lovely despite being so utterly familiar – and favoured Emily with a wistful look.

"I'm your best friend, and I will be till the day I die. The rest," Emily added, in somewhat less high-flown tones, "you get plenty of elsewhere."

"Oh darling …" Lena echoed with a sigh.

Someone had finally moved into the house at Fields Corner that had been empty for so long, but it was a week or two before Lena had any mail to deliver. Eventually a letter arrived, addressed to a Miss Cawkwell. A pity the newcomer was a Miss rather than a Mrs, but then so many good things were in short supply these days. Lena mentally revised her route, and rode down there in a state of some curiosity.

She slowed as she neared the bend of the road that would take her to the house – not because the bend was an uncompromising ninety degrees, but because Lena glimpsed movement through the hedgerows, and wanted to scout the lie of the land. She came to a gentle halt, balanced lightly with the ball of one foot on the ground, and peered around the end of the hedgerow. Miss Cawkwell was standing in the overgrown front garden, staring in perplexity at a nanny goat who was cheerfully – one might even say cheekily – munching on weeds. The goat tore off another bunch and lifted her head to gaze placidly back at Miss Cawkwell, stalks sticking out of her mouth in every direction, with yellow flowers bobbing at the end of each.

Miss Cawkwell took a step towards the goat; the goat took a jaunty step back. Miss Cawkwell edged to her left as if considering trying to circle around; the goat danced to her right. Lena's smile quirked as she reflected that the goat was the more graceful of the pair. Miss Cawkwell stalled again, and put her hands on her hips – apparently in confusion rather than consternation. Confusion or not, though, the young woman was not backing down.

Lena took in the sight of Miss Cawkwell, though of course she still suffered the disadvantage of being a Miss. There were so many reasons for Lena to prefer women with other commitments. Apart from which, Miss Cawkwell was too tall, all long limbs and angles, as if she would never quite grow out of the colt stage. Her hair was flat and mousy brown, clumsily cut in a short bob, with a couple of pins failing in their task of fixing back the longer strands. She wore a shapeless gingham dress, with a long apron tied over it, and a pair of overly practical shoes. Miss Cawkwell was, in sum, not the sort to entice interest. Though Lena couldn't help but notice that Miss Cawkwell had a long lovely neck, a pale shapely column that provided her only element of elegance.

Finally, long moments later, Lena pushed off and coasted the bicycle to the front gate. "Hello!" she called.

Miss Cawkwell looked around distractedly, saw Lena – saw the satchel, and the letter in Lena's hand. "Hello," she replied, in an appropriately coltish voice. She strode over to the gate, not neglecting to swing a hand against a nettle on her way, and almost trip over a tuft of grass. There was already a nettle rash running up the tender side of one forearm. "Are you the postman, then?"

Lena grinned. "I am," she replied, handing over the letter. "I used to help my Uncle Bert anyway, so when he enlisted I took on the job."

Miss Cawkwell nodded. After giving the letter a cursory look, she tucked it unopened into a pocket.

Lena found she wasn't ready to be dismissed yet, so she tipped her chin towards the goat. "I see you have your gardener in, helping you clear the weeds."

That drew a laugh from Miss Cawkwell. It was an odd kind of laugh, beginning with a honking snort and ending up as a peal of bells. After a moment, Miss Cawkwell said, "My intention is to milk her."

"She's not cooperating?"

"And I don't understand why. I went to fetch her yesterday evening from Mrs Doherty. Being away from her kids overnight – Well," Miss Cawkwell concluded with a slight hint of confusion at this intimate subject, "she's supposed to welcome the milking."

"Yet she'd rather eat weeds."

Miss Cawkwell smiled a little, ducking her head shyly. "Perhaps she's naturally mischievous."

"Stubborn," Lena countered, able for the moment to gaze her fill at Miss Cawkwell's lovely neck. When Miss Cawkwell looked up again, Lena got off the bicycle and propped it against the thick hedge which was haphazardly sprouting new growth. "Let's see if we can't outwit her. Lena Pearce," she introduced herself, holding out her hand.

"Sylvie Cawkwell," Miss Cawkwell responded, going to open the gate, then shaking Lena's hand instead, and then barking her shin on the gate as it belatedly swung free. Sylvie grimaced – but not heatedly – as if she were used to this sort of thing.

The two of them strolled with a fair pretence of nonchalance towards the goat – who considered them with a bright eye while still munching away – and then as they finally drew near, she skittered off out of reach. This despite the obvious fact that her udder was full.

"I don't think she'll mind very much if we trick her into it," Lena said. "I think she'll be grateful."

"She'll forgive me, then? She'll let me milk her again? Mrs Doherty said I could have her every other day."

"Yes, I think she'll forgive you."

"Ideas?" asked Miss Cawkwell.

"Well …" Lena considered for a moment. "You're the one who has to make friends with her. Why don't you gather up a large bouquet of those yellow flowers she likes so much, and tempt her hither – while I circle around behind, and give her a push in the right direction."

Miss Cawkwell looked at Lena with frank admiration. "A master strategist."

She smiled in response, unaccountably bashful. "Let's see if it works first!"

By the time Miss Cawkwell had gathered an armful of flowers, Lena had managed to nonchalantly sneak around behind the goat. With a nod they each indicated they were ready – and Miss Cawkwell brandished the flowers at the goat while Lena grabbed the goat's hips and shoved. The goat obligingly took a step or two forward and stretched in hope of a mouthful of flowers. Miss Cawkwell stepped back at just the right moment, the goat took another step, and they all three progressed from there in fits and starts.

"Does she have a name?" Lena asked, aware of her breath beginning to pant from the effort.

"Christabel."

Lena let out a laugh. "Ha! A pretty name for such a stubborn thing. What was Mrs Doherty thinking?"

"I don't know –" As Miss Cawkwell leant down to gather more of the weeds while still backing away, she abruptly overbalanced and landed on her rear. She didn't even take a moment to huff a breath before scrambling back up to her feet, ungainly and yet endearing in her determination.

"Are you all right?" Lena asked.

"Yes, thank you. Come on, Christabel …"

"Not bruised?" Lena cast an eye towards the rounded curve that could just be discerned under the gingham.

"Oh! Yes, probably! Never mind." Miss Cawkwell gathered more of the flowers as she went, no doubt so as not to leave any as distractions in the goat's path.

Lena smiled at her, and gave Christabel another shove. "Where are we heading?"

Miss Cawkwell gestured behind her. "There's a shelf for her to stand on just inside the shed." This was announced with rather a lack of authority, and so Lena concluded she was needed for the duration. She was torn between silently castigating Mrs Doherty for leaving Miss Cawkwell to manage things alone, and quietly singing her thanks. For Lena was having fun.

Once they were out of the old flower beds, Christabel stopped being so difficult. Soon she was daintily stepping up the slope that led to the milking shelf, eagerly pursuing the bunch of weeds that Miss Cawkwell placed in the feeder.

"Shall I show you … ?" Lena offered.

"Please," said Miss Cawkwell.

So Lena helped Miss Cawkwell add grain to the feeder, then wash Christabel's udder, and inspect a cup's worth of milk before placing the bucket beneath the goat and settling into the task. Lena showed her where to sit, and in what posture, and how to avoid Christabel kicking at her in irritation. She helped guide Miss Cawkwell's hands on Christabel's teats, encouraged her towards a rippling rhythm of fingers. Miss Cawkwell soon had the idea of it, even if her fingers wouldn't quite coordinate. All the while, the two women and the goat were close and warm and … and Lena at least was feeling a little inappropriate. Judging by Miss Cawkwell's slight blush, there was a chance that she felt somewhat the same way, even if it were only modesty that heightened her colour rather than desire.

Once the process was over and poor Christabel's udder was looking suitably shrivelled, Lena carefully set the bucket of milk out of the way, and then showed Miss Cawkwell how to massage the udder and clean the teats. Christabel seemed satisfied to the point of smugness, munching away on the grain and what was left of the flowers.

"Right," Lena finally announced. "I think we're done."

"Thank you," said Miss Cawkwell. Her cheeks were red and her demeanour was flustered, but her neck remained cool and pale and elegant. Miss Cawkwell lifted a hand to try to brush back the longer strands of her hair which had come loose. "I'll walk her back to Mrs Doherty."

"Do you have a lead?"

"Oh. Yes." Miss Cawkwell went to fetch it, and by luck managed to fasten it to Christabel's collar just before the goat decided to leap down to the ground – stepping on Miss Cawkwell's foot in the process, though it was Christabel who bleated a protest.

"Would you like company for the walk?" Lena cleared her throat. "Just in case she gets stubborn again."

"Oh, no. No, thank you. You've helped me so much already, Miss Pearce."

"Lena."

"Lena." Miss Cawkwell blushed even harder. "I'm sure you have the rest of your round to finish."

"Well …" Should Lena confess that she'd left Miss Cawkwell until last? Perhaps not.

"Thank you. I would have been quite lost without you."

"Oh, you're so –" *lovely.* "Welcome." Lena smiled. "You're so very welcome. Sylvie."

They accompanied each other and Christabel to the front gate, navigated this obstacle with difficulty, and then suffered through clumsy farewells – not helped by Christabel circling them and winding the lead around their knees. At last Lena managed to disengage, and climbed onto her bicycle so that she could escape down the road in an ecstatic kind of agony.

"If only she weren't a Miss!"

Emily laughed, recumbent on the sofa as usual, with her bare feet on the pouffe. Lena was aware of Emily watching her as she paced back and forth, too skittish to settle. Emily was about to speak, then seemed to change her mind. When Lena turned again to pace towards her, Emily remarked, "It's true, my darling, she doesn't seem at all your type."

"Single."

"And not pretty!"

Lena stopped, and ran wondering fingers across her own throat, remembering … "She has the most elegant neck you will ever see."

"Ah …" Emily sounded sceptical.

Lena laughed, and faced her best friend. "Am I so shallow, then?"

"Yes, my dear, I'm afraid that you are."

She laughed again, and wandered off, this time to gaze sightlessly through the window into Emily's back garden. "But she was so … Sylvie was so …"

"Sylvie, is it? Not Miss Cawkwell?"

"She was so … tenacious."

"Tenacious!" Emily pushed up to sit a little straighter. "And that trumps pretty now, does it?"

Lena was looking at neat rows of fulsome cabbages, and remembering a mess of nettles, and weeds with yellow flowers. Remembering Sylvie facing down the placidly mischievous Christabel. Lena felt she had known from the start who would win the confrontation. "It's as if she faces challenge after challenge every day of her life, and she never lets it defeat her."

Emily lifted her brows in surprise.

"Well, all right, maybe some of those challenges are just bruises or tripping over a tussock or having to wear a ghastly gingham dress … but she sails smoothly on. Yes!" Lena cried, the correct simile finally occurring to her. "She's like an ugly duckling who hasn't quite transformed yet into a beautiful swan. She has the neck, though. She really does have the loveliest long pale neck. And maybe none of the rest of her will ever quite catch up – but she has the attitude, too. She sails on through all the things that the world throws at her, and she remains her own true self."

When Lena finally got to the end of that, she pushed her hands into her trouser pockets and turned to face Emily with at least a pretence of defiance.

Emily was staring back at her, apparently stunned. "Well," she said eventually. "Perhaps it's just as well that she's a Miss."

"Why?" asked Lena. "So I won't attempt her seduction?"

"No, so that you can let her seduce you right back."

Lena coasted along the lane on her bicycle, knowing just when to push the pedals through a half-turn to maintain her speed. The air was warmer today, though still fresh against her face as she glided past hedgerows and transformed the road's turns into elegant curves. She drew near the woods and then slipped silently through the living cathedral of arched branches, swept to the left, eased into the side road, and finally drew up to stop the bicycle at Amy's gate.

Lena was smiling, and keen to see Amy – but even Lena knew that her smile was gentler, and her eagerness had changed. Which was just as well, because when Amy answered the front door, she was shining with joy. For a moment Lena's heart thudded in an answering song, an honest panic – and in the next breath she realised that Amy's joy had nothing at all to do with her.

"Oh, Lena, Lena," Amy murmured, slipping onto the front step and closing the door behind her. They were standing so very close to each other, and yet Lena knew that last inch of air between them would never be crossed again. "He's come home. My Robbie's come home."

Lena quirked a grin in genuine satisfaction. "That's marvellous, Amy. That's really wonderful."

"It is, isn't it?" Amy was almost breathless with happiness. Lena had never seen her quite like it. "And he's all right – well, there's some treatment he must continue with, rehabilitation, he won't tell me the details – but even once his leave finishes, he'll be serving in England now. They won't send him overseas again. He'll be here, he won't come to any more harm."

"That really is wonderful, Amy."

"I know. It really is." But then Amy paused, and considered Lena for a long moment. "I'm sorry, Lena."

"You have nothing to be sorry about," Lena protested.

"Are you all right, though? You look … different."

"Do I?" Lena dropped her gaze and turned away a little to ponder that. A long pale elegant neck came to mind, along with the nettle rash on a tender forearm as Miss Cawkwell patiently pushed back a strand of mousy brown

40

hair. "Maybe I am. But don't worry, my darling. It's not about you."

"No?" Amy sounded relieved, and just the smallest bit disappointed.

Lena smiled at her. "I'm so happy for you and Robbie, Amy." She belatedly handed over the letters. "Back to regular deliveries from now on, I swear."

Amy took the letters, and slipped her hand around the doorknob. But before turning it, she looked at Lena and her smile turned mischievous as she whispered, "I want to say thank you, Lena."

Lena laughed, and shook her head in disbelief while stepping onto the path and slowly backing away. "I have to go. Deliveries to make!"

"Have fun!" cried Amy.

"Did you know," Lena asked, pausing for barely a moment at the gate, "that a Miss Cawkwell has moved into Fields Corner?"

Julie Bozza

Julie Bozza is an English-Australian hybrid who is fuelled by espresso, calmed by knitting, unreasonably excited by photography, and madly in love with John Keats.

juliebozza.com
twitter.com/juliebozza
goodreads.com/juliebozza

Inside

Eleanor Musgrove

Alfred Schuchard – Fred, to his many friends and the customers who used to queue into the street for his baked goods – settled down on his bed with a sigh and opened his book. They allowed books in here, which was some relief. He hadn't been sure, when he'd begun throwing things into bags, what he'd be allowed to keep, or whether his possessions would be taken away from him. He'd had no idea what he was doing, actually, or what would happen. Everything that had been happening was so bizarre, he couldn't begin to guess what would come next.

If there was one place he'd never expected to find himself, it was the Alexandra Palace internment camp. He didn't belong here, he knew. Still, he'd had plenty of time to adjust to his new situation since he'd first arrived almost six months ago, so now he simply settled down to read away his allocated free time before dinner. Occasionally, he peered over the top of his book to idly watch as the men on general duties attempted to find room for even more beds in the crowded hall that served as their sleeping quarters. He barely glanced up to nod at them in acknowledgement as they squeezed another little cot in next to his own. People were moved around more often with every passing week, it seemed, and now almost everyone on site seemed to be sleeping in the same large room, trying to pack their meagre belongings in with them. They all simply had to adjust to dwindling living space; not that it had exactly been plentiful before.

He was deeply immersed in his book – it was an old bilingual favourite that his father had learnt English from – when he heard hesitant footsteps draw to a stop near the foot of his bed. He looked up and found himself staring into the eyes of a man whose face would have been simply perfect for a German Army recruitment poster. He was tall, and slender, and couldn't have been more than twenty-five years old. In fact, Fred was only just approaching twenty-four himself, and he strongly suspected that the other man was at least a couple of years his junior. His dark, tousled hair suggested that he had just emerged from the relative luxury of their rather temperamental shower block, and it wasn't until a hint of amusement entered those piercing blue eyes that he realised he'd been staring for too long.

Fortunately, the other man showed no sign of noticing Fred's awkwardness. "*Guten Abend*," he began, and Alfred glanced towards a window with a start. The sky was, indeed, beginning to darken, though there was still a while to spare before he needed to report for his evening duties, and dinner.

"English!" a guard barked from the side of the hall.

"*Guten Abend, Englisch*," he amended, loudly, before holding up both hands towards the guard with a sheepish smile, head bowed. He couldn't be a complete newcomer, then, if he already knew that they were allowed to speak in whichever language they liked among themselves. Still, he was new enough to be nervous about disobeying orders. Alfred hadn't realised they'd had any new internees recently. "It seems," he continued in English, turning back to their fledgling introductions, "I have the bed next to yours."

"*Guten Abend*," Alfred returned politely, unsure of what to make of the stranger. "I'm Alfred Schuchard. Welcome, I suppose, if that's the right word."

The newcomer smiled nervously as they shook hands. "Hallo, Alfred. I am Viktor Schoettmer. It is nice to meet you."

"Likewise, though I suppose you wish it were under different circumstances. We all do."

Viktor nodded distractedly. "Your accent, it is very good."

"Probably because I'm a bloody Londoner, that's why!" This only seemed to embarrass his new friend.

"Ah. I'm sorry. I forgot that most people here have lived in England for a long time."

"I was born here. I assume you haven't lived here long?"

"No. I came to study. When war broke out … I didn't think it would actually happen, and then it was too late. I stopped going to class and hid in my flat, and everyone thought I'd already been caught. Then one of the people I lived with brought a new friend home – two weeks ago, I think – and he told the police about me. I should have hidden better."

"You speak good English, for someone who hasn't been here more than a couple of years."

"One year. I was learning English Literature. Now I am here."

He looked so helpless, Fred couldn't help but take pity on him. "My father was from Mainz. I'm here because they think that means I'd probably be a spy if I was left roaming about outside."

The lad – he could only be nineteen or so, now that Fred got a better look at him – raised an eyebrow at that. "And are you? Is your *Vater*?"

"No. No, I'm not. As for my father, he died when I was fifteen, so if he's spying for your lot it's a bloody good trick." Viktor didn't seem to know whether to laugh or not, simply hovering awkwardly until Alfred took pity on him. "Get comfy, we're here for the duration."

As Fred returned to his book, he was dimly aware of the movement to his right as Viktor unlaced his boots and tucked his meagre possessions – the basic necessities and little else, if Fred was any judge, unless he had more waiting to be cleared – under his bed before sinking tentatively down onto it. The boy seemed lost in thought, and Fred soon got caught up in his reading once more.

The voice startled him, breaking the relative calm of his reading space among the murmurings of other prisoners in the hall.

"Would ... you read it to me? Please? It has been long since I had a chance to read."

Fred considered the idea for a moment, glancing back down at the page before nodding. "English, or German? The book speaks both, see, and so do I."

"*Auf Deutsch, bitte.* It is hard to be so far from home, and familiar things." Then he sat back on his bed and waited expectantly. Fred sat up a little straighter, turned back to the beginning of the story he'd been reading – he'd only just started it anyway – and began to read in soft German.

Viktor hadn't been assigned to a work team yet, so when the guards whistled for the beginning of dinner preparations, Fred left him the book. "That's just my team being called. I'll come back before dinner, you might as well keep reading." It seemed only polite, after all, to offer the newcomer some sort of diversion. He'd be all right, of course, in the big hall with a handful of other men with no interest in whatever the majority were doing with their free time.

Indeed, when Alfred returned to find his new acquaintance, ready for the meal – another team would serve what Fred's had cooked, as on most nights – Viktor hadn't even moved. He was sitting on his bed, feet on the floor, book held loosely in his lap. He seemed to be staring right through the pages, and Fred recognised the signs of a man whose war had just caught up with him. He'd experienced it himself, on his arrival, and he hadn't had the terrifying experience of trying to hide. It was a miracle Viktor had been brought here at all, really, rather than being accused of espionage and imprisoned elsewhere.

"Viktor?" It took him a couple of tries before the young man looked up, those sharp eyes focusing on him with difficulty. He offered up the book, and Alfred took it automatically, tucking it under his pillow before holding out a hand to help him rise. "It's time for dinner. Come on, it's not awful tonight."

Viktor stared at him for a moment longer, then followed him silently to the mess hall.

Later, they stood side by side in the entrance hall for the count, repeated each morning and evening to check that nobody had escaped. As usual, nobody had escaped that day, nor the next day, nor the next. On the morning of Viktor's fourth day in the main camp population, he was finally called to receive his work assignment as soon as they fell out. Alfred waited a few moments – they had a brief period of free time before the day started in earnest – for his return with news. He hoped it might do his new friend good, having a consistent task to work at each day; after the structure of academic life and then the carefully-planned routines of avoiding discovery, sitting around all day could be doing him no good.

Sure enough, Viktor was wearing a tight smile when he returned to his friend. "What do you do here?" he asked, though he'd been told before. Fred had suspected at the time that his new friend had been lost in the fog of his sudden upheaval, but he'd kept talking in the hope that it would help somehow.

"I work in the kitchens," he told him patiently, "like outside. How about you?"

"Gardening," Viktor shrugged. "I know nothing about plants, but the vegetables have to grow, I suppose."

"I'll get myself put on the stock run this afternoon, if you like. Come and see you're getting on all right." He wondered if that seemed strange, clingy perhaps, but Viktor's face had lit up and he couldn't take it back now.

"That would be very nice. I am a little nervous."

"You'll be fine. The lads will show you what to do, they don't bite. You'll fit in."

The day passed quickly, and a runner came at lunchtime to collect sandwiches for the men working the vegetable gardens. It was three o'clock almost before Alfred knew it, and the usual argument began about who had to go and haul the vegetables back from the plots, ready to be prepared for dinner. Fred got some funny looks when he put a stop to the squabble by volunteering, but he didn't much care as he set off towards the vegetable plots. Collecting what they'd requested earlier was no trouble at all, but as he cast an eye around, he couldn't spot his friend anywhere.

"Isn't there a new bloke here today? Viktor? He bunks next to me."

"Oh, yeah – haven't seen him in a couple of hours, though. He went to get a spade; probably sleeping somewhere. It's his first day, and the guards haven't noticed; leave him be."

He nodded, thought about it for thirty seconds, and asked where the spades were.

Alfred approached the little shed with his box of vegetables, and heard muted whimpering noises from inside. He set the box aside carefully before leaning around the doorway. The figure hunched in one corner was Viktor, he could tell, making weak, desperate noises and rocking slightly.

"I'm not, I'm not a spy, I haven't spoken – spoken – to anyone, I don't know anything –"

"Viktor?" He had to step over a couple of trowels that seemed to have fallen from a shelf at some point, but at last he was close enough to reach out and touch his friend's shoulder. He didn't, though, some instinct holding him back. "Viktor?"

The man turned and clutched at his arms, eyes wide and blank. "Seppel? Seppel! Is that you?"

"Viktor … Viktor, it's Fred – Alfred. From the next bed. You're safe, you're safe at Alexandra Palace." It took a while, murmuring soft promises and holding on to his friend's forearms in a strange sort of embrace as Viktor clung back. At last, the other man calmed slightly, wild eyes settling on his friend's face.

"Alfred. Where – ? I … I should be gardening – I should, yes?"

"Are you all right?"

"Yes … Yes, I am not where I thought I was. I should go back to work."

"… All right. I'll walk you back, and we'll talk later."

He took the head of the team aside and briefly explained what had occurred, whereupon the man promised to have the whole crew work in pairs the next day.

"I don't know what happened; he's a civilian, like us. I think perhaps they were rough with him when they brought him in. Will you be careful with him?" The older man's face darkened, and Fred was briefly afraid that he'd said the wrong thing. He needn't have worried.

"I always liked it here in England. I thought the government were good people; I thought we were accepted. My family and I, we were British. Now the longer I'm in here, the more stories … I miss Germany, and I have not been there since I was ten years old."

Fred nodded grimly; he knew the feeling. "I'm sure it's the same there, for British Germans. War makes monsters of us all."

"You're forgiving. I'll look after your friend."

"*Danke.* Well, er … I'd better get back to the kitchens." After a brief exchange of nods, Fred retrieved the box of produce and hurried away.

During free time, they found their area of the colossal shared sleeping hall all but deserted as a hotly anticipated table tennis match began on the other side of the building. Fred simply rolled over on his little camp bed and waited for Viktor to tell him how he was feeling.

"Do not look at me like that," the other man muttered at last. "I am embarrassed."

"There's no need," he assured him. "There's plenty here have nightmares about bombing raids and things." This seemed to both surprise and reassure his friend, and he felt bold enough to press on. "It sounded … it sounded as if you had a different experience, though."

Viktor nodded, staring blankly up at the ceiling.

"You don't have to tell me if you don't want to."

"I'd been hiding, it looked bad," the younger man blurted, "they thought – so they took me in to question." He swallowed hard and turned his face towards Fred's for a few seconds before returning his gaze to the ceiling. "I was so scared. They kept asking – and they didn't believe me. It … it could have been worse, I know." He was silent for a long time, then, and slowly, hesitantly, Fred reached out to pat his hand. It was awkward, but Viktor's gaze gradually shifted back to Alfred's face.

"Perhaps we should see if you can get a transfer to the kitchens with me. Friendly face, and all that –"

"No!" Viktor had suddenly wrenched his hand out of Fred's reach, recoiling as far as he could on his narrow camp bed. "No. No, I will tend the garden. Thank you. I'll … the garden." Then he stood, mumbled something about table tennis and left the room.

Evening count came and went, and still Viktor would hardly look at him. Fred didn't understand it. He might be embarrassed, but surely that was no reason to ignore him so completely? What had Fred done? Perhaps he'd crossed a line when he'd touched his hand, but the younger man hadn't seemed to mind. He'd only meant to reassure him, but that seemed to have backfired rather spectacularly. As they settled in to sleep, however, he made one last attempt to repair their friendship before the problem could spill over into the next day.

"Viktor. I'm sorry, about before."

He seemed surprised. "You did nothing wrong. It's me. I won't go to the kitchens. I'm sorry."

"It's not a problem," Fred assured him. "Just let's stay friends. Are you going to be all right tonight? I mean, are you feeling better?"

There was a moment's silent thought, and then a hand on Fred's arm startled him. "I will sleep. You're here."

He was sure Viktor meant to remove his hand at some point, but when he began snoring softly it fell to Fred to lift his friend's arm, move it across the small gap between their beds, and lay it back across its owner's chest. People would talk about the most trivial things in here.

Viktor, unfortunately, proved that point the next morning, when one of the British guards pulled him aside before breakfast. Fred winced and began moving casually in that direction. Few of their guards had much sympathy for their prisoners, especially the 'more foreign' ones, and they had a tendency to pick people at random to take their moods out on.

"You. What's your name?"

"Viktor Schoettmer, *Herr* – I mean, sir."

"Victor? Is that why you became a spy? To bring your country victory? Didn't work very well, landing yourself in here!"

Viktor frowned, obviously hurt. "I'm not a spy."

"Are you getting aggressive, prisoner? Do you need putting in your place?"

"I'm not –"

"Calling me a liar now, are you?"

Victor began to splutter, but Fred stepped forward and nodded respectfully at the guard, keeping his eyes lowered. "Excuse me, sir, but he's needed for breakfast."

The guard sneered, obviously not fooled in the slightest. "Aren't you lucky your little friend's looking out for you? Get out of my sight, prisoner."

Alfred snagged Viktor by the arm and dragged him away, ignoring the other nearby guards trying to stifle their sniggers and the prisoners trying not to make eye contact.

They sat together at breakfast, the two of them at the end of a table where nobody seemed inclined to talk to them. Viktor, who usually wolfed down anything he was given, was picking at his food in a disgustingly wasteful manner. Fred put his own portion away in record time before regarding his friend worriedly.

"My middle name's Günther."

Viktor looked up at him, puzzled, and Fred pressed on.

"Dad said it meant an army of warriors. That's what he always said, that a baker was worth an army of warriors – *his* sort." He risked the slightest gesture in the direction of the guard who'd given them the trouble that morning, just to make sure his point was clear.

"He's not a warrior. Just … just a babysitter." Viktor muttered it in German, and Fred smiled encouragingly.

"Just goes to show, what's in a name, right? I'm the least brave person I've ever met. Not like you."

Viktor turned bright red, and tried to hide it by lowering his face over his breakfast and rapidly filling it with food. Well, that was something, Fred supposed.

When the outdoor team came back from their day's work, one of them caught Fred's enquiring gaze and grimaced slightly. A glance at Viktor showed why: the man was pale and shaken, sticking close to the man who was guiding him into the hall by a light touch at his elbow. Fred bit down the irrational surge of jealousy – Viktor was *his* friend – and rushed to see that he was all right.

"A man outside the wall, he was shouting very bad things about the prisoners. He took fright," the man told him in German, presumably for Viktor's benefit, "but after, he kept working. You're a brave man, Viktor. Strong. You will survive."

Fred thanked him – Viktor didn't seem to have the strength to do much more than nod weakly – and took over the task of guiding Viktor back to their beds as the rest of the gardening group dispersed.

"Are you all right?" Fred asked, as Viktor slumped back onto the thin mattress to stare up at the ceiling.

"Yes." He sighed. "Are you not needed in the kitchen?"

"No. We got everything ready earlier, it's set out ready to be served cold. We're a bit low on non-vegetable supplies, anyway; it's going to be a lean meal tonight, I'm afraid. Is there anything I can do to cheer you up?"

"I'm fine," Viktor insisted, and then, "… You could tell me about your home. Your family."

"Well, then … my mother runs the bakery now that I'm not there, with my sister, my sister's husband, and their children."

"And you? You have a wife?"

"No. No, I'm something of a confirmed bachelor, and likely to stay that way now I'm stuck in here."

"The war won't be for ever."

Fred shrugged. "Well, I was never much of a hit with the ladies. I didn't really try very hard, to be honest. I was busy working and things. How about you? Some lucky lady waiting at home?"

Viktor shook his head, gaze still firmly fixed on the ceiling directly above him. "No. There have been girls, but none of them were … quite right. Now, who knows if I will see home again?"

They lapsed into a companionable silence after that, each lost in their own thoughts of home.

"Do you miss it?" Fred blurted at last, and then coloured as he realised what he'd asked. "Sorry. Stupid question –"

"Some things, yes. I miss the Germany of my childhood. Things are different now. I think they must be different here, too."

"Since the war started? Yes. Yes, they are, I think, though I've been in here."

"Before the war. Things have been getting bad for a long time. I thought here would be better."

"I wish it had been." Fred hesitated for a moment, then asked gently, "Who is Seppel? You asked me if I was him, when you got scared in the shed."

"It was the noises, I knocked something and then I thought I was being attacked – Seppel is my brother, my younger brother. Joseph, really. I thought – for a moment I thought I was being questioned, and then I thought maybe I was home. But I'm not home. Seppel may be called to join the army there soon – he is sixteen years old. Three years younger. I should be there to protect him."

"And you? Who would protect you?"

Viktor sighed heavily. "I don't know. Perhaps I am better off here. You look after me now."

Fred didn't have the faintest idea what to say to that, but Viktor didn't seem to be expecting an answer. Indeed, judging by the soft, even rhythm of his breathing, Fred suspected that he'd dozed off. Let him, for a moment. He needed the rest, and Fred suddenly had an awful lot to think about.

He had, in a way, been acting as Viktor's protector, his champion, since he'd arrived here. He'd had more quiet words to make sure suspicious residents didn't make trouble for his new friend than he'd ever had on his own behalf, and even before he'd realised the boy was a little broken inside, he'd done his best to make things easy for him – easier than he himself had ever had it, that was for sure. He *was* fond of the lad. He chanced a glance across at his sleeping neighbour and closed his own eyes with a sigh.

Perhaps too fond.

"Fred," Viktor began quietly, several days later, "what is wrong? You have seemed ... out of sorts, lately."

Fred didn't know how to reply to that, so he didn't, keeping his eyes fixed firmly on his book. Perhaps Viktor would just assume that he hadn't heard him. Sure enough, when the other man spoke again, it was in a slightly louder voice.

"Have I done something wrong?"

"No," Fred assured him automatically, before lowering his book with a sigh. "No, you've done nothing wrong. Best friend I've ever had, probably, in fact. I've just been ... well, thinking."

"Ah. Missing outside?"

That wasn't strictly the problem, but there was some truth in it, so Fred seized upon it eagerly. "Yes, I suppose I am. How about you?"

"I miss being able to go where I want, when I want, no guards. I miss my home, my family. But it is better in here than I thought it would be, when I first arrived. I thought I might be sent with all the captured soldiers."

Fred hadn't thought of that possibility. Of course, Viktor was a 'real' German, in the eyes of whoever it was who'd thrown them all in here. He turned to face Viktor properly, to show him he cared. Of course he cared; that was the problem. "Did that worry you?" It was a stupid question, but it was the only way he could think of to keep Viktor talking, to make him see that he had someone to share his burdens with.

"A little ... *Ja*, a lot. They would be from the Front; I heard things, before – and what if they thought I was a traitor? For coming to England, for not going home to fight? What if they thought I was a British spy, just as the British thought I was a German spy? They would hate me. Even here, I thought ... I thought you would all hate me."

"I don't hate you. I don't know how anyone alive could hate you." Fred could feel his cheeks colouring slightly – he'd said too much – but he wouldn't take it back.

Viktor was something special, anyone could see that. Or ... could it be that he was wrong? Were there people here in the camp who'd been making things difficult for him, especially while Fred had barely dared to pay attention beyond the habitual niceties of sitting together at lunch? He'd been so afraid to ruin his friendship with Viktor by – well, he didn't rightly know what he thought he'd do, but he was sure he was doing this whole friendship thing wrong – that he had no idea if his protection of the younger man was still recognised by the rest of the camp. "Why? Have people been making trouble?"

"No. No, I just … well, I made a friend, a best friend, but now he seems … different."

"Who?"

"You haven't even looked at me properly in days, until now. Have I upset you?"

"Oh. No. No, I'm sorry. It's just … as you said. I suppose I'm homesick."

Viktor nodded thoughtfully. "Perhaps there is a friend at home, and you feel bad for spending so much time with a new friend?"

Fred laughed at the thought. "No. No, it's not that. Blimey, I'd love you to meet my mates back home. They'd love you, I know they would."

Viktor smiled at him hopefully. "Perhaps when the war is over, I could visit you at home?"

"Yeah. Yeah, you should." The warmth in his voice surprised even him, but suddenly all he could imagine was Viktor, sitting beside him at the bar in their local, laughing as Dave and Pete battled it out for the affections of the barmaid. Perhaps he would even join in – but the idea hurt to think about, and Fred didn't want to try to work out why that was, so he gave up altogether. "You definitely should. So, how's the gardening been going?"

"Ah. My back is sore. It is not like studying from books; it has been a long time since I went digging, until now." And with that, conversation became easy again, just as long as Fred didn't think too hard about the warmth spreading through his chest and the smile he couldn't keep off his face.

Several weeks went by, relatively pleasantly by camp standards, before Fred decided that enough was enough and went in search of one of the camp's worst-kept secrets, an Austrian-born gentleman whose interests did not, particularly, lie with the fairer sex. It wasn't that Fred was similarly inclined – of course it wasn't, he hardly needed any more trouble in his life – but perhaps a man who'd experienced the full range of feelings towards his fellow men could help Fred understand where on the scale his feelings for Viktor fell. Perhaps he'd be able to tell him that all this was nothing to worry about; perhaps this was simply the sort of protective feeling one might experience towards a younger brother – perhaps the way his heart leapt every time Viktor smiled at him was just a glow of pride at the way he'd settled in so quickly. That was, surely, all it was?

Fred found the older man sitting on his bed, absently watching the comings and goings of his fellow residents as they sought out friends and began card games. He stepped hesitantly into his line of sight and nodded politely. "Excuse me? *Herr* Pichler? Might I have a word?"

"Yes, of course! Please, call me Leonhard. I'm sorry, I don't –"

"Schuchard. Fred Schuchard."

"May I call you Fred?"

"Of course. I, er, I wanted to – er, that is – um, people say –"

Pichler fixed him with a shrewd look and gestured to a chair beside his bed. "You've heard I know something of the love that dare not speak its name."

"Er … yeah. I think so. I mean … you prefer the company of – ?"

"Yes, we're talking about the same thing. And you, perhaps, have questions?"

"I … yes. I'm not – I mean, I don't want you to get the wrong idea, I'm not … I don't know how you survive, it's bad enough in here without worrying about that sort of thing … but I thought you might be better at feelings. About men. And I … I don't quite understand my feelings."

"About men? *A* man, maybe?" Pichler sat up a little straighter. "Go on, I'm listening. Can't promise I'll be any help, but tell me what's on your mind, ask what you want to know, and I'll keep your secrets."

Fred stared at the floor for a few more moments. He took a deep breath, and let it out slowly. "… Yes, a man, I suppose. I just … I want to rule out anything untoward. I've never really loved anyone, let alone a man, but … you have. You know … well, you know how that feels, and how it doesn't, and I'm hoping you'll set my mind at ease."

Pichler raised an eyebrow. "Are you looking for comfort, or truth?"

Fred hesitated. Did he dare risk hearing something he couldn't cope with? "… I'm hoping the truth will be comforting. But … the truth of your opinion, please."

"Very well. Tell me about this man of yours, then."

And, though Fred was afraid of what he might reveal, he did. "He, um … Obviously, I'm not going to name names, but he's younger than me, perhaps

I just feel as if he's a younger brother to me or something, I've never had a –
but yes, he's younger. And he looks like a poster for Germany or something,
he's very handsome, and all that, if that … I mean, if it matters. But it
shouldn't, should it, because I'm not – I don't – He's just … I want to protect
him, and look after him … I want him to be happy. And he's not, and that
… it hurts. I can't keep him safe from all the things in his head, I can't
change what he's been through."

"And if you found out he was … inclined as I am?"

"He's not. He's a nice boy, of course he's not … is he?"

Pichler barely even seemed to register the slight; Fred hadn't realised how
rude he sounded until he'd already spoken. "I don't know. But if he was, how
would you feel?"

"I – Scared, I suppose. Because then … then I'd really have to decide.
And, well, I suppose … I mean, if he … I'd be a bit flattered, I think."

"Well, then. Perhaps you harbour more feelings towards him than
brotherly or friendly feelings, or perhaps you don't. But the way you speak
of him … I don't mean to cause offence, or speak out of turn."

"Please, tell me."

"… If, as I suspect, you're talking about young Schoettmer, I've seen you
with him. It would take eyes open to the possibility to see it, but … I'd say
you've got it bad for the boy."

Fred blanched. Was that how it was? Was it so clear to this stranger, the
answer that had eluded him?

Pichler was studying him intently now, a calculating look on his face.
"I can't say I blame you; he is pretty."

"*Stay away from him.*" He couldn't explain the sudden fury boiling in his
chest, but Pichler obviously thought *he* could, judging by his satisfied smile
as he sat back. "I'm not jealous," Fred spluttered, "I just – don't want you
corrupting him. Anyway, who said I was even talking about Viktor?"

The Austrian shrugged. "Just my opinion, of course. Come back and talk
to me any time you need."

By the time he got back to his own bed, the gardening crew had long since
returned from their duties. Viktor was sitting on his bed, glancing between
Fred and Pichler, whose bed was just barely visible at the other end of the
row opposite theirs.

"Afternoon," Fred greeted Viktor as casually as he could, expecting his usual friendly reply.

"Afternoon," Viktor repeated, sounding a little puzzled and slightly distant. "You are friendly with Leonhard Pichler?"

"Never spoken to him, really, until today. Just happened to get chatting. Why? Do *you* know him?"

Viktor lay back on his bed and fixed his eyes on the ceiling. "I have heard of him. If you don't mind, I am tired. I wish to rest."

Fred could understand that ... but when he left to start taking the food out of the ovens, Viktor was still awake, still staring resolutely up as if he could just *almost* see the answers to all life's mysteries, carved into the ceiling high above him.

A week after his conversation with Pichler – which Fred still didn't much like the conclusion of – a runner from the gardens was sent to the kitchens.

"I'm covering for you, you need to go and get Viktor out of the shed. The door slammed shut on him in the wind and now we can't get it open again. He's barred it, or something. Either way, we can't distract the guards talking about cabbages for much longer, he might listen to you."

"Me? Why – ?"

"You're his best mate, you've got more chance than anyone else."

"I – right, yeah. All right. On my way."

There was a sizeable crowd gathered around the little potting shed by the time Fred arrived, and for a while the sound of their anxious chatter obscured the sounds coming from inside the shed – but then he heard it. A broken voice, sobbing. He pushed through the crowd to join the foreman of the gardening crew, who stepped back from the door when he realised Fred was there.

"You're going to have to try," the foreman muttered quietly. "Get him to sick-bay or something, cos if the guards find him skiving –"

"I know." Fred stepped up and tapped gently at the door, which only prompted a slight scuffling noise and a groan from the other side. "Viktor?" There was no response, so he got a little closer to the door and tried again. "Viktor, it's me, Fred. Are you all right?"

Seconds crawled by before a small voice answered. "Fred? It ... is dark."

That surprised a small chuckle out of him. "I bet it is. Are you hurt? Can you remember which way the door is, for me?"

Again, the response was slow to come. "... Yes. I can."

"Good, that's good, you're doing well. Can you tell me what you can see in that direction?"

"It is dark. They ... they will come, they will say –"

"Viktor. Viktor, listen to me. They won't come. I promise you that. Concentrate for me. Is there anything in the way of the door?" Fred took advantage of the younger man's hesitation to turn to the nearest bystander. "Here, clear this lot off, will you? Guards'll see this a mile off, and he doesn't need the audience, either." The man nodded, and Fred turned his attention back to the shed. "Viktor? Anything in the way?"

"A ... yes."

"Can you move it for me, Viktor? Without hurting yourself?"

"... Yes. But they will get in –"

"No, they won't. Just me. I'm the only one coming in. I promise, Viktor, it's just me. Can you move it so I can come and help you?"

"I ... I think I can."

"Okay. Don't get hurt."

"No. You won't let me."

Fred winced; that was placing a lot of trust in him in a situation he couldn't actually control. "I won't. Just be careful, yeah?" There was a terrible scraping noise, and then a low whistle from somewhere behind him. A guard approaching; the signal wasn't hard to decipher. The shed door cracked open a fraction. "Right, I'm coming in."

He slipped inside the little wooden hut and pulled the door half-shut behind him, enough to shield them from view without alerting the guards to any strangeness. Viktor was curled against one wall, peering timidly up at him like a frightened child. If his young nephew had looked up at him like that, Fred wouldn't have hesitated to scoop him into his arms; he had the same reaction to Viktor's vulnerability. "Shhh, shh. It's all right, I'm here. What happened?"

"They shut me in, in the dark ... I blocked the door so they couldn't get in."

"It was the wind, Viktor, just the wind."

"Shouldn't you be in the kitchens? Are ... is this a dream?"

"Shh, it's all right, they're covering for me. Just ... keep it down, yeah?

We don't want people coming to check on us." Fred pulled away from his friend, reaching down to take his hand instead. "Do you want to come home with me, sit in the kitchens in the warm?"

"I … no, I … would they mind?"

"Well, if they do, you can plead sick and go to bed. Nobody's going to send you back to work in this state."

"I'm pathetic –"

"Oi. Stop it, that's my friend you're insulting." That raised a very wobbly smile, and Fred decided that they weren't going to get a better chance to move. "C'mon. You can decide where we're going on the way to the door."

"But Stefan won't –"

"The foreman? He said to get you out of here, get you settled, no problem there." Still, if Viktor was worrying about his boss, that had to mean he was more aware of his surroundings than he had been before. Fred helped him to his feet, kept a tight grip on his arm, and had them out into the weak London sunlight before the younger man could protest.

The head of Fred's team had no objection to Viktor sitting with them, especially when five minutes of sitting in a warm corner made him restless enough to come and lend a hand. He stood shoulder to shoulder with Fred, watching carefully and copying what he did to make sure that he didn't get anything wrong.

"Not cooked much, I take it?"

"Not much, no. Is it so obvious?"

"You're doing fine. Just stop worrying so much about it, yeah? Here, tell you what, have a good knead of that bread over there. Always makes me feel better."

Viktor obediently turned his attention to the dough in question, and Fred watched him for a while to make sure he was doing it right. He found himself mesmerised by Viktor's hands as they worked, gingerly at first before he began to gain confidence, and Fred forced himself to return to his own work.

For a while, they worked solidly, until Fred realised that there were loud thumping noises coming from his friend's direction. He turned to find Viktor kneading the bread as if it had personally offended him, wincing and grunting softly. He moved over to take his hands, guiding him into a gentler rhythm, but the younger man remained tense and unresponsive until the head of the kitchen glanced over and dismissed them both, telling Fred to get Viktor settled while the rest of the team finished making dinner. Viktor clung to his arm all the way back to their beds.

"You're all right now," Fred told him, as he glanced furtively around before tucking him in under his blanket, smoothing his hair back from his forehead with a tender, almost motherly air. "Tucked up in bed with nothing to worry about. Get some sleep before dinner, all right?"

"Stay with me?"

Viktor sounded so afraid, Fred couldn't bring himself to say no to him. Besides, the younger man had hold of his arm, and seemed to have no intention of letting go any time soon. He sat carefully on the edge of the bed and hoped nobody would come in and see them like this. "I'll stay. You sleep now, all right?"

With a final squeeze of his hand, Viktor obeyed.

When the rest of the men returned for free time, they were lucky that Pichler and a friend of his were the first back in. Pichler gave Fred a thumbs-up and a grin when he saw him, then headed back to his bunk before Fred could correct his assumption. He moved back onto his own bed, laying Viktor's hand gently back on top of the blanket. When dinner was announced, he shook his friend awake but made no mention of the afternoon's stranger moments. Things were complicated enough without dwelling on what Pichler thought of them, or whether he was right about Fred's feelings ... and if they weren't going to talk about Fred's feelings, it seemed only fair to let Viktor choose whether to talk about his fears or not. They sat a little closer together than usual at dinner, perhaps, but for the most part Viktor seemed determined to put a brave face on things and recover, and Fred was more than happy to let him do so.

When they settled back into their beds after the evening's count, however, Viktor reached out in the darkness to squeeze Fred's hand. "Thank you for today. I have been trying not to bother you about things, but today was very bad."

"That's all right. You can always bother me, if you want to tell me you've had a bad day. We're friends."

"You are a good friend, Alfred. Thank you." There was a long silence, and Fred thought Viktor had fallen asleep until he spoke again, so softly that even from the next bed, he barely heard him. "More than a good friend."

Fred waited, straining his ears for more, but the next thing he heard was a gentle snore that told him Viktor was sleeping at last.

Fred had no idea what to make of it all. Sleep refused to come for some hours.

When Fred opened his eyes the next morning, Viktor's bed was empty. He panicked, for a moment, afraid that his fears had overwhelmed him again – or even that he'd been taken off for more interrogation – but as the room came into focus from beyond the lingering veil of sleep, he realised that he could still see him, off at the far end of the opposite row of beds, deep in conversation with Pichler. He couldn't hear what they were saying, but Viktor's posture gradually changed from slightly hostile and defensive to give him a slightly more relaxed, if disconsolate, appearance. Pichler said something, and suddenly they were both looking in Fred's direction. Embarrassed to have been caught staring, he looked away, but not before he glimpsed a knowing grin on Pichler's face and a blush colouring Viktor's cheeks as he turned away too. When he next dared a glance, the boy was nodding sheepishly and Pichler was patting him on the shoulder. Fred slumped back down onto his bed and stared up at the ceiling.

Viktor and Pichler? He hadn't seen that coming. Could Viktor really be – ? Well, it seemed Pichler had got his wish. Why should Fred care? He had no interest in that sort of relationship …

Oh, God. He couldn't fool himself any more. He liked Viktor altogether more than he should. And now it seemed that Viktor himself might not have been averse to the idea, if only … if only he hadn't met Pichler. Apparently he preferred an older gentleman. Well, that was … perhaps that was for the best all round. Fred didn't have a clue what his emotions were doing, to say nothing of the complications of illegally courting a man in an internment camp. He would have to keep an extra eye out for Viktor and Pichler if they were going to risk everything with some sort of illicit affair.

This careful awareness got off to a bad start when a hand landed unexpectedly on his shoulder.

"There you are. You were miles away." Viktor himself was standing in front of him, looking faintly nervous. "Will you come to get the vegetables today? I need to talk about something."

For a moment, fearing that he was about to get a long speech about how, regardless of the moral value of homosexuality, Pichler made Viktor happy, Fred considered refusing. His own conscience kicked in before he could, however; what if Viktor wanted to talk about his traumas, or just needed support? "Yes. Yes, I'll come this afternoon."

Viktor nodded and, uncharacteristically early, disappeared off to get washed and ready for the day.

The day passed in a sort of gloomy haze of dread for the baker as he worked away in the kitchens, and when the time came to go and collect the fresh vegetables, he volunteered with a heavy heart. Perhaps if he hadn't been so slow to realise what he wanted, he wouldn't have to watch Pichler steal the man who'd, completely unexpectedly, stolen his affections. Now, however, there was no helping it. It was too late, and all Fred could do was try to make sure Viktor didn't get hurt. He made his way to talk to Stefan, the garden foreman, and was hardly surprised to hear that Viktor had just taken the produce they needed to the shed to get it out of the sun. Fred slipped inside – sure enough, his friend was waiting there – and half-closed the door. "You wanted to talk?"

Viktor seemed a little taken aback by his tone, and Fred realised this was going to be more difficult than he'd expected. "Are you well? Is this not a good time to talk?"

"I'm fine." Fred made a conscious effort to soften his tone, and tried again. "I'm fine, really. What do you want to talk about?"

Viktor hesitated, and Fred decided to help him get started.

"Is it anything to do with your conversation with Leonhard Pichler earlier?"

Viktor blushed just as deeply as he had then. "Oh. Well … yes. Yes, it is, but it is a very delicate matter … the law …"

"If you and he are having … some sort of affair, that's all right. I don't need you to explain, I'll keep your secret –"

But Viktor was frowning at him in obvious confusion. "Pichler? I am not having any affair with Pichler!"

"Oh – I'm sorry, I just assumed you knew he was a –"

"Homosexual. I know he is, yes. But that does not mean I am involved with him – I thought *you* were with him –"

"What? No, I'm not –"

"I know that. He told me, this morning, when I asked him about it. He, er … I told him why I wanted to know and he said I should talk to you about it."

Viktor seemed to be speaking in riddles, and as happy as Fred was to hear that Pichler and Viktor were nothing more than nodding acquaintances or perhaps even friends, he didn't much like being confused. "I don't understand."

Viktor took a deep breath. "You are a good friend, Fred. I do not wish to lose this friendship. But … I fear you may hate me for what I say."

"Doubt it," Fred told him, "unless you keep me in suspense. Or it involves murder."

Viktor didn't even smile. "I have … feelings for you that are not friendship. Feelings like those I have when I become close to a girl, but … I never wanted to risk everything for those girls. I did not really know them. You … I care very deeply about you."

Fred couldn't believe his ears. He had longed to hear such sentiments expressed by his best friend, but in his wildest of dreams he hadn't been able to truly imagine it. Now his heart felt as if it was too big for his chest, expanding painfully as his pulse pounded in his ears.

He realised he'd been speechless for too long as Viktor spoke again, obviously embarrassed. "I am sorry if this offends you. I hope –"

"Viktor … I've never been in love. I dunno how it feels. But I know spending time with you makes me happy, happier than anything, and … and I don't think it's just being mates."

Viktor's eyes widened. "You are not upset – ?"

"I'm not upset. When I went to talk to Pichler the other day – I went to ask him about my feelings about you. I was so … I was determined not to think of you this way, to feel about you the way I do, cos you're a bloke. But then I saw you blushing at him earlier and I just … I was so jealous, Viktor, I … I'm afraid I might be the jealous type."

They stared at each other for a moment, trying to catch up with the situation, and then Viktor spoke once more. "So … what do we do now?"

Fred glanced towards the door; they couldn't have much time. "Er … do homosexuals kiss?"

That made Viktor laugh, and it took him a moment to compose himself enough to answer. "Yes. I think they do. Do you want to?"

Fred had never kissed anyone before, let alone a man. It was a little awkward, bringing his hand to Viktor's cheek to gently hold him still and then leaning in to brush his lips against the other man's. Viktor, he dimly noted, had his hands resting gently on Fred's upper arms, and the moment Fred pulled back Viktor leant back in, chasing his lips and taking control, kissing him firmly.

They broke apart sheepishly after a few moments, and Viktor smiled again. "I have not kissed a man before."

"Me neither," Fred told him, "but if you've no objection, I'd like to make a habit of it."

Fred had always been told that homosexuals were wrong, that God would strike them down and send them to the pits of Hell, but now he didn't see how a kiss like that – how *anything* between himself and Viktor – could possibly be wrong or bad. "Yes. Yes, that would be … acceptable."

Viktor beamed widely at him, and Fred beamed back before realising that they'd been in the shed for far too long to be inconspicuous. "Oh, God, I've got to go back to the kitchen like this. I'd better be off – I'll see you tonight?"

"Of course." Viktor managed to dive forward and peck his cheek before Fred could leave, the pair of them blushing furiously. At least it was a hot day; they could explain away their flushed faces easily enough. It was time to get back to work.

When Fred returned to his bed before dinner, hoping to spend some time with a good book, or Viktor, or some combination of the two, he found Leonhard Pichler sitting on a small trunk, waiting for him. "Leonhard. What brings you to this side of the room?"

The older man raised an eyebrow. "Has Viktor spoken with you?" Fred could feel himself blushing, and it seemed Pichler noticed. "Ah, I see he has. I was going to warn you to be nice to him, but I suppose it's too late."

"Be nice? Why would you need to tell me to be nice to Viktor? I'm always nice."

"Well, you made it quite clear how you felt about, you know …"

"I've … reconsidered. When I saw him talking to you, I thought … and I was jealous. And then he said … Well. You needn't worry about any hearts being broken."

"You thought what? That we were courting? No, no. No offence to the pair of you, but neither of you are my type – besides, my very special friend would kill me if he thought my eye was wandering."

Well, that was a surprise. Fred hadn't known Pichler was seeing anyone. It did, however, offer an opportunity to ask a question. "How do you do it, Leonhard? I mean … being as you are, in here where there's nowhere to hide."

The man shrugged. "It's easier on the outside. I'm not the best to ask about hiding, being an open secret and all, but my friend prefers to be more anonymous. It's hard. You can't get away with much, and you have to snatch your tender moments when you can. But all you really need is to be together, right? Anything else is just a bonus. I hope, after the war, things will be easier. We'll never be *allowed*, but people in here seem happy to keep anything quiet from the guards, and some are quite tolerant. Maybe outside … people might be the same."

"I just wish I could be a simple, normal ladies' man."

Pichler shrugged. "Perhaps it would be easier. But you would not have Viktor, and I would not have my love. In some ways, maybe we are lucky. Women we love are kept from us while we are in this camp. Our friends are here."

Viktor returned at that moment, along with a couple of other chaps who slept nearby, and joined the conversation. "Hallo, Leonhard. Has Fred told you how his day went?" After the brief moment of frankness they'd been granted at the end of their deserted row of beds, they were back to speaking in code.

"Yes, he has. I am glad you both had good days."

With that, Viktor smiled brightly. "Very good days. I thought we might play cards. Would you like to join us?"

Leonhard seemed surprised, but pleased – Fred knew he wasn't especially popular, probably due to his romantic leanings – and accepted the invitation with alacrity. Fred called over to the nearest men, convincing a few to join, and it seemed as if they'd barely started playing when dinner-time came and they were forced to stop. That being said, Leonhard had won three hands and another man at least four, so they must have been playing for a while. As they all went to take their places at the dinner tables, Fred didn't regret the lost time with his books at all.

"I'm glad you didn't move to the kitchens," Fred admitted sheepishly as he pulled Victor a little closer in the darkness of the potting shed, "or we couldn't use the shed."

"I am glad too," Viktor agreed, head resting on Fred's shoulder, "although the only reason I didn't want to before was …"

He trailed off, blushing, and Fred grinned in anticipation of an interesting new piece of knowledge. "Why?"

"… I was afraid I might … do this." He darted forward and captured Fred's lips with his own, smiling as Fred kissed back. They'd been courting secretly for several weeks now, and their opportunities for kissing hadn't been as frequent as either of them might have liked. Fred couldn't help but marvel at his own thoughts: not so very long ago, he couldn't have imagined wanting to kiss anybody, never mind a man – the thought had never entered his head. Now, he couldn't seem to kiss Viktor enough, and it was frustrating that they couldn't walk hand in hand together as other couples did.

"Ah," Fred conceded as Viktor pulled back, "perhaps that was a good choice. I wouldn't mind you doing it again now, though."

"It is your turn, I think," Viktor teased, and Fred pulled him back into his arms to press his lips to his mouth, his jaw, the side of his throat –

"Just going in to get a spade, mmhm, just a spade, that is all –" The unusual song gave them just enough time to break apart before Stefan swung the door open and reached for a spade without making eye contact. "Still here, Fred?"

"On my way out now. Just asking Viktor if he thought there'd be strawberries this year."

"Doubt it, we've not planted any. See you at dinner. Viktor, could use your help over on the corner plot."

Then he was gone, leaving them to exchange guilty looks.

"That was close," Viktor said, and then, "He must know. The song –"

"Warning us he was coming, I know. Good of him, though. He still can't know for sure. And it doesn't seem as if he'll tell anyone."

"No, he will keep our secret. Still, we must be careful." Fred nodded and picked up his crate of vegetables. "I ought to run back to the kitchen with these." He risked a brief kiss on the cheek, despite the open door of the shed, and smiled at the younger man. "See you at dinner."

"I look forward to it," Viktor told him, picking up a trowel and leaving the shed with a spring in his step. It didn't seem as if he was going to let their near miss upset or worry him, and Fred decided that he would strive to follow his example as he returned to his own work.

Their love wasn't easy, but it was too good to lose.

Eleanor Musgrove

Eleanor Musgrove is a recent graduate of the University of Kent, and the great-great-granddaughter of a civilian internee from the First World War. She is currently working towards publishing her first novel, and has many more tales to tell.

eamusgrove.wordpress.com

Break of Day in the Trenches

Outside, the storm raged. Not thunder and lightning, despite the sound and look of it, but iron and steel and high explosive. For all that, the air around them was warm and stale and motionless; if air could ever be stagnant, then this was. His face was pressed into the wool of his greatcoat sleeve, damp with the condensation of his own breath; the rest of him into the gritty, mud-laden rubble that had once been one wall of the dug-out. The body that lay on his back was also warm, and heavy. As if –

This is altogether not the time to think about – that. "Are you all right, sir?" he asked.

"Much to my surprise, I think I am. There's a beam or something across my shoulders, but no damage." A sudden heave of movement. "I might even be able to get off you, if I'm careful. Ah … Sergeant Carter, isn't it?"

He took a deep, rather shaky breath. "No, sir. Second Lieutenant Lewry, 13th Battalion East Surreys. Was the other man Sergeant Carter? Because if so – one of his hands is sticking out of this lot, but the rest of him is underneath. He's dead, I'm afraid."

The man above him grunted. "Damn. I mean, not about you –"

"I know, sir."

"He was a good man." The weight at Lewry's back slumped. "Captain Barnes, 11th King's Own. Captain Russell-Hansford-Barnes if you believe the Army List. Are *you* all right – Lewry, did you say?"

Be serious. But sometimes laughter was the only response he could muster that didn't involve screaming. "Crushed under the weight of your hyphens, sir."

There was a moment's silence; then a chuckle.

Lewry would have wriggled in embarrassment if he could. "I'm sorry, sir."

"Don't worry. It would help if something really could take our minds off this, wouldn't it?" The breathing in his ear intensified briefly. "I wonder whether I should try to move. It would be a shame to get half out and then have it all fall in again."

As if someone had been listening to his words, the air filled with the shriek of an eighteen-pounder. Their muscles tensed; they could not run, but it was something to be ready. The shell landed close by; earth and air shivered, and a scatter of gravel fell from overhead. Both men held still for a moment, then relaxed.

"Our own shells, too," said Lewry. "Serve us right for picking this time to come back over." His sleeve was beginning to chafe his face. The front of his uniform was soaked from hours of hasty crawling from one shell-hole to wait in another, head down, seeing nothing but the sergeant's boot-soles in front of his face, until the heavy fire had started and they had dived into the nearest offer of safety that there was.

"What were we supposed to do, walk all the way to Ostend and cross there?" Captain Barnes shifted again. "Serve the Boche right for taking us prisoner. But then, if I hadn't been so busy watching everything they did – and damn well they do it too – I might have thought of getting away earlier. And we wouldn't have been caught in this lot."

They lay there, not speaking. Something – sand? water? worse? – dripped like a ticking clock in the dark. The thunder of the barrage rolled over them, passed, returned, faded.

"I think they're losing interest," Lewry said.

"Good. Though I hope someone's still interested in the prospect of our return."

Before he could stop himself, Lewry said, "The machine awaits the return of the cog."

"I beg your pardon?" Captain Barnes said at last, rather stiffly.

Lewry opened his mouth, but he could have spoken no words even had he known what to say. *I never knew silence could feel like that.* He couldn't draw breath through the dense mask of his sleeve. Instead he coughed. "Nobody waiting for me, sir."

"I believe we might dispense with the sir, you know. And of course someone's waiting for you." There was a scuffing noise: a hand, unexpectedly, gripped Lewry's upper arm.

"Only the army. Or the bullet with my name on."

"Don't be –" But the captain didn't go on. "No family? Really?"

"Zeppelin. We lived on the third floor, but the whole house was destroyed. My mother was at home. Nothing left." Lewry pushed his head harder into the crook of his elbow.

"And – your father?"

"Joined up. Nothing else to do. All his money went. He kept it under the bed, you see. Besides – he's not interested in living without my mother." There was more than condensation on his sleeve now, but he had learned long ago to hide the tears from his voice. "I was their only one. They moved from Sussex to Croydon to send me to a better school, then university. And along comes the machine and chews me up."

"I'm sorry."

He sounds as if he means it. "Thank you. It's hard not to feel crushed, sometimes."

The hand gripped a little tighter, and withdrew. "Speaking of which – hold still a moment." Barnes breathed hard, and the weight on Lewry's back lifted a fraction. "Now, be honest. Are you *sure* you're not hurt?"

"Quite sure, s– Captain Barnes."

"Good. Because I might lean on you by accident, and if I can do that without worsening any damage I shall feel a lot happier."

For a few minutes there was noise of scuffing boots and sliding cloth, a rattle of soil and breath and creaking wood. Once a hand landed square between Lewry's shoulders, pushing him farther into the piled rubble, but a moment later the weight, all the weight, was gone.

"There. Can you sit up?"

"Yes, thanks." He pushed himself up on his arms, then twisted into a sitting position. He hadn't seen Barnes without his cap before; his hair, cropped short, gleamed like a horse chestnut in the – "Why," Lewry said. "It's still light outside. I thought we'd been in here longer." *Lord, he's good-looking.*

Captain Barnes was inspecting his watch. "So did I. But I'm embarrassed to say that my watch must have stopped quite some time ago, and I never noticed. So much for navigating by the sun." A smile twitched at the corner of his mouth, and then flattened. "*Damn.* If I had noticed – Carter might still be alive."

"Or something else might have had his name on." Lewry shifted round, so that he couldn't see the curled, dead hand where it projected from the fallen wall, and rubbed the damp grit from his face. "So have we been going along no man's land, instead of across it?"

"I'm afraid so; once we were through the wire, anyway." Captain Barnes sighed again. "I suppose this must be a Boche dug-out, then. I always heard theirs were better built than ours."

"That may have been true at the beginning, but our side has improved." *A man can get through a lot of dug-outs in nearly two years.* Lewry felt in the pockets of his greatcoat. "Oh, good. Brandy, sir?"

"If you're offering me brandy when I've led you into this mess, you should *certainly* stop calling me sir. My name's David." Barnes took the small flask, swigged a mouthful and screwed the cap on again. "Thanks. I hope I've left enough for you."

"As much as I need." Lewry drank, and coughed. "I'm still not used to it, but it does help. Er – my name is also David. I get called Lew, mostly. I ended up on the wrong side of the line a few days back, but nobody found the time to send me on to a camp." The flask was empty; he stowed it away again. "I believe my battalion was due to relieve yours later today."

"Thereby liberating us to roam the exiguous flesh-pots of Sailly La Bourse." Barnes chuckled. "I don't want to miss that. Shall we go, do you think?"

Lewry turned round and squinted into the light that poured down the truncated flight of steps. "Sun like a spotlight behind us; lovely target for the Boche, we'll be. Our lot won't see anything for the sun in their eyes, and they ain't keeping their fingers that careful on the trigger. If I may say so to a senior officer."

"Going by the book, you probably shouldn't, but in practice I'm glad you did." There was a pause. "I haven't been out here very long. I'm sure I did actually learn these things at Staff College, but in the stress of the moment –"

Is exactly when you shouldn't forget them. "You'll remember next time," Lewry said. He was not, himself, much given to asking personal questions, or answering them; but Barnes had caught him unawares, earlier. Now was the time to level the balance. "Have you got family, s- I'm sorry, I'd rather call you sir. Calling you David don't feel right."

"Oh. Well, if you're Lew … could you call me Russ, perhaps? You, ah, needn't pronounce the hyphens."

Lewry found himself startled into laughter. "All right. Russ."

"Good. And the answer to your question is, yes. Two parents and a sister, waiting for me in a sandstone Gothic horror in the deeps of Dorset, unless Fran has persuaded my dear mama to open the cage door and let her train as a nurse."

"Nobody else?"

"Nobody," Barnes said cheerfully. "You?"

"I already said."

"Of course. I'm sorry." The captain glanced in his direction. "Well. So. If we should wait till dark, I'll catch up on some sleep. Unless you think that's a bad idea."

"Don't let them know you asked a second lieutenant for advice. They'll laugh you out of court." Lewry watched the flush mount and fade on the captain's face. "I shouldn't have said that. I was about to ask if I might do the same. Of course it's a good idea, sir."

"Russ."

He shrugged. "Russ, then."

"Thanks, Lew. Sleep well."

And so Lewry did, for a few hours, before the nightmare woke him to a darkness full of the sound of his own pulse. He sat up, shivering, and wrapped his arms round his knees. At last his breathing slowed and the smell of mud and damp chalk grew less like the smell of death; but he could not banish the picture of the dead hand crawling away from the rubble on its own.

Beside him, Captain Barnes was sleeping quietly. Outside, a distant locomotive, on which side of no man's land he could not tell, trailed its disconsolate rumble across the night. The moon, in its last quarter, shone through a crack in the roof; the pale light washed all colour from clothes, skin and hair, turning khaki and flesh and chestnut to white and grey and black. Slowly, cautiously, Lewry brushed the back of his hand against the captain's hair; then he lay down and went to sleep again.

When he roused the night was only a little lighter, but enough to show him the captain peering at the back of one hand. "Morning, Lew. God, my knuckles hurt."

"You fetched that German corporal a hell of a punch before we ran. Do you want a dressing on it?" He felt in his pockets again. "My water bottle's still full, as well."

Barnes chuckled. "First brandy, now bandages. Medicinal comforts all round. You should be in the Corps." He fumbled in his own pockets. "I have my own water bottle, but I can offer an apple. Not much, but better than nothing. You have first bite."

"Thank you."

Their fingers touched briefly as the apple was passed from one to the other; they ate it, share and share about. Barnes took the core at last, and threw it over his shoulder. "Who knows? When all this is over, maybe there'll be an apple tree."

"I'd like to think so," Lewry said, smiling a little. "Here's the dressing – let's see your hand."

Barnes held it out. "None too clean, I'm afraid."

"You'll survive." Lewry taped the dressing and looked up. The smile widened to a grin. "I hope so."

"So do I. Actually, I more than hope so. Because if I don't, I shall spend eternity complaining to a higher authority about being redrafted before my time."

The dressing was finished, but Lewry did not let go the damaged hand. "That sounds more like Hell than Heaven. In fact it sounds pretty much like being in the army."

"You really don't like it, do you?"

Lewry did not look up. "Of course I don't. I should have been in Sussex, ploughing, if my father had had more sense. Or keeping accounts for some firm or other." He shrugged. "But never mind that. How do your knuckles feel?"

"Sore, but the better for being covered. Thank you. I hope my sister makes as good a nurse as you do, if she gets the chance."

"With all due respect, sir ..." *No, don't.* "It doesn't matter; forget I spoke."

Somewhere in the grey dawn a bird twittered hesitantly, and fell silent. Quietly, Captain Barnes said, "Lew."

"What?"

"You're still holding my hand."

"I know." He smoothed the dressing, very lightly. "I'll apologise if you want me to – Russ." At last he looked up.

Captain Barnes was smiling, very slightly. "Do I gather that you're not interested in my sister?"

74

"Meaning no offence. I'm sure she's wonderful." He swallowed. "Of course, I ought not to be interested in – anyone. Apart from anything else, there's a law against it and no chance and no privacy and I don't know why I'm saying this to you now, except that a yard in the wrong direction and I'd have been where Sergeant Carter is now, and to be honest it would be *bloody wonderful* to have – to know – someone was waiting for me. But forget I spoke. Forget forget forget, whenever you like."

"You're right about it all, of course. But I won't forget. What's more, I don't want to forget. Because – if there was the chance, and the privacy –"

"Stop. Stop right there." Lewry was breathing hard. "I don't so much as want to think about making plans until we're the right side of the right line. So let's go. Sir. If you don't mind. Before it gets any lighter."

"Yes. Of course." Barnes climbed the stairs slowly. He looked back over his shoulder and called down, "We're in luck. Fog. But I can hear bells."

"Church bells? How many?"

"Just two, and one of them cracked."

"Sailly, then. I hope the fog doesn't play tricks round here." Lewry scrambled up beside him, and listened. "Come on – this way."

"Sure?" Barnes whispered.

"Quite sure." He stepped off the top of the stairs, swung to his right and began to pick his way across no man's land. By some trick of the barrage, shells had fallen mainly in the dips in the rolling terrain; seen at this level, close at hand, the land was deceptively green under the low grey silence.

Captain Barnes caught up with him in a moment. Together, crouched low, half-running, but not so fast as to fall into unexpected wire or shell-holes, they picked their way over the hummocky grass. The fog was as thick as ever, but a gathering brightness spoke of daybreak, without revealing the exact point on the horizon where the sun rose. The bird that had sung so hesitantly earlier suddenly launched into full song.

"Who goes there?" A narrow, dark face barely to be seen below the parapet; a London voice startled to a high, questioning pitch, but still whispering. "And mind the rat, whatever you do. He'd bite King or Kaiser, that one." Even as he spoke a large, sleek and particularly dusty rat leaped over a splintered plank and disappeared into the grass. On the plank were two stems of poppies, petals scattered, the dust on them smudged by the dew.

"Friends. Captain Russell-Hansford-Barnes, to be precise. And Second Lieutenant Lewry, 13th East Surreys. Where should we come down?"

The man in the trench saluted. "Private Rosenberg 22311, sir. Glad to see you back." He was wearing a fresh poppy tucked behind his right ear. "Fire-step just along to your left, sir, best place to come over," he went on in a low voice. "The 13th are champing at the bit to come in, but Major Bromilow insisted on waiting for you. He was dead certain you'd fight your way back through any number of Germans."

"Did better with Lew here to help me, I can tell you that." Captain Barnes moved along the parapet, clambered down, and held up his unbandaged hand. "Come on, Lieutenant."

"Thank you, sir. I suppose I'd better ask for someone to link me up with my people."

"I suppose you had." Barnes looked up and down the trench. "They're all asleep, poor buggers. Hard night digging, I dare say. I'll take you along to Corbeau, he's our liaison officer."

They looked at each other. Private Rosenberg, a few yards along the trench, whistled mournfully over a bucket fire and a canteen of something that might eventually be tea, given a little faith and encouragement.

"This way." They walked away from the fire and the tea, through the communication trench, towards the reserve trench and Lieutenant Corbeau of the Armée de Terre.

"Almost there," Barnes said at last, and, as if by common consent, they stopped before turning the last corner.

"See you again," they said to each other. "See you again."

"If we only get the chance," Lewry whispered.

"We'll get it. I'll see to that." Barnes drew a deep breath, and stepped forward. "Lieutenant Corbeau, good morning. You know where the 13th East Surreys are? Excellent. Will you kindly escort Second Lieutenant Lewry that far? They'll be glad to see him, I hope."

They saluted each other and turned away, leaving the communication trench deserted except for the growing light and the shadow of poppies in the wind.

Only a live thing leaps my hand,
A queer sardonic rat …

Isaac Rosenberg
'Break of Day in the Trenches', June 1916

Jay Lewis Taylor

Despite having spent most of my life in Surrey and Oxfordshire, I now live in Somerset, within an hour's drive of the villages where two of my great-great-great-grandparents were born. Although I work as a rare-books librarian in an abstruse area of medical history, I am in fact a thwarted medievalist with a strong arts background.

I have been writing fiction for over thirty years, exploring the lives of people who are on the margins in one way or another, and how the power of love and language can break down the walls that we build round ourselves.

twitter.com/jaylewistaylor
jaylewistaylor.livejournal.com

Per Ardua Ad Astra

Lou Faulkner

30 June 1916

The guns had been firing almost continuously for a week now. The thunder and vibration went on, and on, and on, filling everyone with dread; only high in the air was there the slightest relief from it. Even here, the shells pursued them. Peter Mitchell kept a grim eye on the rest of 'A' Flight, and the wrecked earth of the Lines under the lower plane, watching for the flashes amidst the rolling smoke that meant that another shell was on its way. Meanwhile, he trusted his observer to protect them both, and somehow do the job that they were here for: to photograph this sector of the Lines for the brass twenty miles away.

At this height, the evidence of a big push in the offing was everywhere, though the columns of marching men moving up from the green fields to the churned hell of the trenches were lying low, since it was bright daylight. The ammunition trains had, for now, ceased bringing up supplies to the new gun emplacements that Mitchell – a former artilleryman – could easily recognise. But these things were happening on the other side of the Lines, too.

"The Hun's not stupid, he knows something's up," mused Mitchell, as he saw Hooper transfer his attention from the sky to the camera bolted onto the cockpit's side. Instantly Mitchell glanced up, then back over his shoulder, past the whirling propeller; roofed over by the top plane he could not see directly overhead. He counted the seconds until Hooper – Vince – would have changed the plate, flicked his gaze forward again and met a grin and a thumbs-up.

Another glance to either side. Yes, the two other tough ungainly machines of 'A' Flight were where they should be. Half a dozen black anti-aircraft bursts close on his right caused him to bank slightly, and then the formation turned to make its final run along the sector. Vince swayed with the tilt, and once they were flying level again, glanced back over the top plane. Their gazes met for the briefest instant; a smile just touched Vince's lips and Mitchell felt his own mouth quirk in response. Then they were back at their tasks, Mitchell keeping them in the air and watching for danger from below, and Vince watching the sky and taking the photographs that were the real reason for this patrol.

At last Vince yelled "Finished!" and stowed the final plate hastily in his cockpit.

Mitchell shouted, "Right, we're going home!"

He signalled to the other two machines to turn back, and as the formation changed course, Vince flung his arm up to the sun. The black archie died away.

Mitchell snatched for the Very pistol and sent up a light: the signal to circle. Vince was already standing on his cockpit coaming, obscuring Mitchell's view ahead, as a monoplane's shadow flashed above them and the top Lewis gun spoke. Bullets flicked through the top plane. Mitchell gritted his teeth, held the FE2b in an even bank for two seconds. Then Vince let go of the gun and slammed down into his seat again. A snatched glimpse of a Fokker plummeting sideways across his vision. Then the Fokkers – three of them – were gone. He glimpsed them far below, one blazing like a comet. They'd dived on the formation as it made its turn and run for home when it showed its teeth.

Vince was replacing the drum of ammunition, and the archie started up again, black evil-smelling smoke fifty yards ahead. Mitchell banked, twisted, and snatched quick glances to left and right. The two other Fees were still there, though one was trailing a thin plume of smoke. Andrews, the pilot, cut the engine and put the nose down. He'd make it over the Lines, all being well: it wasn't the urgent plunge of a machine about to become a fireball. Shapley on the other side signalled that he'd escort them to safety, side-slipped down to sit on Andrews' tail, and their flight-commander swerved again and set course for home with the all-important photographs.

Five minutes more and they were over the Lines, and Mitchell began picking up the landmarks for St-Matthieu Harcourt. There was the chalk-pit, the gun-emplacement that he could only see because he knew it was there; there was the cattle-wade, and Paternoster Wood, three large copses close-strung like beads along a stream. They were almost home. He skimmed a hedge, their shadow leaping it too, and came in to land on the home turf of 168 Squadron with scarcely a bounce, taxied to the apron in front of the hangars and switched off.

They sat for a moment in silence, drinking in the stillness, the lack of vibration, and, dear God, the safety of home. Then Mitchell took off helmet and goggles, half-stood and shrugged out of the bulky jacket and chucked it onto the concrete. Vince's joined it a moment later.

The air was warm and damp on Mitchell's face, after the chill of the upper air; somewhere high above, where they'd been just a few minutes ago, a skylark was singing.

"Your landing's improving," said Vince judiciously.

"Thank you, O gracious one." And Mitchell sketched a half-bow before clambering out onto the wing-step, from where he jumped to terra firma.

The first time he had come in to this airfield after his initial familiarisation flight, he had made one of the worst landings that ever a man walked away from. A sudden gust of wind, an up-draught from the line of trees that had not yet been felled, as the airfield was then so new; the squadron's old BE2c had been tossed up thirty feet and he'd tried to side-slip the height off instead of going round again.

"Bloody Australians!" his flight-commander had roared as he scrambled out from the twanging wires and creaking undercarriage of the all but undamaged machine – "D'you always have to fly upside down?"

After which he gathered his new chicks about him and took them into the Mess out of the cold wind and the snow underfoot, and over hot cocoa he explained the art of staying alive in the skies of France. Mitchell listened and took notes – literally, the habits of Oxford died hard – and went over those notes that same evening and put them into practice in the sullen dawn the next day.

Rawlinson was long gone, fallen to Immelmann, who had fallen in his turn just a fortnight ago, but Mitchell was still here, and Second-Lieutenant Vince Hooper had watched his progress from the lofty height of a week longer at the squadron; and at the end of the second month, they had gravitated towards each other and had flown together ever since.

"Not bad, for a colonial," reiterated Vince affectionately as they gathered up coats and photographic plates, while O'Keefe, their mechanic, started going over the Fee.

Then it was report-writing, in a quiet corner of the Mess. The table they used was their habitual one; as the longest-serving members of the squadron they had that privilege. Hampton, the steward, brought a pot of coffee without being asked, and for half an hour or so they were busy – *Left ground at 6 am. Wind light, gusting stronger, from the west. Cumulus at 5,000 feet. Possible gun emplacement, corner of Peacock Wood ... new communication trench ... attack by Fokker Eindeckers ...* It was a chore after a tiring patrol, but as always, Mitchell felt better after writing the experiences out.

Meanwhile there were sounds outside: the mechanics doing something which involved a lot of hammering. There was a sudden interruption as Len Andrews came in. Mitchell sat back and called out, "What happened?"

"Holed the tank, and someone else shot through a rudder-line, the bastard. If one of you hadn't been there – was it you?" He looked at Vince.

"It might have been."

"Well, thanks. You saved our bacon – and so did John and Clement. If it hadn't been for them covering us – they had engine trouble, they'll be in later –"

"What about Jacky?"

"He's all right, but he's got a broken leg. I got us down almost in one piece this side of the Lines, but went over the edge of a shell-hole. The machine's probably still arse-up in the mud, if it's not being used as target practice –" Len was garrulous, eyes sparkling with annoyance, his curly hair seeming to crackle with indignation. "I got a tender back, and Jacky's probably in a field hospital by now, surrounded by pretty nurses. He asked me to give you all his love, lucky devil." Jacky had been with the squadron three weeks, and was shaping up well.

"Good for him. Look, I'll order lunch; you need a bit of ballast after that, your report can wait."

"Lunch? I need a drink!"

"Not just now, Andrews." That was Captain Mitchell speaking, and Len subsided with ill grace, but was distracted by the appearance of John and Clement with a tale of their engine cutting out. They had made it back to 174 Squadron, then limped home, but had talked their mechanic into replacing the entire engine, hence the racket outside.

The five of them occupied the end of the long mess-table, and, over bacon and sausages and a pot of tea, relaxed a little. Mitchell sat back at last, with, he knew, a satisfied air. "That's more like it. Vince, I'm off for a kip. You?"

"Yes, I'm about ready. Len, glad you're back! – and you two, of course!" He slapped the lad on the shoulder, lightly – it had been a close shave for him – and together they left the long, raftered hut that was home for them all; or, Mitchell thought, you could call it a waiting-room.

The squadron, though it had been here six months, had no sleeping-huts yet. There were tents instead, set in Evensong Wood at the perimeter, dotted here and there as space allowed. Major Sansom had decreed that pilot and observer should share accommodation – "You need to be able to talk things through" – and Mitchell and Vince could attest that it helped. It was as peaceful there as anyone was likely to get, this close to the Front. There were even birds chirping among the branches.

"Too green," grumbled Mitchell. "Trees should be grey or blue, and have parrots in them." Three years he'd been in Europe, a year at Oxford and two in France, and it was still his perennial complaint.

"Not green enough. One day I'll take you to Sherwood Forest ..."

Cups of tea in hand, they ambled to their tent, which was set a little beyond a stand of holly, and put the cups down on the battered chest between the beds. Mitchell shifted the framed photograph from home a little to accommodate them: his elder brother, standing in front of the family's High Victorian mansion built with gold-rush money, wife at his side and little son in his arms (who they said was the image of his uncle, though Mitchell couldn't see any resemblance apart from the dark hair). Cavalry horses, the successors of the racehorses that had once lorded it over the property, and the black boys who looked after them, were visible in a paddock in the background.

Vince's photograph was taken in a studio, because his family didn't have the money to bring a photographer to their red-brick terrace, and who would want to anyway? His parents were posed beside a potted palm, and his two younger sisters were in a state of well-combed primness, which he said made it difficult to recognise them. Mitchell lay on his camp bed, his eyes on the trees visible through the open tent-flap, and said, "I'm sure Sherwood Forest would be improved by a few parrots," and Vince sleepily replied, "I'm sure it would."

That afternoon, Mitchell taxied their machine to one side of the apron and switched off. Vince scrambled up after him. O'Keefe handed up the Lewis guns, and left them to it. They regarded each other from a distance of a couple of feet.

"Hun above, five hundred feet, starboard. What do we do?" asked Mitchell.

"Zoom and turn." Vince tipped his hand up at an angle, stood up in his cockpit, and grabbed the upper gun.

"One, two, three!" Mitchell opened the throttle and kicked the rudder bar. "Four, five!" Vince grabbed the top Lewis gun. "Six!" And Vince sprang up on his cockpit rim, and swept the gun barrel from side to side. "Eight!" He was back in the cockpit, and Mitchell pushed the throttle forward and applied rudder again.

"We got him!"

The imaginary engine roar at Mitchell's back increased as he counted on, and zoomed again to shake any pursuers. They both scanned the sky: Mitchell below and in front, and Vince above them and to the rear, his fair unhelmeted head gleaming in the sun as he glanced from side to side.

"Fokkers attacking 'C' Flight!"

"One, two!"

The practice session continued; they went through their routines slick as any circus team, taking it in turns to call out the threats.

When they finished, Mitchell swept his fingers over the ignition, and he and Vince grinned at each other. "Home, sweet home."

"Good old St-Matthieu …"

There was a burst of applause below them. Startled, Mitchell peered round a strut and down. There was a group of four young men – no, boys just out of school – in neatly-pressed uniforms.

"Enjoy the show?"

"Good Lord, yes! I don't suppose you could run through it again, sir – or even just a part of it?" The speaker was from Yorkshire, Mitchell thought, surveying him benignly. This one might survive, since he was already asking questions.

"We will, but we'll explain what the Fee can do first. What's your name, sonny?" The boy was all of three years younger than Mitchell.

"Benson, sir."

"Well, Benson – and the rest of you –" He and Vince climbed out of their seats and jumped to the turf. "I'm a Hun, and Hooper here is one of you …" The two of them started making passes with their hands, demonstrating what each machine could and couldn't do, and the youngsters attended with fierce concentration. Then he took them to the Fees that would be theirs and ran them through some simple exercises, while a hundred yards away, 'B' Flight took off in a crescendo of engine noise.

Another of the newcomers – this one, Fortescue, had definitely been to Eton – had a camera with him, and at the end of the session he took photographs of his new comrades to send back to Mater and Pater. There was one of Mitchell and Vince, arms slung round each other's' shoulders and laughing into the lens.

It was a good afternoon: apart from the never-ending voice of the barrage.

The evening patrol, the third of the day, went well too; everyone came back, which had begun to happen more frequently now that Immelmann was gone. They only went a short distance over the Lines, and the Germans were, for the most part, keeping well below ground level, so the only artillery they had to worry about was their own – and indeed in the front cockpit the Etonian, Fortescue, became very thoughtful as shell after shell ripped past, some close enough to rock the Fee. But he took care with the photographs, noting down times and positions with great thoroughness while, from the front cockpit of Benson's machine, Vince guarded them; and Fortescue seemed to have absorbed Vince's instructions and watched, watched, watched the skies in between exposing the plates. Vince, twenty feet away, was standing in his cockpit, not on the coaming, not with a new pilot. Mitchell watched them all, splitting his attention half a dozen ways at once.

They were up for an hour, then turned to fight their way back against a wind that had begun to gust from the west, with the sun springing out from the stratocumulus now and then to dazzle them. Smoke raced over the hollows of no man's land; out of that smoke he could see, now the light was going, the greenish gleams of rifle-fire, while every so often a shell from the barrage tore past, or black puffs of archie exploded on either side without warning. The air was mercifully clear of Fokkers.

The Lines behind them, they were back over fields and little woods and farmhouses. Fortescue relaxed, turning to grin up at his captain, who thumped the fuselage – "Keep watching!" he yelled, and the lad jumped and resumed his guard. A few minutes later, Mitchell spotted Paternoster Wood up ahead in the dusk, bumped over it, and nudged the stick forward. Two more copses, the hedge, and the turf of the landing-field tilted up to meet them. Fortescue braced himself – Mitchell thought, "He's got his eyes closed, I'll bet!" – and the machine touched, barely bounced, touched again and rolled to a halt.

"Are you still with us, Mr Fortescue?" he enquired mildly, pulling off helmet and goggles.

"Ah. Yes."

"Good man. But don't ever relax until we're back on the ground."

"No, sir." He was chagrined, for sure, but he'd remember the lesson. Mitchell opened the throttle slightly once more, and took the machine to the apron.

It was getting chilly, and the wind had picked up, so Mitchell climbed down, coat and all. O'Keefe came up, followed by the small tan-and-white form of Florentina, the squadron dog, and Mitchell exchanged a few words with him. Vince and Benson joined them, and the four of them made their way over to the Mess, and shut the door on the noise of the barrage.

After dinner and a sing-song, there was an energetic game of rugby in the Mess that night. The CO and his senior officers played whist with a fierce concentration while the action roared up and down the hut, passing barely a yard from their table. Florentina took refuge in one of the armchairs that had been pushed to the wall, and after a few minutes, Mitchell said, "It's time we turned in, do you think?"

"I'm too old for this. Let's go!"

They left the mess-hut, letting the door swing closed on the uproar, and strolled past the hangars, arm in arm, to Evensong Wood. It was a clouded night, light rain and no moon, and they paused on the edge of the wood and turned to the east. The dark horizon was punctuated by the periodic flick and stab of searchlights.

"Poor buggers." Vince swept his hand along the horizon, taking in with impartial sympathy the men in the trenches, the grounded balloons, the scattering of night-scouts.

"Poor us, come tomorrow."

"Yes."

They reached their tent and set the candle on the chest of drawers. "Which bed?"

Mitchell considered the draught that found its way in through the fastening of the tent. "Mine, I think."

A weary undressing, and Vince blew the candle out, and climbed in with him. They clung together. Vince put his nose into the warm space between Peter's neck and shoulder; Peter's own nose was tickled by that fair, floppy hair.

"Good set of lads today. Benson's a decent pilot," mumbled Vince.

"Yes, they might last longer than last week's." Peter's breath caught. "Oh God, Vince. The big push is coming soon. I've got to lead them into the thick of it."

"I know. I know. I've got you."

They wound their arms tight around each other and stayed like that for a full minute, then Peter relaxed. "Sorry, Vince."

"If we go, it'll be together. There's that."

"Yes. There's always that."

Eventually they slept.

Once, Peter cried out in his sleep, clutching at Vince to stop him from falling, falling from his stance on the coaming of the Fee's front cockpit; but that wasn't unusual. It was that little incident that had brought them together, after all, and Vince still maintained that he could have scrambled back to safety without Peter's desperate grab and iron hold: though that wasn't what he had said right after Peter had nursed the stricken Fee down to land in a field.

Such night-time cries were not entirely uncommon in the tents of Evensong Wood.

1 July 1916

Their batman woke them with a respectful "Mr Mitchell, Mr Hooper," from outside the tent, and a few moments later, a couple of mugs of hot coffee appeared through the tent flaps. Vince grunted, "Thank you, Stevens," and reached out a wiry arm from his camp bed to take them. Mitchell struck a match and lit the lantern, and they consumed their coffee in gulps while dressing.

In company with the other flying officers, they trudged across the dark hazy aerodrome (a half-moon showing to the east, Mitchell noted automatically) to the briefing room to hear today's orders: which were to bomb, and strafe, and – "This is it, isn't it?" asked Andrews, and Major Sansom said, "Yes. This is it."

The Fees were already lined up on the apron when they emerged, and O'Keefe and the other mechanics were arming bombs and fitting them to the bomb-racks. Mitchell and Vince glanced at each other, shrugged and clambered up to their cockpits. Flying together, this time, leading the squadron, since *this was it*. The lights from the squadron sheds cast their radiance over the misty apron, sending leggy shadows out to people the perimeter in the pre-dawn darkness. Over there to the east the searchlights still flickered and swung now and then.

Behind Mitchell, O'Keefe swung the propeller. Once, twice, and the engine caught; all along the line of machines the roar was echoed. O'Keefe ducked under the boom and away, and Mitchell took the Fee out onto the grass, and taxied to take-off position. The ground-mist covered the aerodrome, but he could see Mars shining sullenly through it. Higher up was Capella. There was Pegasus, flying high. Away beyond the Lines, the sun was climbing to the horizon.

It was time to be off. Vince turned his helmeted head back for a moment; each gave the other a private smile. Then Mitchell opened the throttle. The Fee sped across the grass. A longer run than usual, but she was carrying a heavy load, of bombs and ammunition.

Then the air took her, and she was up, eager, through the mist; climbing towards the stars, climbing towards the light.

Lou Faulkner

I live in a little house with a big garden in the far south of the world, and most of my life has revolved around books: selling them, lending them out, and more recently, writing them. Apart from bibliophilia, I've done a variety of different things, including years spent learning falconry, and I enjoy trying hands-on pursuits that might give me material for my stories: blacksmithing, tall-ship sailing and flying. I will attempt things in my writer's persona that I would never contemplate as myself: this does not, however, extend to bungy-jumping.

Notes

There is a photo in the Wikipedia entry for the Royal Aircraft Factory F.E.2, about a third of the way down the page, that inspired this story. I took one look and thought, "Dear God, did they really fight like that?" And they did.

en.wikipedia.org/wiki/Royal_Aircraft_Factory_F.E.2

The Man Left Behind

Eleanor Musgrove

Henrietta Lawson had mixed feelings about her first name. On the one hand, it didn't suit her and she hated it. On the other hand, it did make a few things easier.

"Henry," she'd told people, when she started her first job after leaving school. "Call me Henry. I can't stand Henrietta." Some of the customers of that little village shop had been more accommodating than others in that respect.

"Oh, but Henry's a boy's name, dear," her Auntie Meg from down the road had told her, "and Henrietta's a beautiful name. Young girls these days are always shortening their names, for some reason."

Henry had handed over the bag of items her aunt – her mum's friend, really – had bought and gave her her very sweetest smile. "Thank you. Have a good day, Auntie Margaret."

The older woman had pursed her lips disapprovingly, but made no complaint as she left. Henry had lost her job to the return of the owner's newly-widowed daughter not a year after the incident.

That had been the beginning of the war, the war they'd all thought would be over by Christmas, despite the knowledge that it had already changed a local family for ever. Now, however, it had been going on for two years, and more men than ever had left their sleepy little home. Many, Henry knew, would never come back. She wasn't sure whether she was relieved not to have to go out to fight and die in the trenches, or humiliated and frustrated by being one of the few men left behind.

Of course she knew that Henrietta was a girl's name, and she knew that she was, at least in appearance, a woman – she was treated to a lovely reminder of the fact every month, after all – but the truth was that she had never really felt like a woman. Even as a child, she had delighted in running off into the fields with the boys to play tag and climb trees. Sometimes, when she was very little, she used to borrow a pair of Peter's shorts and scoop her hair under a flat cap in order to make sure the lads included her; eventually,

91

she'd had to give that up due to parental scoldings, and had settled for arguing her way into the boys' games despite her feminine attire. The only concession she had won to her true self, to the way she felt inside, was becoming known as Henry.

She'd always thought that Peter was lucky, growing up – he'd got to play at being a builder and carpenter in his younger years, while she was stuck scrubbing floors and washing clothes. Then her older brother had been called away to war, and Henry had wanted to go with him.

"No, Henry, you can't," he'd told her, when she'd mentioned her intention to enlist.

"I should be out there, the same as all the other men –"

"I know," he interrupted. Peter, of all people, had always listened to her and seemed to understand the fundamental difference between how she looked and who she was. "I know, but Henry … the medical examination. There's no way … they won't let you."

She faltered; she hadn't thought of that. "But who will watch your back?"

Her brother had sighed. "I'll have my friends. But I need you to look after our parents for me. Promise?"

She nodded. "Don't get killed."

"I'll do my best."

He'd marched off to war just a few days later, but before he left he'd pulled her aside.

"I've spoken to Mr Dixon. He's too old to come with us, and he needs some young people to help him on the farm. Strong people. I put in a word for you, told him you're as strong and hard-working as any boy. You go up there and talk to him, they're all talking about taking on women as labourers now. They'll take you, too. Proper man's work." He'd hugged her to cut off her profuse thanks, told her to borrow anything of his she needed while he was away, and then before she knew it he was gone.

Mr Dixon hadn't been sure about hiring her at first, but he couldn't deny he was short-handed. Henry was the first female – though she rankled at the label – to be offered work on Dixon's farm, but she hadn't been the last. Peter's old boss seemed pleased with her work, and raised no objection when Henry pointed out that skirts weren't the most practical attire for farm labouring and asked if he'd mind her wearing trousers instead. Taking her brother at his word, she borrowed a couple of pairs of his old trousers – he'd no doubt have grown out of them by the time he came home, so she took the liberty of altering them to fit her properly – and wore them proudly to work the next day. She made sure to work twice as hard as usual, and old Mr Dixon nodded approvingly. Soon, many of the girls were following her example, though they were all clearly a little uncomfortable in the male attire. Henry made non-committal noises of agreement whenever they complained about it, afraid to admit that this was what she should have been wearing all along.

Rosie changed all that. Working together in the fields one day, the girl had told her that she was getting used to the trousers – itchy though hers apparently were. "How about you, Henry, are they growing on you yet? Dead practical, you have to admit, and they really suit you."

Henry had shrugged. "Always felt more like a bloke anyway. About time I got to wear the clothes." She'd looked up, startled by her own admission, to find Rosie watching her with simple curiosity rather than malice.

"So … you feel like a man? What does that feel like?"

Henry shrugged. "Difficult. As if my body … it doesn't quite fit right, it doesn't look the way it should. I feel like … like a man, in here." She pressed a hand to her heart. "I know you'll think that's wrong."

"You're not the only one who's ever felt wrong. But knowing that you feel that way … it makes me feel better. Is that a horrible thing to say?"

Henry frowned at her. "No. Why does it – ?"

But Rosie only blushed, a pretty pink colour tingeing her cheeks, and turned away to return to her work. That was well enough, Henry supposed. Girls should be allowed to have their secrets, after all, and there was plenty to be done.

For all the other girls she could have spent time with while working on Dixon's farm, Henry found herself working alongside Rosie almost every day. It was Rosie who seemed to catch Henry's eye and smile, Rosie who Henry sought out. She found herself watching the other girl cross the farmyard more often than not, seeking out the opportunity to brush their fingers together as Rosie handed her a mug of tea. Henry knew that the female form was attractive to her – it only made sense, in her mind, given all her other masculine inclinations – and she also knew that society would never allow her to court a woman, let alone take a wife. Not that she wanted to *marry* Rosie; they were just friends, could only ever be friends. So when

Rosie glanced over her shoulder one day and caught Henry staring, Henry looked away, stubbornly ignoring the way the other girl's cheeks turned pink once more. Rosie might be the first person Henry had ever truly considered bringing flowers to, but she could never know, and would never feel that way in return. Rosie couldn't even bear to meet her gaze without turning red, it seemed.

It wasn't until several weeks later that Henry finally got to find out what the blushing was all about. Humming merrily as she wandered into the cowshed with a pitchfork ready to clean the place out, she was surprised to hear Rosie call her name from just outside the doorway. By the time she turned, the other girl had already stepped inside. Henry swallowed hard, trying to ignore the attraction she'd found developing for her friend over recent weeks. She'd always been able to tell Rosie everything, things she'd never have dreamed of telling anyone else, but recently she'd had to keep something from her. The girl was beautiful, there was no denying that, at least in Henry's eyes, but the more they talked – thrown together in a way they never had been – the more she realised they had in common. If Henry had been in the body she deserved, she thought they would probably have been courting by now. At least, they would have if Henry had had her way. *His* way, as it would have been. But that was just idle wishing, and that did nobody any good.

"Is it news from Peter?"

Rosie shook her head. "No, I'm sorry. I'm sure he'll write soon. You'd have heard by now if anything had happened … No, I just wanted to talk to you." She picked up the wheelbarrow abandoned by the door and moved closer as Henry began to shovel muck into it. There was no time to be idle on the farm, and Henry didn't trust herself to meet the other girl's eyes for fear of revealing improper feelings.

"What's on your mind?"

Rosie hesitated. "You," she admitted at last. "I mean … what you told me about being Henry really, not Henrietta … Was that true?"

"Only on the inside, sadly," Henry confirmed, still afraid to meet her eyes, but now for entirely different reasons. Had Rosie decided that she was disgusted after all? Even Henry sometimes found herself feeling like an abomination against the laws of God and man, cursing her body for being wrong, cursing herself for being wrong for it. She was stuck with herself;

Rosie wasn't. Working together or not, she could cut off that friendship in a heartbeat.

"... I thought I was unnatural. I didn't understand how I could feel this way."

At that, Henry paused to lean on the end of her pitchfork, regarding her warily. "Which way is that? You feel like ... a man, too?"

Rosie laughed, that lovely blush covering her freckled cheeks once again. "No. No, I just ... Goodness, I'm being so forward, I – You'll think me silly."

"Of course not. We're friends, aren't we? You can tell me anything."

Rosie took a deep breath, then nodded. "You're right. Well ... I, er, I met someone. Someone I really like."

It took a moment for the emphasis to hit home, and Henry felt her grip tighten on the pitchfork, bitter frustration and disappointment coursing through her body. She did her best not to show it as she spoke. "Oh? Who's the lucky fellow?"

"Well, that's just it ... I thought – that is, everyone thinks he's a woman." She lowered her eyes to fix her gaze on the straw beneath her feet. "That is ... I thought I was falling for another woman, but you're a man in a woman's body, and it makes sense, I suppose, but people would never accept –"

"Me? You like *me*?"

Mortified, Rosie nodded, blushing ever deeper.

Henry couldn't let her think she'd done wrong, not for a moment longer. She reached out and touched her arm gently, causing her to look up. "Even ... as I am? You could feel that way for me?"

"Exactly as you are," Rosie told her sheepishly, "but I under-"

Henry leant forward, acting without thought for propriety or common sense, and kissed Rosie bashfully on the cheek.

Only when Henry stepped back, appreciating the way Rosie's lips had curled up into a slightly flustered smile, did Henry remember where they were. "Well ... this is romantic."

Rosie blinked, startled out of her slight daze, and cast a look around herself at the filthy cowshed before laughing. "I suppose we could have picked a better place for this."

"And what is this?" Henry asked, hoping against hope that the answer wasn't 'a mistake'.

"... The start of something?" Rosie looked as hopeful as Henry felt, and

Henry had never felt better or more comfortable in her life.

"Yes. Only the start."

Rosie grinned and mumbled something about finding another pitchfork, leaving with a distinct spring to her step.

With a smile, Henry turned back to her task and began shovelling again.

Eleanor Musgrove

Eleanor Musgrove is a recent graduate of the University of Kent, and a one-woman word machine at least one month out of the year. She is currently working towards publishing her first novel, and has many more tales to tell.

eamusgrove.wordpress.com

Notes

With thanks to Alex Jacobs, whose help in beta reading for me was invaluable.

And with apologies if any reader is offended by the pronouns in this story; they are as they are in an attempt to seem true to the time.

Hallowed Ground

Charlie Cochrane

For those who still lie in the corner of some foreign field.

There was me, the padre and a packet of Black Cats. And bugger all else except the pitch dark night. Me, the padre and a packet of Black Cats we didn't dare light any of, because the Germans might have spotted the glow and that would have been that.

I wasn't even supposed to be there, but I guess neither of us were. He'd been out to take church parade for the lads and wanted to return to base so he could do the same for another poor group of sods the next day. I'd given him a lift from the casualty clearing station, and we were both heading back, when a shell took a fancy to the piece of ground just to the left of us, the little strip we'd played cricket on just two weeks previously, before the Germans moved further forward. Up went me, the padre, the car and all, including Stevens, the poor injured lad we were taking back with us. The lad who was at present scattered all over the field, with his legs at third slip and his head lolling around square leg, if you follow me.

The padre was pretty cut up about it: he'd not long been in France and nothing he'd heard or read had prepared him for the reality of modern war. He wanted to bury Stevens there and then but he'd have ended up getting the three of us buried.

I got him settled into an old shell hole. At least, I got his body settled, because his mind took a bit longer. He kept saying that Stevens would have survived if we'd stayed put, but that was just the shock talking. I know that; I'm a doctor. That's how I also know that Stevens would have had no chance if we hadn't moved him and a pretty slim one even if we'd got him back. That's why we'd taken the shorter way – my decision – because time was one thing Stevens didn't have. I got that through to the padre eventually, but he was still uneasy. Maybe he was guilty that he'd survived and Stevens hadn't. It happens.

Me, the padre and the Black Cats. Until I noticed my pack, which by

99

some miracle had been thrown through the air and landed – pretty well intact – about twenty feet from where we were. I reckoned I could crawl over and get it, so long as I stayed quiet. There didn't seem to be any of the enemy out on night patrol, but the padre wouldn't have it.

"It's not worth the risk," he said, "whatever's in there."

"You might not think that come the middle of the night when you'd be grateful for a wee drop from my hip flask. Think of it as medicinal," I added, because you never know with these clergy types. Some of them seem to think Jesus turned the water into wine so everybody could wash in it. "I've got some chocolate creams, too."

That seemed to settle the matter, although halfway across those twenty feet – which felt like a hundred yards – hearing a nearby crump made me wonder if I shouldn't have argued. Although I suppose if your number's going to come up it can happen as easily in a hole as in the open. I kept going, grabbed the bag and headed back. The look of relief on the padre's face, seen by a Very light's timely illumination, was a picture. You'd have thought I was the Archangel Michael himself, come to bear him up to safety on a fiery chariot or something.

I got myself comfortable again, comfortable being a bit of a loose term given the circumstances, and broke out a bit of the chocolate. The rest would have to be rationed out. He had a canteen of water and we both had our greatcoats, so all in all it wasn't so bad. Stevens would have been glad to swap his conditions for ours. I remembered the padre had mentioned playing a bit of cricket, and thought it might help him if we chatted about it. Quietly, of course, although there was plenty of noise to cover our whispers. It turned out we'd played some of the same teams, before the war put an end to all sorts of innocent fun. We'd faced some of the same bowlers, been smote hip and thigh by them. I was proud of that joke, and he'd laughed at it, but not even talking sport was helping him keep calm.

I suggested we try to get a wink of sleep, because it wasn't going to make a scrap of difference to whether we survived the night, although I didn't tell the padre the last bit. I doubt he'd spent the night under fire before.

The shells kept falling, on and off. Now closer, now further away. And while I managed to grab a bit of sleep in between them – I've always had the ability to drop off at will – the padre was as stiff as a board. In my profession, you get to see plenty of men at the extremity of their life, men who want to find some solace before they go to their long home. It's not quite the absolution of the confessional, divesting themselves of a secret they've carried a long while. You get to recognise the look they wear. The padre must have known that look, too, from his profession. I wondered if he also knew he had it plastered all over his face then, and whether he was hoping I'd take the hint.

"If you can't sleep, at least try to relax," I whispered. "It'll be a long time till dawn and it'll go no faster if we worry ourselves through it. Have faith." I hoped he could see my grin, especially if he thought his number had come up. What was it he wanted to get off his chest?

"I have faith. I didn't realise how easily frayed it could get under such circumstances." He sounded as if he was trying to be chipper, hiding a deep fear. I'd heard that tone of voice in others, too.

"Nip of whisky help?"

"No. Keep it for when we really are *in extremis*." He managed a laugh with that. "I suppose you're used to this sort of situation?"

"Not exactly. I normally spend the night under some sort of cover." I *had* passed long hours similarly, but I didn't want to admit the fact. He'd have asked questions and it didn't make for an edifying tale.

He was quiet for a while, and I almost dozed again, but a still, small, unsteady voice, which I bet he never used from the pulpit or lectern, said, "Have you ever had the feeling these will be your last hours?"

"No. Never." It was an honest answer. I'd heard of men being sure they were "for it" and that prophesy coming true the next day, but my belief was that the feeling contributed to the outcome. Maybe if they'd convinced themselves that the end was nigh, they were more reckless in action or something like that. Psychology had never been my strongest suit.

"You're fortunate." I didn't need to ask the padre what was on his mind: his voice made it plain.

"They're nothing to be ashamed of, those thoughts," I said, for want of anything more comforting to say. "And they don't always come true. I know people who think every day is their last." That might have been stretching the truth. "One day they'll be right, I suppose, but they'll have had a miserable time of it up till then."

"Yes. Yes, I suppose it's the worst thing, lacking courage."

"I wouldn't say it's a matter of courage." Not as I'd understood it in the past. "I suspect that the most courageous men are the ones who are most scared, but who still go up that ladder or into that wood, braving the unknown in the cause of duty, despite their misgivings and fears."

The padre chuckled. A nervous, constrained chuckle but one nonetheless. "I seem to have found myself in a shell hole with a philosopher. Who'd have thought it?"

"I'd never have guessed I'd be spending the night with a man of the cloth." I stopped, suddenly agonising over whether I'd invested that joke with any hint of another, more private, more uncomfortable meaning. I hoped he'd take it at face value, although I didn't find out immediately, because an exchange of bullets and a ghastly scream, maybe half a mile away but clear as a bell in a night which had turned deathly quiet, focused our minds on things other than jokes.

"Do you think that was one of the lads at the service?" he asked, eventually.

"It came from the right direction, but there's no way of telling at the moment."

"Yes, of course." His voice had a wavering edge, again. "They all seemed so young."

"Too young," I agreed. No point in trying to deny the obvious. "At least, though, if it was one of them they'd not have died unshriven." Confession, absolution, comfortable words – they'd all been included in the service, which had been surprisingly simple and suitable to the troops' needs. Whatever else was bothering the padre, he should have felt proud of what he'd done for them. I told him so.

"That was just doing my duty, as they do theirs. Nothing particularly special, in the circumstances." He went quiet again for a while, eventually breaking the silence to say, "Do you think it makes such a difference? To die when you've just received absolution?"

That was a whole other debate, to be had with earnest fellow students late at night over cocoa or port. What man or woman ever died in such a state? Who could go from one day's end to the next without making a mess of things somewhere along the line? And in this particular *line*, it was an hourly occurrence. We didn't exactly offer Fritz the left cheek when he smote us on the right.

But it struck me that his question had seemed more personal than theological, and it needed a personal answer.

"I believe that you have to commit yourself into God's hands and believe His mercy's greater than we'd be inclined to dish out, were we the COs for the operation."

"I do that every day, believe me. I pray it's enough."

What did he have on his conscience that was worthy of such contrition? I wondered if he might even have murdered somebody, given the sombre tone of his voice. Surely it couldn't be that bad?

"Would it help to talk? I know that a problem shared isn't always a problem halved."

He laughed, bitterly. "Sometimes it's a problem doubled."

"It's your choice." It didn't always help to air one's baggage, but in this case it felt like the right treatment. "I promise I'll regard anything you say as coming under medical confidentiality."

"Does medical confidentiality cover immorality?"

"I expect it does." I had plenty I could have said about immorality – or what people termed immoral.

Had he been committing adultery with the verger's wife?

"Hmm." He must have been mulling things over – you could almost hear the wheels of his mind turning, grinding his emotions small – until another explosion, closer this time, seemed to decide things for him.

"I have these desires." This wasn't the quietly confident, reassuring voice he'd used during the service. "Sinful desires. I don't put them into action, but they gnaw at me." He swallowed hard. "Even now, even here, at the end of all things."

"You don't know if it's the end. It's like young Stevens: only God would know if he'd have survived the journey, anyway." If it were possible for a man to die of despair, the padre sounded as though he was heading in that direction.

"If it *were* the end, I'd die happier if I could tell you about things. You'll detest me."

"Really? How bad can these temptations be?"

"How bad? The unforgivable sin, perhaps. I want other men. To lie with them."

I had to bite my tongue, the temptation to say, "Is that all?" being so strong.

He continued. "It's terrible enough for any man to be consumed with such desires, but for a man of the cloth …"

I bit my tongue again. So much I could have said, so much I had to keep in. I wanted to tell him that I understood, that I shared his inclinations, although I didn't feel the burden on me so much. I'd been extremely fortunate in the character – and discretion – of my lovers. I wanted to say that he shouldn't fret so much, that plenty of men, good, decent men, felt as he did, and still kept their faith intact. But that would have sounded platitudinous, if not downright callous. Every man's conscience is his own and makes its own demands.

Yet I had to say something, and fast, or he'd think I was disgusted. I tried, "I've always believed there are worse things a man can feel."

"Really?" He sounded surprised.

"Of course. I fail to see how your desires hurt anyone, apart from yourself."

"But you know that scripture says it's wrong."

Scripture. That was a red rag to this particular bull.

"No point in quoting scripture at me if it's any place in the Book previous to Matthew." I tried to keep a civil tongue and a level head. The Old Testament got used too often to defend the indefensible. "These feelings of yours. Do they make you judge where you shouldn't judge, or cast the first stone? Or anything else which is *really* wrong?"

"No, I suppose they don't." The uncertainty in his voice belied his words. "But I can't ignore the traditional teachings. I'm a clergyman."

"Yes, I see that. Caesar's wife should be above suspicion." I remembered a particular clergyman I'd once spent the night with: we'd got as little sleep as the padre and I were having *that* night although the reasons had been much more enjoyable. *He* hadn't been particularly bothered by Leviticus. "I'm not sure how you've coped, though. It must be hell."

More like hell than even this place was. At least the men were given regular periods of withdrawal from the line and the chance of leave if they survived to enjoy it. You couldn't get a rest from your thoughts and desires; I knew that for myself. It was time for that nip of whisky. I expected him to sip the tot I poured him but he knocked it back like a hardened veteran.

He said, "The answer's not in this, I know that from experience, but I do appreciate the comfort it brings. Thank you."

"That's all right." I wished I could offer him some more substantial comfort, but all I had was more whisky – which didn't seem a good idea – and words. "Desires of themselves aren't anything to be ashamed of. Even the Lord was tempted in the wilderness. It's what you do with them that makes the difference."

And even then, there were degrees of difference. I'd never countenance murdering a man in cold blood, but if the Germans were attacking the hospital I'd not think twice about picking up a gun to defend my patients.

"Perhaps," he said, then went quiet again. I shut my eyes, thinking of my lovely young curate who'd lit up the last April bar one. I made sure my greatcoat was drawn close to me, in case my body reacted at the suddenly vivid memory.

Later – half an hour, an hour, two hours, I couldn't tell – the padre said, "Perhaps I should have given in to these desires. Given in, confessed, allowed myself the chance of absolution. Then I wouldn't risk dying not knowing."

"Not knowing what?" I replied, still half stunned from sleep and only realising as I spoke, how I'd encouraged him onto dangerous ground.

"Not knowing what it would be like to realise those desires. Whether it would be the door to hell or the door to heaven." He shuddered, evidently horrified at his own confession.

I could have given him an honest opinion on that. Whether I had the courage to do so was another thing. Funny how I could face the shelling but was still reluctant to bare my soul, even though we might have been at the end of all things. His shivering helped make up my mind. I put my arm around his shoulders, and drew him closer, a conscious drawing of our bodies together rather than the forced proximity we'd already shared.

"If you want an opinion that's neither medical nor theological," I said, going into action, if only metaphorically, "I'd say that it all depends on the quality of your lover. And whether it means something or whether it's just to scratch an itch. Like the men seem to want to scratch all their itches when they get into town."

He leaned into the hug. "Are you saying that from experience?"

I swallowed hard. No going back now. "I am."

"Would it be impertinent to assume that it's directly relevant experience?"

"It isn't. Rude," I added, just to clarify. "I know the feelings you speak of. The only difference is that I've not fought them. Not since I learned how to give in to them gracefully."

A distant explosion – the first there'd been in a while – punctuated the calm of the night. Perhaps it was going to be the start of a barrage, supposedly clearing the way for a surge forwards at dawn. In which case, I thought, maybe I should offer the padre a chance of eliminating that risk of dying *not knowing*. I supposed you could do it in a shell hole by dark as effectively as in a bedroom with white linen sheets, but I reckoned that would put him off for life.

So I just took his hand in mine: it felt slender, full of sinewy strength.

"If we make it through tonight, remember this. If we make it through the next few months or years or heaven knows what, remember this." I felt the pressure of his fingers on mine. "When this bloody war is over, then please find me. We'll carry on this conversation. I'll give you my honest opinions. You can trust me, I'm a doctor."

A convenient Very light lit up the sky, and the padre's face. I'd never understood what beatific might really mean until I saw his smile, then. He wasn't bad-looking to start with but in that illumination he was beautiful. I couldn't have done anything but kiss him, could I?

He leaned into it, then broke away, his smile rueful now. "Thank you."

"My pleasure." I ran my fingers down his face, along his jaw. "Shame we didn't meet back in Blighty, before this bloody thing blew up."

"I have to disagree." He took my hand again. "I'd have run a mile. This business focuses the mind."

"It does." Time for another nip of that whisky and a bit more chocolate. That was the safest way forward, given that the faint light in the sky couldn't still be the lingering rays of the Very light, and must be the herald of dawn. I raised my flask to make a toast. "Home. Beauty. A clear mind and a clear conscience."

"All four." He drank after me, our fingers touching again on the little flask. "It's a mess, isn't it?"

"A bloody nightmare," I agreed. "Still, it doesn't sound like we're getting a barrage today. Maybe we can even grab a gasper in a while. The sky's brightening."

"I should say Morning Prayer," he said, patting the pocket where he carried his missal.

"We'll say it together. My patients could do with a word put in for them

106

and I wouldn't refuse a bit of comfort, too."

He must have started saying the words mainly from memory, as the light was still a touch too dim to read by. I joined in where I could, the familiar words even more applicable given our situation.

O Lord, our heavenly Father, Almighty and everlasting God, who hast safely brought us to the beginning of this day: Defend us in the same with thy mighty power; and grant that this day we fall into no sin, neither run into any kind of danger; but that all our doings may be ordered by thy governance, to do always that is righteous in thy sight; through Jesus Christ our Lord.

When he reached the end, we sat in silence, sharing the last of the chocolate, until the sound of an approaching vehicle put us back on guard, but it was only one of our lads, sent out to find us. I gave the padre's hand a final squeeze, and a whispered, "When the war's over, find me. Remember?"

"I'll remember."

"We thought you were all goners, sir," the driver said, as he came to a stop and just remembered to salute.

"Only poor Stevens. They've not beaten me yet," I said, hitching up my pack and waiting as the padre got into the car. "Anyway," I tipped my head in his direction, "I had an advantage. That foxhole was hallowed ground."

The padre looked at me, as if he was about to argue, then broke into a grin. "Hallowed ground indeed."

Charlie Cochrane

As Charlie Cochrane couldn't be trusted to do any of her jobs of choice – like managing a rugby team – she writes, with titles published by Carina, Samhain, Bold Strokes, MLR, Riptide and Lethe.

She's a member of the Romantic Novelists' Association, Mystery People, International Thriller Writers Inc and is on the organising team for UK Meet for readers/writers of GLBT fiction. She regularly appears with The Deadly Dames.

facebook.com/charlie.cochrane.18
twitter.com/charliecochrane
goodreads.com/author/show/2727135.Charlie_Cochrane
charliecochrane.livejournal.com
charliecochrane.co.uk

A Rooted Sorrow

Adam Fitzroy

These days, when Mrs Mercer's nerves were strained to breaking-point, Miss Woakes was often the only company she could bear. When Miss Woakes came to the cottage they would drink tea and talk about their gardens, their knitting, Church – in short, any subject but the one uppermost in both their minds.

"Mrs Jessup looks tired," said Miss Woakes, one Thursday in August. They were in Mrs Mercer's tiny, faded parlour; outside the window, past the towering hollyhocks, the pale brick village slept in the sunshine like a basking cat. "It's such a long way there and back every weekend – and it's not as if she didn't have her hands full the rest of the time. I believe her sister should send over one of those daughters of hers to help out, but I expect she'd say she needs them all at home with Alfred to look after – and of course their maid's taken herself off to London to work in munitions, silly creature."

Mrs Mercer's eyebrows lifted only a fraction. Mrs Jessup's absence from Church had been commented on in the village, and she had been disconcerted by the vicar's reluctance to do anything about it.

"At least," he had said emolliently, "she hasn't gone over to the opposition. I've no doubt she'll return in due course, Mrs Mercer, and meanwhile we must make allowances." And, since the vicar was a man of whom Leonard had approved, Mrs Mercer supposed him to be right.

"He must need a great deal of nursing," she said now, although it was not a matter to which she had given much thought before; Alfred was, if not in the bosom of his family, at least within reach – rather than in some grave on a battlefield, like Gifford Peverell, or languishing in hospital like her own dear boy. Alfred had been grievously wounded, which was a shame, but he had returned to the village; therefore, Mrs Jessup could have little cause for complaint.

"So I understand." Miss Woakes stirred her tea. "He can't do much for himself with his hands so badly injured – and his eyes are completely gone, of course. The Baxters do everything for him – wash and dress him, feed him with a spoon, lead him everywhere; it's a truly Christian endeavour, to my mind."

"No doubt." Yet, however dependent Alfred might be and however onerous her other duties, Mrs Jessup had the privilege of visiting her son occasionally – a privilege Lady Peverell had not been granted, and neither had she. One might almost, she thought, be disposed to envy her.

"I understand he sometimes mentions Simon," continued Miss Woakes. "They were such friends, of course. I remember seeing them together, riding that pony of Simon's – Japheth: he was quite a favourite in the village, wasn't he?"

Japheth had gone when Simon was fifteen and away at school. Leonard had objected to housing and feeding a beast of no practical use, and Simon had returned to an empty paddock and the pronouncement that Daddy thought it was better that way. Whether he had cried about it afterwards, Mrs Mercer had never been permitted to learn.

"They used to go looking for owls and things," she said. Simon had filled notebook after notebook with observations of rabbits, roe deer, badgers, kestrels. He had made casts of foxes' footprints and drawn the shapes of clouds. Leonard had been pleased with this focus on the natural world, although he'd chosen to view it as a preliminary to the *real* work of Simon's life – which was, of course, to be medicine. Simon, however, had had ideas of his own.

"How is Alfred getting along, do you know? Is he … feeling a little better?" How difficult even to frame the question! There was no hope of recovery for Alfred and it would be foolish to ask – no man 'recovers' from having the eyes blasted out of his face, or from losing the use of his hands. "Is he settled, now that he's at home?" Although to be accurate he wasn't at *home.* Caring for him as well as helping to run a busy public house would have been beyond Mrs Jessup, and village life had been thought too distressing for Alfred, so he lived with his aunt and uncle, the Baxters; their farm was close enough for Mrs Jessup to walk to every Sunday, yet far enough not to be troubled by visitors. There, surely, Alfred could be comfortable and quiet and devote himself to his convalescence.

"I believe so. According to Mrs Jessup they try not to talk about the war in case it sets his nerves off, but he does sometimes ask about the vicar's boys. Otherwise, he seems to want to forget the whole business."

Mrs Mercer could sympathise with that. What was there to discuss, after all, about Gifford Peverell, killed leading his men 'over the top'? Or Simon Mercer, his spine crushed when his horse rolled on top of him? That they were young, and that their lives were over? It hardly needed putting into words.

"His main concern at the moment," went on Miss Woakes, "seems to be a badger sett he and Simon found in the corner of Four Acre Wood. He's keen to know whether it's still there or not, and of course nobody can tell him. Mr and Mrs Baxter are run off their feet, and what would Mrs Jessup know about badger setts even if she had time to look for it? But apparently it means a lot to him, so his cousin Madeleine says she'll go when she has an afternoon free. She's very fond of Alfred," Miss Woakes concluded, wistfully. "I wonder if there isn't something romantic in the air?"

Mrs Mercer considered this at length. Madeleine was the free-spirited one of the Baxter girls: Celia was always helping with baking and laundry, while Lucy had scarcely left school when the war began and seemed to have been busy sewing ever since. There were few men available to work the farm now, and no doubt all three had to do their share of labouring; it was hardly a promising backdrop for romance, but no doubt where there was affection love would flourish. Like a flower, she thought, thriving despite the poverty of the soil.

"I believe ..." Miss Woakes began again, delicately, "Alfred's injuries were above the waist. Mrs Jessup hasn't given up all hope of grandchildren. And there must be some work he can do, Mrs Mercer, only nobody can think what. It would be awful, though, wouldn't it, to have to live on charity for the rest of his life?"

Mrs Mercer could think of worse things, but having to rely on the goodwill of others would certainly always be galling.

"I'm glad he's in good hands," she said, as cheerfully as she could. "Do you think he'd like to borrow Simon's notebooks, to remind him of their days out together? Perhaps someone could read them to him, since he can't do it for himself. Does Lucy read well, do you know?"

"She does," replied Miss Woakes, indignantly. She remembered every child and adult she had taught during forty years as village schoolmistress, including Mrs Mercer herself. "All of them were good readers when they were at school – but they're busy with other things now, so I shouldn't think they get time for reading. I'd be more than happy to visit the poor boy myself – but it's a long way, and I don't walk as well as I used to."

"Of course." Miss Woakes could hobble around the village with her stick well enough when the weather was fair, but to expect her to cover four miles to the Baxters' farm and four back was out of the question. And, now that Mrs Mercer thought about it, Simon's handwriting would be indecipherable to anyone who didn't know him as well as she did – and even she sometimes struggled. "Well, perhaps *I'll* walk over to the farm and read them to him," she said suddenly, hearing her own words almost with astonishment.

Leonard would have been horrified, she knew. As the village doctor he'd considered it his duty to treat even the lowliest resident, but otherwise he rarely even exchanged a nod with them on the way to Church. The trouble with the Jessups was not just that they were in trade; it was the nature of that trade which made them unacceptable. As publican of The Peacock, Dr Mercer had held George Jessup responsible for every example of drunkenness and bad behaviour in the locality: when Tom Garger drowned in the duck pond it was Jessup's fault for selling him too much beer; when unmarried girls found themselves in the family way it was Jessup's fault for encouraging licentiousness.

Leonard, however, wasn't there to object – and in his absence Mrs Mercer felt that, just this once, she could let compassion rule her rather than the precepts of a man who'd been dead for several years.

"Oh, Mrs Mercer, would you? I'm sure Mrs Jessup would be grateful – she says everybody's so careful not to trouble Alfred he must feel like a pariah. His nerves are delicate, and no wonder, but if you talked about the past, about what used to make him happy … and I know his friendship with Simon made him happy, even after Dr Mercer sent the pony away."

Such a tactful euphemism – they both knew what had befallen Japheth – but what was the fate of one pony when the sons of millions of mothers faced the same extinction every day?

"Dr Mercer didn't approve of Alfred," said Mrs Mercer. "He didn't consider their friendship suitable and he said Simon ought not to encourage it. I sometimes feel Dr Mercer wasn't a particularly sympathetic man." She had felt it often in the past, but had rarely allowed herself to give expression to the thought.

"He was a particularly *upright* man," Miss Woakes replied. "He set

112

standards for himself that other people found difficult to meet. That meant he was always disappointed in somebody or something, and I think it made him angry. He didn't have any time for fools, did he?"

"He most certainly did not." Mrs Mercer stared at the pattern around the rim of her teacup. "When would it be convenient, would you say, for me to visit Alfred? Wednesdays and Thursdays are easiest for me."

"Perhaps next Wednesday?" suggested Miss Woakes. "I'll speak to Mrs Jessup, and she can let the Baxters know to expect you. They look after his body well enough, Mrs Mercer, but they have no idea what to do for his mind … and what interests the girls doesn't interest him, of course. They really have very little common ground, though bless their hearts they do their best."

Mrs Mercer could imagine it clearly: Celia with her baking and Lucy with her sewing would be creatures of a different world to Alfred, domesticated and tame, and he would never speak to them about battles and fear and death. Madeleine, though … Madeleine would make him a good wife, since she was willing to go off searching for badgers on his behalf. Mrs Mercer might cultivate Madeleine Baxter's friendship, she decided; Madeleine clearly had something out of the ordinary about her.

"Wednesday, then," she replied. "Unless the weather turns, of course." Nobody would expect her to walk eight miles there and back in the rain, she knew. "And if I cut through the corner of the Old Hall estate, I can look for the badger sett along the way."

After Miss Woakes had gone, Mrs Mercer went up to Simon's room. She had sat there frequently in the first weeks and months after he was injured, when she had been on tenterhooks for the next budget of news from one hospital chaplain or another as he passed slowly through the system. They must have been hard-working and conscientious men – staying up throughout the night attending deathbeds, praying over the sick, writing notes of consolation to mothers and wives – and she was grateful to every single one of them.

It had always been a source of comfort that Simon's nature notebooks were where he'd left them – where his own hands had touched them last – each covered in brown wrapping-paper illustrated with Simon's own drawings. Here in 1900 was Japheth tied up to a gate, a year later two out-of-proportion rabbits, and the year after that a delightful sketch entitled 'Chaffinchs Nest' in Simon's twelve-year-old handwriting; at some later date, Leonard had officiously inserted the missing 'e'.

This, however, was the first time Mrs Mercer had taken the books from the shelf. Now she spread them on the bed and looked at them, remembering the fair-haired earnest boy with the round-framed spectacles who had tramped all over creation in his school holidays and come back in the evenings to write his notes. They had lived at The Lodge in those days, with servants and a carriage, and Leonard had been kept busy with his patients. Mrs Mercer had had a household to run, calls to pay, and the demands of an ailing mother to meet, so to all intents and purposes Simon had been allowed to run wild. Leonard had, of course, blamed his wife for the boy's lack of discipline but she had pleaded his case wholeheartedly; of their four children he was the only one to have achieved even a fifth birthday and therefore she was inclined to indulge him. This was the closest she had come to defying Leonard throughout the entirety of their marriage.

In due course Simon, too, had given evidence of an independent spirit. Medicine – insofar as it affected human beings – was not for him; he proposed to enter into *veterinary* medicine instead. Leonard, considering a vet little better than a farrier, had been met with such a series of well-constructed arguments that at length he'd agreed a compromise: if Simon could secure a place at the Royal Veterinary College by his own efforts, Leonard would continue funding his education.

Simon had been in the final year of his veterinary studies when the war broke out.

Simon's notebooks had begun at the turn of the century when his grandmother had given him a diary for Christmas. He had started out in the usual way, recording who had been to dinner at The Lodge and what they had eaten, but at the end of January he had found a pattern of footprints in the snow and traced them back to discover a foxes' earth. From that moment on, nothing had existed for him but the animal kingdom in all its many forms and guises.

Alfred Jessup's first appearance in the diary was in 1904, when he would have been about ten. Both 'only children' in a village which generally ran to large families, they had somehow gravitated together – Mrs Mercer did not know precisely how – and after that, whenever Simon was at home, the boys had been inseparable. When Simon was away at school, observing a chaffinches' nest from his dormitory window, there were occasional mentions in his notebooks of letters from Alfred detailing the progress of village animals. At an age when the majority of boys almost had to be whipped to write at all, Alfred had voluntarily maintained a correspondence with Simon – one of whose existence the school had not seen fit to advise his parents, and of which she and Leonard had therefore been unaware.

Mrs Mercer turned the pages slowly. If Simon and Alfred had observed a badger sett in Four Acre Wood, as Miss Woakes believed, there would undoubtedly be a drawing or a sketch map to enable her to find it.

"People do such dreadful things to badgers," Simon had said once. "They're harmless, and quite intelligent, but the farmers dig them up and torture them purely for amusement – and it takes them a dreadfully long time to die," he'd added, with a catch in his voice. "Why would anyone do a thing like that to an innocent animal?" And she had been unable to answer him: cruelty was arbitrary; he had known it as well as she had, even then.

Walking anywhere was one of many things Leonard had considered vulgar. A lady, he had informed her, did not walk: she either took a carriage or waited for company to come to her. Well, the days of the carriage were long gone – so, indeed, were the days when company might be expected to call – and Mrs Mercer still had, she thanked Heaven, a strong constitution and a serviceable pair of walking shoes. Nevertheless it was some time since she'd walked any distance, and the path to Four Acre Wood was overgrown these days. Perhaps, as a child, she'd been smaller and better able to slip through the gaps – or perhaps she'd simply been less careful of her clothing back then.

The path wound uphill beside a fence on the other side of which was Old Hall, Lady Peverell's domain. A gamekeeper patrolled these boundaries with a shotgun over his arm; he had been to the war, it was said, and come home injured in some unspecified way. Gifford Peverell had asked his mother to find the man a job, but beyond that and the fact that he was generally considered an unpleasant individual who regularly drank himself insensible at The Peacock Mrs Mercer knew little about him. Now she saw him at a distance, watching her almost in contempt, and then she saw him turn and walk away; clearly he felt she was beneath his notice.

The gate in the corner of the field was higher than it had been in the past, and she saw that it was padlocked shut. Beyond, however, the path was clear – and further up the hill were four beech trees, just as there had been in Simon's drawing. He and Alfred would have come to this gate, either on foot or riding Japheth, to observe the badger sett. She wondered whether they, too, had found it barred against them, and what they would have done if they had.

"We'd have climbed over it, of course." She could almost hear the words. They'd been young lads, all long legs and enthusiasm; they wouldn't have let a little thing like a locked gate stand between them and their objective.

Mrs Mercer took a look around her. The gamekeeper had dropped behind the shoulder of the hill, his steps almost idle, and now only a few hedge sparrows and the occasional blackbird stirred. The field she had crossed was yellow with ripening wheat; in a week or two it would be loud with reaping, but now it was completely silent. If there were field mice and hedgehogs, if there were beetles and butterflies – and she was sure there must be – then they were taking as little notice of her as she was of them.

As a girl, she used to bundle her skirts around her waist and climb over obstacles with her underthings on display. Mother had said it wasn't ladylike – but she hadn't *been* a lady at that age, she'd been a child; she'd been scatter-brained Maisie Turnbull right up until the moment her father's cousin had asked to marry her. Father had always told her what to do and she'd obeyed him, in this matters as in others; marriage to Leonard would mean her orders coming from a different source, that was all.

It would never have occurred to Mrs Mercer, the respected doctor's widow, to hitch up her skirts and climb over a gate. She was delighted to learn, however, that for Maisie Turnbull it posed no difficulty that could not be resolved with undignified scrambling and a copious expense in perspiration. She reached the other side with one torn glove and marks on her sleeves and skirt, but leaned back to get her basket with an overwhelming sense of triumph.

"There, Simon," she said aloud. "You didn't think your mother could do that, did you?"

She was glad the gamekeeper had been going in the opposite direction and there was no-one to hear her, but Simon's imaginary laughter was clear and bright and bell-like in her mind. The fact remained, however, that she was several decades removed from the scapegrace child she'd once been; sudden weakness in her legs assailed her and she looked around for somewhere to sit, just for a moment, until she got her breath back. The tussocky bank appeared clean enough; she perched as if on a misericord and waited for her knees to stop shaking.

It really was a pleasant little corner, badgers or no badgers. Simon's book was in her basket and she took it out and opened it at the drawing of the sett, trying to convince herself that her object in sitting down had only been to identify the site. Four beech trees in a straggly line – three almost touching and one set conspicuously apart – were markers of the location, as was the shape of the land, although the vegetation was deeper than it had been when Simon was here. He'd noted lords-and-ladies, brambles, wild garlic, the greenery of abandoned places; now, where the ground was not bald and scuffed, the site was rank with nettles. Or perhaps Simon had seen only what he wanted to see: the dignified and interesting plants. Perhaps even then he'd been editing his experience – just as, latterly, his mother had so carefully edited her memories.

That solitary beech was quite a character. Evidently at some point in its history it had grown out at an unusual angle, stifled by some larger and more dominant tree which had since been felled. Its bark was scarred and abraded in many places; it would have made a fascinating study for any artist or photographer who had the time to sit and examine it in detail; she could see how its warped outline would have appealed to Simon – he had always had compassion for things which were not quite as they should be. Simon would undoubtedly have loved this tree.

Getting to her feet, trusting her legs to be slightly stronger now, she looked at the tree more closely. Some of the scars on its surface, she saw, were not accidental but the results of human intervention. People had carved their initials into it, which struck her as both a wickedly cruel and an absurdly sentimental thing to do. Surely couples only carved their initials into tree trunks when there was some danger of their being parted? When romance progressed along its predetermined path, to marriage and children, there was no need for memorials; there was a living record, clear and public, and everyone acknowledged it. Those who defaced nature with a record of their affair must surely be aware of its ultimate impermanence; she had always thought of it as a last testament to doomed love, something left behind when there was nothing else on earth to record that the moment had existed.

In the circumstances, Mrs Mercer really should not have been quite as surprised as she was to see Simon's initials carved into the trunk of the tree.

She had recovered her composure by the time she reached the Baxters' farmhouse later that morning, was ushered into the parlour and treated as an honoured guest.

"Oh, Mrs Baxter, you really shouldn't have gone to all this trouble!" By the best chair a low table was set with splendid old china and a vase of colourful pansies. She dropped into the chair gratefully, her feet throbbing inside her sensible shoes.

"Nonsense. We don't get many visitors." Which seemed all the excuse Mrs Baxter needed for making a fuss of this one; within minutes Mrs Mercer had been served with a cup of tea and a piece of seed cake.

"How is Alfred?" she began, uncertainly. "I wasn't sure whether he would be ... downstairs?"

"Bless you, he keeps his room most of the time," said Mrs Baxter. "The sun shines in there, which he can feel even if he can't see it. We go up whenever we can," she added, as if expecting to be censured for not doing more.

"Oh," responded Mrs Mercer, "I'm sure you take the best care of him anybody could – but your days must be so full ..." She trailed off, unwilling to imply that their attention to their nephew might be found wanting in any way.

"It *is* a lot of work," conceded Mrs Baxter, which Mrs Mercer was certain was the closest she came to complaining. "But we're glad to do it, of course – and there's people suffering worse wherever you look. Mr Baxter sometimes used to go on at me about not having a son to take over the farm, but now he says he's grateful our girls won't be sent to fight – though what they're to do for husbands when it's over I can't imagine." She'd settled on a footstool and was looking up at Mrs Mercer deferentially, the habit so ingrained she probably didn't realise she was doing it.

"Of course."

"He's a sad sight these days, Mrs Mercer. Not at all the boy he used to be."

"No. I wouldn't expect it." A robust, thorough-going village lad with coal-black curls and a cheeky grin, Alfred had been a contrast to Simon with his poetic looks and tumble of pale hair which could never decide if it was blond or light brown. "He was such a strong young man in those days, wasn't he?"

"Still is," said Mrs Baxter. "Not that it's done him any good. I mean, wouldn't it have been better for him ... maybe for everyone concerned ... ? What kind of life has he got to look forward to, after all?"

"Ah. I see what you mean." She knew what Leonard would have said. Had said, in fact, on more than one occasion. "But I don't think that's up to us, is it? It's God who makes those decisions, and I'm content to leave it all to Him; that's why He's God, after all, and why we're not. Perhaps He's got a purpose in mind for Alfred that we're just not capable of understanding." Although, now that she put it into words, she wasn't certain she believed it herself. That God could choose to slaughter His creation wholesale was beyond all possibility of question, but it was very difficult to think of a sensible reason why He should.

Later, having finished her tea, Mrs Mercer gathered her self-possession and walked up the narrow staircase to Alfred's room.

"Alfred? It's Simon's mother. May I come in?"

"Yes. Please."

The room was sunny with a window overlooking the farmyard and the bed positioned to be seen from outside. In the bed, his face bandaged, his tousled hair seeming afire in the glaring daylight, Alfred sat wearing pyjamas and a pullover. On his lap was an old-fashioned school slate, and one of his ruined hands was casting about in the bedding for something he had lost.

"My chalk," he said. "I think it's rolled under the bed again."

Mrs Mercer put down her basket and got to her knees, burrowing under the bed. There were two or three pieces of chalk there, and as she hauled herself upright she couldn't stop herself holding them out to him in triumph. "Here!" Then she recollected that he could neither see what she was doing nor take the chalk from her outstretched fingers.

Alfred seemed to sense her confusion. "There's a box," he said. "Somewhere."

"Ah, yes." She dropped them in with their fellows, and then without waiting for an invitation seated herself on the bedside chair.

"I've been writing," said Alfred. "Can you see it?" His speech was thick and a little slurred; there were clear signs of injury and healing scars around his mouth, and he appeared to have lost most of his teeth.

Mrs Mercer looked. Faint across the surface of the slate she could detect a line of letters ... A-L-F-R-E-D ... although the R was tilted and looked more like an ampersand.

"It passes the time," he continued, "but I need somebody to tell me if it's any good."

"Well, I think it is," she answered with conviction. "How long did it take you?"

Clearly this was the wrong thing to ask. "All morning," Alfred admitted. "But I've got to do something or I'll go out of my mind." It was almost an apology.

"Well, I've come to entertain you," Mrs Mercer told him briskly. "I've brought some of Simon's books to read to you ... for amusement, you know." She drew to an uncertain halt; the expression on his face, insofar as she could judge, seemed quite at odds with the sunny morning. "Of course I won't if you'd rather not."

"No, please ..." He struggled to speak, and to give him time while he marshalled his reserves she laid a hand on his arm and learned that beneath the bulky pullover he had the stick-thin limbs of a man of eighty, which was no doubt why he was wrapped up so warmly even on a lovely summer day.

"I've been to see the badger sett in Four Acre Wood," she went on, in an effort to distract him. "Your mother told Miss Woakes you were concerned about it. I found the place, but I don't know what to look for to tell whether or not the badgers are still there. If you'll explain it to me, I can go again on my way home and give you the answer when I see you again." And for the next few minutes she listened to a set of very careful and detailed instructions about paths, claw-marks, snuffle holes and dung pits.

"You might find a clump of hair, if you're lucky," said Alfred, in conclusion. "It's about four or five inches long and feels rough when you roll it between your fingers." Mrs Mercer looked up sharply but there was no discernible emotion on his face, although the action he was describing was one he would never again be able to perform. "It'll be caught on the underneath part of the gate, if it's there at all."

"Very well, I'll be certain to check," she assured him, calmly. "Now, would you like me to read to you? And if so, what? I've brought Gilbert White and W.H. Hudson as well. Simon was always very fond of those."

"No, thank you. But we can talk about Simon if you like. Have you brought any of his letters from hospital?"

"I haven't." Not that it hadn't occurred to her, but she had carefully not shared those letters with anyone – not even Miss Woakes. They were so private as to be almost sacrosanct, the only contact she still had with her severely-injured son, although every single one of them was in someone else's handwriting. "But I can remember everything they say," she told him, brightly, "almost word for word. At first he was in a temporary hospital in the grounds of somebody's chateau, in a big wooden hut, and he had a window. He said it was just like being back at school, only warmer, and there were rabbits on the lawn." Simon's enthusiasm for the rabbits, blissfully oblivious to international politics and the conflict raging around them, had conveyed itself even through the tortured handwriting and formal phraseology of the hospital chaplain. "They would never have allowed rabbits on the lawn at school," she observed, wryly.

"No," said Alfred. "The headmaster would have shot them himself from his study window."

"Would he? I had no idea he did that."

"Oh yes! Simon said he would probably have liked to shoot a few of the boys, too, but somehow he restrained himself."

"Fortunately," replied Mrs Mercer, with a laugh. That had the ring of authenticity; it was exactly the sort of thing Simon *would* have said. Then again, how many of those boys had since met a similar fate under the guns of the German army? Potted at, like rabbits: innocent, easy targets. "Well, after that," she continued, "they put him on a train. He didn't say anything about the journey, so I suppose he must have been drugged, but it was more than a hundred miles. He went to another hospital – a proper French hospital in a proper town, and the nurses were all nuns. He didn't have a window, but they used to wheel him outside sometimes in a … in a basket." Inevitably her eyes were drawn to her own basket where it stood on the floor beside her chair: woven strands of willow, so delicate while they were growing yet so strong and reliable when harvested and dried. She'd seen crippled men being pushed about in wicker baskets by wives and nurses, and she'd often imagined herself pushing Simon in such a way. "He said there was a swallows' nest in the eaves of the building, and that he'd watched them flitting in and out."

"He must have been longing to write about them," said Alfred, sympathetically. "He'd hate being indoors all the time, without any animals to look at."

"Yes," replied Mrs Mercer. "And I'm sure you're just the same. Can you at least hear the birds singing from here?"

"I can." And he told her about a family of blackbirds and a flock of starlings, and one strident crow which sounded like his old sergeant major. "I'd love to be able to tell Simon my observations," he concluded, sadly.

Mrs Mercer blinked. "Well," she said, "at least you've told me. That's very nearly as good, isn't it?"

Alfred seemed to be making an heroic effort to smile. "Of course it is," he told her, gallantly apologetic.

"And I could write it all down, couldn't I? I could write a nature notebook of my own, and add it to Simon's collection." She wondered why it had taken so long to think of it, except that the natural world had never really been one of her interests. She knew a mallow from a marigold, could identify any number of cultivated plants, but ask her to distinguish between a moorhen and a dabchick and she'd be powerless; her childhood wanderings had all been in the cause of playing boys' games, rather than observing the wonders around her.

"Yes," said Alfred. "I think he'd like that."

"He would, wouldn't he?" It was clearly an idea that entertained them both.

After half an hour it was obvious Alfred was becoming tired, but he seemed disinclined to let her leave. When Mrs Mercer hinted that she must not trespass on either his or his aunt's goodwill he introduced yet another subject to keep her in her chair. This delaying tactic, subtle at first, steadily became more blatant.

"Oh," he said at last, "I wish you didn't have to go!"

"Thank you, Alfred," she responded, gently, "but I shouldn't tire you; Simon would be cross with me if I did."

This produced the closest Alfred had yet managed to a smile, and with it what sounded like a gasp of exasperation. "I like the way you talk about him," he said. "It makes it seem as if he could walk into the room at any moment." Yet Simon's days of walking anywhere had been over even before his journey from hospital to hospital had begun. "I'd give anything for that to happen, you know."

"Yes, dear," said Mrs Mercer, reaching out and carefully squeezing what remained of Alfred's hand. "So would I."

Leaving Gilbert White and W.H. Hudson behind – on the basis that at least nobody in the household should have difficulty reading the *printed* word – Mrs Mercer took her departure a short time later. On the way out of the farmyard she turned to look back at Alfred's window; this was where she would have paused to wave and smile if he could see her – and, although in the sensible part of her mind she knew he couldn't, the inclination was still there. To her surprise he was leaning across the window aperture, one ruined hand on each side of the frame, his head tilted as though listening for the gate-latch. She obliged by being as obvious about her departure as she could, and calling out to him.

"Goodbye, Alfred. I'll visit again next week."

A sketchy wave was the only response this offer elicited before he moved away from the window. Mrs Baxter, standing in the doorway, exchanged glances with Mrs Mercer.

"I think it's done him good," she offered, tentatively.

"I hope so." Mrs Mercer was on the point of setting off to retrace her steps to the corner of Four Acre Wood when honesty compelled her to an addendum. "I think it's done me good, too."

"Yes," concurred Mrs Baxter. "I thought perhaps it might."

These words were Mrs Mercer's accompaniment as she commenced the journey back. It had honestly never occurred to her that she had any motive other than altruism, but now she realised she'd derived considerable benefit from her excursion – even just from being in the fresh air and taking exercise. As long as the weather continued kind, she saw no reason not to visit Alfred regularly – assuming he was amenable. Once winter set in she would no doubt find it tiresome, but perhaps she could come to an arrangement with someone in the village to be given a ride in a cart or a motor car: the vicar, for example, might find it convenient to drive her part of the way when he was visiting his parishioners. Thus, in all but the most inclement weather, she should be able to maintain a routine of visits as rewarding to herself as to Alfred.

This prospect kept her amused until once again she reached the barred gate giving entry to Four Acre Wood. There she paused to check for badger hairs caught under the lowest rung, and retrieved five or six long grey strands which she folded into her handkerchief. Logic suggested they had arrived since the latest rain and were thus no more than a week old, so – in the absence of dung pits and snuffle holes and other things she couldn't imagine identifying if she found them – Mrs Mercer was satisfied that badgers were still using this path, and probably also the sett. Nevertheless she'd promised Alfred to search thoroughly – and, acting as Simon's proxy, she considered herself duty-bound to be as diligent as her son – so she put her foot onto the lowest bar of the gate and her gloved hand onto the top, and this time despite her tiredness it was easier to swing her body over and into the sheltering green.

"Well." The voice, alarmingly close at hand, was accompanied by the sound of a shotgun barrel being closed. "I thought you'd be back. You'd better have a bloody good explanation for trespassing."

"Oh!" Caught at a disadvantage, Mrs Mercer could do nothing but gape into the shuttered face of the gamekeeper. "Oh, I beg your pardon," she said, flustered. "Yes, of course there's an explanation – but whether or not you'll think it's a *good* one …" And she stopped, pink with embarrassment at such babbling inanity. Leonard would have been mortified: a wife unable to string a sentence together could be no sort of asset in a civilised society.

"You're Simon Mercer's mother," the man continued, his tone of accusation unchanged.

"Yes." It wasn't easy to respond graciously when she felt she'd been caught with her hand in the till. "Are you an acquaintance of my son's?"

"I used to know him," the gamekeeper replied, seeming to consider for a time before breaking his gun again, setting it against a tree trunk, and folding his arms in a conciliatory gesture. "Back when he had that pony, my father used to shoe it for him."

"Oh, then you're one of the *Rawnsleys*?" She had vague memories of a large family, a drunken father, a traumatic eviction on Sir Gilbert's instructions … and after that nothing but an enigmatic silence.

"Joseph Rawnsley," he confirmed. "I served with Mr Gifford Peverell in France."

"Did you?" This seemed a safer topic. "I'm so sorry; he was such a dreadful loss to the village."

Rawnsley shrugged, and there was emptiness behind his eyes. It happened that way often these days: mention of the war brought about an awkward silence followed by a change of subject – even in those who had reputedly done well – as though, irretrievably altered by it, everyone was trying to forget the war had existed in the first place. "So what are you doing? You know as well as I do this is Old Hall land."

"Yes, although I'm certain Lady Peverell wouldn't object." In fact it had never occurred to her to ask permission, although perhaps it would have been wise.

"I don't know about that," he grunted. "But you don't *look* like a poacher, so you tell me what's going on and I'll know if I need to mention it to her ladyship or not."

Mrs Mercer sagged back against the gate, glad of an opportunity to explain her apparently eccentric actions. "It's the badgers," she said. "I found some hair under the gate, but I wanted to know whether the sett was still active. Can you tell me, Mr Rawnsley, by any chance?"

Rawnsley sniffed. "Oh yes, the buggers are still here all right," he said. "You see 'em sometimes, 'specially at night – mother and father and a handful of kits. They don't do no harm, except when they get into the wheat – and that isn't a lot, anyway. Fond of badgers, was he then, your Simon?"

"Well, I expect you remember how much he loved all sorts of animals … He was so kind-hearted as a boy." Although that wasn't, of course, the whole story. "And I've just been up to visit Alfred Jessup, who asked me if the sett was still here and if the badgers were using it. It seems important to him to know, although I'm not sure why."

"Maybe he just wants to know something normal's going on," grunted Rawnsley, sourly. "And if there's honey still for tea." Then, in answer to Mrs Mercer's uncomprehending look, he elaborated. "It's from a poem – about homesickness. Mr Gifford used to read it to me sometimes; he knew the chap that wrote it, when he was at Cambridge."

"Honey for tea," repeated Mrs Mercer. "A metaphor for everything normal? Yes." And how necessary for the young men out there in those awful trenches, under the mouths of the dreadful guns, to be reminded of the old-fashioned England they were fighting to preserve. It was a quiet kind of patriotism that valued such trifles as the presence of honey on a tea table, she realised – although at the Baxters' farm the equivalent would no doubt have been seed cake.

"And anyway," said Rawnsley, "this was a special place. Didn't you see where Simon carved his initials on the tree?"

"Yes, I did." But her brows furrowed. "It seems rather unkind to the tree, somehow."

"But that's a matter of degree, though, isn't it?" returned Rawnsley, combatively. "Whatever we do in this world we're being unkind to somebody or something, but there's hurts and then there's *hurts* – and some of them don't matter, but some do. Dr Mercer passed away a few years back, I heard?"

The sudden tangent was almost enough to take Mrs Mercer's breath away. "Yes, he did." She was not expecting, nor did she receive, even a conventional expression of sympathy. "Nearly seven years ago, now."

"Well, then, maybe it's time for you to see something. Come on over here a moment and have a look."

It was an alarming suggestion – a man she was at least a little afraid of, encountered in a lonely wood, uttering words no sensible female would hear without a qualm. This was how innocent women were lured to their doom, or so she had grown up believing. On the other hand she was twice his age and her looks had faded; if indecency was what he had in mind, he could surely find a worthier object than herself.

Inwardly trembling, she took hold of her courage and stepped closer.

"No, here," he said, gripping her hand roughly. It was in her mind to resist, and she almost did, but he pulled her over to the beech tree and laid her palm upon its trunk. "Feel that?" he asked. "Something carved into the other side?"

"Oh!" Of course. When she had encountered Simon's initials she had looked no further; perhaps she had assumed he was here alone when he carved them, or that the identity of any companion wasn't her business … but then she'd always known who it was that came to this secluded corner with her son. "A.J. Alfred Jessup. Well, they were only boys, of course – and I'm quite sure they were fond of each other. Very fond indeed."

"They wasn't just fond," said Rawnsley, and although he left it there his tone implied rather more. Much, *much* more, in fact.

"I suppose not." In her heart of hearts Mrs Mercer was obliged to concede that something about Simon had always suggested he would never marry, and that grandchildren of her own were out of the question. "They were … ?" But it was no good; she couldn't quite summon the detachment to ask, although in her mind's eye the picture of the fair head leaning against the dark was perfectly explicit. Had the two boys kissed each other in this glade, she wondered? Had they made promises of eternity here? Had they found a safe, clean corner where they could stretch out together on the ground, limbs wrapped around limbs? Somewhere inside her soul Mrs Mercer hoped it had been so, although Leonard had always insisted that sort of thing was vile beyond the power of language to describe.

"You're not shocked, are you? Not even a little bit!" There was quiet approbation in Rawnsley's tone, and he took a step back and gazed at her as though impressed. "Most mothers would shout and throw a fit if I told 'em something like that about their precious only son."

"I'm sorry," smiled Mrs Mercer, quietly amazed at her own composure. "Were you hoping to shock me? I don't really think I'm the shockable type, I'm afraid – and anyway, I love my son. I haven't always understood him – but that doesn't matter, does it, when one loves?"

"No, it doesn't. There's a lot wouldn't see it that way, though, I promise you. Lady Peverell, for example. Treats me like I'm a bad smell under her nose, she does, and I wasn't half to Mr Gifford what your Simon and his Alfie were."

Mrs Mercer looked up sharply. The gamekeeper was beetle-browed, intense, with the palest eyes she'd ever seen and the apologetic remnant of a beard half-forgotten on his chin; he didn't look like the perfumed, indecisive boys generally considered That Sort – but then neither had her beloved Simon nor his dearest, damaged friend.

"Poor Alfred!" she exclaimed, suddenly. "How he must have hated my visit! I truly didn't wish to remind him of anything that might be painful."

"Don't talk daft." Leonard would have spoken precisely so in rebuking her – and her father, too – but somehow Rawnsley managed to make it less insulting. "You'd remind him of *everything* – the good, as well as the bad. We take it all on, don't we: the sickness, the health, the richer, the poorer and all the bloody rest of it?"

"Forsaking all others," she added, following his lead. "As long as ye both shall live."

"Aye, well – that's the problem," he went on. "What do you do when one of you dies and the other one doesn't? Only I promise you Alfie Jessup'd have been a lot happier dead, and I reckon he's up there now wondering what to do about it. I know that, because I'm down here wondering much the same." His glance strayed portentously to the shotgun, propped against the trunk of the twisted beech.

Mrs Mercer bit her tongue on the platitude which sprang to her lips. The men who'd been to war and survived it, she thought, had as much right as anyone – more, indeed – to decide for themselves when it came to life and death. The power of decision-making had been taken from them as long as they were serving their country but some of them had now regained it – and it would scarcely be surprising if they chose to take advantage of it.

"Of course," she nodded, comprehendingly. "Although I hope it won't come to that, for either of you."

"We'll see," was the gamekeeper's desolate response. "We'll see."

"Ah, yes, Joseph," said Miss Woakes, the following morning. "Always such a scamp – and then, of course, there was the eviction; his poor mother, I was so sorry for her." She didn't elaborate but stared into the distance, spoon hovering above her cup, forestalled by memory in the midst of stirring. "I had no idea it was him; he doesn't speak to anyone in the village much."

Mrs Mercer could understand that; the village had done little to help his family when the bailiffs turned them out. They'd last been seen clutching their few belongings – their clock, their bundles of clothing, their black and white cat – on the tail of a receding cart, and afterwards been forgotten entirely. In retrospect it was a scene of almost mediaeval cruelty yet it had been less than a decade ago – and Leonard was adamant that Rawnsley senior had brought it on himself. No one had spared more than the occasional thought for him or his family since that day, though, and the return of one of the exiled Rawnsleys seemed only to counterpoint the absence of the rest.

"He showed me where Simon and Alfred had carved their names on a tree," she said, in an attempt to lighten the mood.

"Indeed?" Miss Woakes' voice was studiedly neutral.

"He said how sad it was for one of a couple to die and the other not to," Mrs Mercer went on. "It made me wonder whether I ought to have felt that way about Dr Mercer, but of course I didn't; I was just glad I wouldn't have to run around after him any more. Was that wicked, do you think?"

"Not wicked," said Miss Woakes, carefully restoring her teacup to a level surface having made no attempt to drink from it, "but human. In your generation and mine, Mrs Mercer, we married or not according to our parents' wishes rather than our own – and we put up with the consequences, whatever they might be. People of Simon's age – and Joseph Rawnsley's too – are rather less bound by tradition than we were."

"Of course. Although perhaps that freedom doesn't extend quite as far as …" Deliberately she left the sentence unfinished, allowing the inclination of her head to convey the innuendo.

"I doubt it will *ever* extend that far," replied Miss Woakes. "Fondness between boys is all very well, but when they become adults they have duties in the world; clinging to one another after a certain age could be considered rather selfish, don't you think? Although perhaps in times of war allowances can be made," she added, in a more conciliatory tone.

"That was what my husband was afraid of, wasn't it – that Simon would become so fond of Alfred he'd neglect his duty to marry and father children, and might prevent Alfred doing so as well? That was why he wanted to discourage their friendship … and why he sent the pony away. He thought Simon was turning into some kind of weakling, or perhaps even a …"

"Sodomite?" Miss Woakes suggested, her face flushing an angry pink.

"Yes – that would be the word he'd use, of course; he had such a hatred of anything irregular. I wonder," Mrs Mercer added, astonishing herself with the twist of malice in her heart, "whether even at this very moment he might be spinning in his grave?"

Miss Woakes seemed to be making a determined effort to dismiss this distracting image from her mind.

"More to the point," she said, "since Dr Mercer is no longer in any position to express an opinion, is what you think of it all. Do you actually believe what Joseph Rawnsley told you? He might, after all, simply have wanted to make trouble for Alfred … for some unkind reason of his own."

"Oh, I hadn't thought of that!" But it had all rung perfectly true, and there had been something almost envious in the way Rawnsley had spoken about Simon and Alfred's friendship. "I believe he may have seen them there together," said Mrs Mercer. "And he certainly implied …" Although perhaps it would be better not to say what he had implied about himself. "It wasn't said in an unkind way," she concluded shakily. "Not in the least. And supposing I had any choice in the matter, Miss Woakes, I would be perfectly willing to accept my son as a sodomite – even a *murderer* – as long as he was still alive. Surely a living sodomite would be more agreeable to any loving family than just a … a total absence, a place where a person ought to be but isn't any more?"

"Ah," responded Miss Woakes, "indeed. When one tries to strike bargains with the Almighty, it often leads to such outrageous conclusions."

"Is it so outrageous?" Mrs Mercer was beginning to wonder whether tears might not be somewhere in the offing, although as an adult she had studiously avoided them. Losing that first baby in the early days of marriage had inoculated her against tears, she felt, when Leonard had so callously insisted she would be ready to try again soon. She had tried again and failed, and he had been sure it was her fault. How much surer would he have been, faced with a son who – to his way of thinking – was not truly a man? He would no doubt have blamed the mother for mollycoddling the boy and condemning him to an outcast life. "My darling boy, alive, on any terms?" Heaven knew she had willed it so with all her might: refusing to consider any other possibility, even in her own mind, had been her last defence against the aching emptiness of the only future she had the power to envision.

"We have no right to ask it of Him," Miss Woakes told her firmly, "which is just as well; who knows what anarchy would follow, if we could?" However a gentler mood seemed to take hold of her at the sight of Mrs Mercer's discomfort, and she adjusted her voice accordingly. "Mrs Mercer, you know nothing in the world can bring Simon back. You've never mentioned to anybody … That is, we understood in the village that he'd reached England safely on a hospital ship, that he was on his way home, and we were all preparing to welcome him – and then he didn't come, and you've never really said why not."

"Of course not." Although it would be difficult to explain, even to so dear a friend as Miss Woakes, that as long as she didn't speak the words it was possible to deny it, to cling to the hope that there had somehow been a ghastly mistake; one heard of such things from time to time, of men wrongly declared dead who walked back into their families' lives months later and wondered what all the fuss was about. "It was the train," she admitted at last, simply glad to be ridding herself of the burden. "He arrived at Dover safely, and he and some other men were put on a train to take them to a hospital in the Midlands ... and during the night it hit some cows that had strayed onto the railway line and the engine was derailed. Most of the men must have been badly injured already, of course, and the accident was too much on top of everything else – although I like to think Simon was so heavily drugged that he didn't wake up at all, that he never realised he was in pain or dying. He was less than a hundred miles from home, too, which makes it all seem so much crueller; I would have been able to visit him later in the week, or perhaps the week after that. He was so close, you see, I could nearly reach out and touch him – but now I know I never will again."

"I'm so sorry." Although the words scarcely impinged on Mrs Mercer's consciousness.

"I don't think he'd want me to get upset, though," she continued, squaring her jaw. "You see, he'd done what he set out to do – his duty, as he saw it – and if other men were dying at the same time, and animals too, he'd probably think he was in good company. Of course he'd be sorry not to say goodbye to the people who loved him."

Miss Woakes made an inarticulate sound of sympathy, and reached over to rest a hand on top of Mrs Mercer's. "Please don't distress yourself, my dear."

"Oh, I'm not at all distressed." And nor was she, Mrs Mercer realised to her own surprise. "A life well lived is all a mother can ask of her son, and his was." Until this very week she'd been unaware of any connection between herself and Alfred Jessup except that he had been a friend of her son's. Now, although she'd be denied grandchildren of her own, she might – as long as she maintained the connection with Alfred – vicariously enjoy the offspring of his marriage to his cousin. Whether that marriage was exactly what Alfred would have chosen – whether, if the war hadn't intervened, he would have elected for a life with Simon rather than with Madeleine – Mrs Mercer could not guess, but neither did she need to. Their lives had all been remade – and now it was simply a question of living with what one had, rather than wishing for what one had lost. Simon was gone, and along with him the future he might have had; his mother would never cease to regret that loss, but would not allow it to deny her a future of her own.

"Atta girl, mother!" Simon's voice sounded in the back of her mind. "Pick yourself up and take one step at a time, as you always do. Look after Alfie, will you, and let him be as happy as he can? He does deserve that, poor boy, even though he doesn't believe it yet himself. Oh – and keep an eye on the dear old badgers for me, too, of course …"

Mrs Mercer smiled. It was so like him, the words so clear and jaunty, that she didn't doubt their origin for a moment – although whether emanating from the shade of Simon in some spectral realm or from the Simon who would remain enshrined for ever in his mother's memory she neither knew nor cared. She knew now what he wanted her to do, and that had always been enough for her before.

As he had so often in the past, Simon had once more shown her a way of going forward.

"Now, Miss Woakes," she said, feeling the calm of new purpose settling comfortably around her shoulders like a cloak, "would you care for another piece of seed cake?"

Adam Fitzroy

Imaginist and purveyor of tall tales Adam Fitzroy is a UK resident who has been successfully spinning male-male romances either part-time or full-time since the 1980s, and has a particular interest in examining the conflicting demands of love and duty.

adam-fitzroy.blogspot.co.uk
twitter.com/AdamFitzroy

At the Gate

Jay Lewis Taylor

"I wish someone would shoot that utter bastard – he's pinched my cheese sandwich."

"Shoot him yourself, Davis. It was your sandwich. Besides, you shouldn't have left it lying around."

The ship rolled violently to starboard; in the trophy store a faint clinking indicated that the wardroom silver was on the move, and a heavier clunk that one of the decanters had shifted.

"Something more humane, then. What about an overdose of morphine? You're the doc, after all; you should know." John Davis glanced at his left shoulder, and rubbed the single curl of very new gold braid, perhaps in the hope of darkening it; there had been remarks passed in the mess concerning the canary on his shoulder. "It's always *my* sandwiches he pinches," he said plaintively. "Have pity on me and share yours? Even sub-lieutenants have to live."

"I'm not so sure about that!" But Surgeon Lieutenant-Commander Alan Kershaw, RN, was smiling. He wedged himself more firmly between the wardroom table and the bulkhead, used his left elbow to pin down the pile of letters for censoring, and pushed his own sandwiches across with the hand that was holding a pen. "Here. I shall be sea-sick if the Slug keeps rolling like this; no point in wasting them. And how do you know it was he?" He took a letter from the top of the pile.

"Well, who else?" Sub-Lieutenant Davis sat down on the other side of the table, just in time to catch the plate of sandwiches as HMS *Arion* rolled the other way.

Kershaw deleted a reference to 'heading south' and said, "No. I meant, he might be she."

"Of course not. All rats are he. Same as all ships are she."

"Never heard that one before." Kershaw grabbed at his sliding inkwell. "Put the fiddles on, Davis, there's a good chap. I'll hold the plate for you."

For a moment there was as much silence as there can be in a light cruiser ploughing across a Force 8 gale in the North Sea. Davis, his mouth full of cheese sandwich, was tightening the screws on the battens. Kershaw, elbow now weighting the plate as well as the letters, was keeping a tight hold on pen and inkwell.

"There. Done," Davis said. "Do you really not want those sandwiches?"

"Really not. Thank you for taking them off me – saved me a bollocking from Cooky, I dare say." Kershaw set down the inkwell. "I must finish these. Do excuse me."

The scratching of his pen cut through the larger noises: the alarmingly solid crash that *Arion* made as she hit the waves; the humming throb of the engine; the combined howl and whine and roar of the wind in the air and the rigging. After a while Kershaw said again, "Excuse me," shot precipitately to his feet, and left the wardroom. Davis finished his sandwiches, put the plate on the pile of letters, and leaned back with his ankles crossed, resting his feet on the stretcher of the table.

When Kershaw, white in the face but not noticeably shaken, came in and sat down again, Davis said, "The rat's around, you know."

"Oh?"

"That scratching noise, I thought it was your pen, but it carried on after you left. You all right, by the way?"

"I'm fine. Where is he?"

"In those drawers." Davis pointed. "I can't hear him now."

"Damn." Kershaw stared at the drawers. "I keep some of my things there, it's too damp in the cabin. I don't really want to know … no, I don't. I'll finish this job, and then the mail can go ashore at *Ganges* when we tie up alongside." *Arion* pitched, corkscrewed, and briefly juddered like a traction engine crossing a railway track without the benefit of tarmac. Kershaw dipped his pen in the inkwell and said, "*If*. And if the bloody Slug doesn't drive me quite berserk."

"Been meaning to ask," Davis said, "why the Slug? I mean, everyone calls her that, always has done as far as I can tell, but why?"

Kershaw finished working on one letter, and sealed it away. "Launched by an admiral's lady. His lordship thought *Arion* was good, Arion and the dolphin, that legend."

"I know it. Classical education, me."

"Well," Kershaw said, "her ladyship had been to Girton – a scientist, believe it or not. Specialised in gastropods after Cambridge."

"What-pods?"

Kershaw raised an eyebrow; Davis smiled, shrugged, and said, "So, classical education don't stretch that far. I was only at Balliol, meself. What are gastro-things?"

"Slugs and snails," Kershaw said. "Turns out that there is a creature called *Arion ater*, European black slug to you and me." He laughed. "Her ladyship was quite vocal. Amused, but vocal. So that's the story: the Ships' Names and Badges Committee having an off day." He lifted his head at the sound of knocking. "I'll give you ten to one that's for me."

"I'll find out." Davis got to his feet.

Kershaw could not see the new arrival behind the open door, but he recognised the voice of his senior Sick Berth Assistant. Resignedly, he began to stow the letters in his briefcase.

"Ten to one and you were right," Davis said. "SBA Maskell, says there's an urgent case in the sick-bay."

"Hey, bloody ho." Kershaw fastened the briefcase clasps. "Wonder who's lost his dentures overboard this time … which watch are you on tonight?"

"Last dog. See you at dinner!" John Davis called to the retreating back. Then he sat down again, and pulled out the latest letter from his girl, Helen, who was still, somehow, enthusiastic about the novelty of scrubbing floors in a convalescent home.

Kershaw wasn't at dinner, nor in the mess when Davis came off watch two hours later. The clock in the almost-deserted wardroom was showing 2300 when at last he closed the door noiselessly behind himself, and sank into the mess's one armchair.

"You've been a while," Davis remarked. "Was it lost dentures?"

"No. Appendicitis." Kershaw wiped one hand across his forehead. "Hope I don't have to do that again in a hurry. I prefer my operating tables to stay still."

"Does it take that long?"

"No … I didn't feel too good, so I went to lie down afterwards, and fell asleep."

Davis nodded. "You do look a bit green around the gills. Brandy?"

"Please. Chit it to me, though." Kershaw smiled at Davis's protest. "No,

I mean it. My pay can stand it better. Besides, your uncle told me not to let you spend all your money on drink."

"Not even when I'm buying for someone else?" Davis put the stopper back in the brandy decanter. "Which uncle would that be?"

Kershaw's indrawn breath was sharper than he had meant it to be. "Grant Hamilton. Your mother's brother. He wrote to me when he knew you'd be joining."

"Oh." Davis looked hesitantly at his senior officer. "You know he – ?"

"Yes, I know."

"Jutland."

"Yes."

The silence was broken by an intermittent, light scratching. For a moment both of them sat motionless. Then, abruptly, Kershaw stood up. "That *bloody* rat. All right, let's look at him." He snatched the drawer open. There was a frantic scrabble of claws and a whisk of pink-skinned, slightly scabby tail. Davis jumped back, but the rat was going the other way, through a gap in the panelling and behind the bulkhead lining.

Kershaw remained where he was, staring into the open drawer.

"Much damage?" Davis asked.

Kershaw's voice was as cool and measured as if he were mustering sick-bay supplies. "Half a tin of chocolate biscuits, most of the cover of 'Treves on Operative Surgery', a bit of picric acid dressing and part of a camera case. There's also a fair dent out of 'First Aid in the Royal Navy', and much good may it do him. Not to mention the smell, and traces of excreta." He pushed his hands into his pockets. "Grant – your uncle – would have found that very funny."

"Picric acid?" Davis said. "Isn't that an explosive?"

Kershaw nodded. "Did Grant tell you that? He liked things to – to go with a bang. But it's also an antiseptic." He reached into the drawer for the camera in its case.

"Made a mess of that, hasn't he?" Davis said, and then fell silent. As Kershaw turned the damaged case over and over in his hands, gilt letters glinted briefly in the lamplight: G.D.M.H. "What did the D.M. stand for?" Davis asked. "I – I never knew him so very well, you see. He was a lot older than me, even though he was Mother's younger brother."

"Douglas Murray," Kershaw said. *Remember that night you signed the register at The Swan in Minster Lovell? You weren't Grant Hamilton then.* "Your mother thought I might like this. I hope you don't mind."

"No, of course not." Davis pushed the drawer gently closed. "I hadn't seen him for years, but he was why I joined the Navy. He was everything I wanted to be, when I was eight."

And maybe something else besides. "That's kind of you to say so. We were good friends, he and I."

"How did you meet?"

"We were both up at Oxford, before I finished my medical training at Guy's. Met in the Exam. Schools." *That was where we first saw each other, yes, but not where we really met.*

"You a Balliol man too?" Davis asked, as a man does for whom Oxford is his birthright.

"St John's." Kershaw had been a scholarship boy. *October it was, we were walking back from The Trout at Godstow, all in the dark and the rain. It came down hard in St Giles, and we ran from tree to tree to keep as dry as we might. Nobody else there at all, or I should never have dared, when you stopped to get your breath outside The Lamb and Flag under the chestnut trees, between lamplight and leaf-shadow, to cup your face in my hands and –*

Kershaw coughed. *Two deep breaths. Three.* "Right. What shall we do about this bloody rat?"

"Are the rest of the biscuits edible?"

"Not fit for human consumption, I should think. Some danger of Weil's disease, if what I read in the 'Journal of Experimental Medicine' is true."

"Tell you what, then," Davis said, opening the drawer again. "Bait. Prop the tin up over them, on a stick or something. Rat wants biscuits, rat knocks stick, tin drops, bingo."

"What are you, Engineering Branch or something?" But Kershaw was smiling. "You share Grant's technical bent, obviously."

"Any bent I have of any kind is a very minor deviation from my natural tendency to think in straight lines," Davis said. "That's why I'm a navigator." He wrenched the tin open, and knelt down. "I'm glad I'm not trying to balance a round tin, here."

Your hands are so like his. "I'll leave you to it," Kershaw said, "and go and see what the galley can offer by way of late dinner. If SBA Maskell knocks and it's the appendix, tell him I'm either there or in my cabin. He's to rouse me out even if I'm asleep."

When morning came, the tin was flat to the deck, and the book on which it had been propped was beside it; but the trap contained no rat. Over the next two days the other members of the mess flung themselves into the Ratbane Plan with gusto, and with equal lack of success. Alan Kershaw, smiling and holding himself slightly aloof, began to keep a book on who would be the successful rat-catcher.

Arion reached Harwich, and the crew had a run ashore, although Kershaw's consisted mostly of passing the mail to the registry at HMS *Ganges* for franking. He also shopped for more biscuits, not as bait, but so that he could store his books and camera in the tin, which he took the added precaution of taping shut. *Arion* sailed again on the dawn tide, with no more than the usual complement of sore heads.

"Well, she ain't going to sink," Davis remarked cheerfully.

"What makes you say that?" Kershaw poured himself a second cup of tea.

"The rat hasn't left. I heard it first thing."

Captain Linscombe, who had appeared to be deeply engrossed in his breakfast, looked up. "What, still no advance on the Ratbane front? Come, come, gentlemen: honour – or at least a certain amount of coin of the realm – is at stake."

"Sorry, sir," Davis said cheerfully. "It's a devious beast. Probably German-trained. Field-grey, you know."

"Ah." Linscombe prodded his egg cautiously. "Kershaw, do tell me – has the Navy been feeding depth charges to the nation's hens? It's the only thing I can think of that would account for the exact texture of this scrambled egg."

Kershaw, chewing toast, paused for a moment to swallow. "You know I don't believe in indiscriminate use of purgatives, sir," he said, to suppressed chuckles from more officers than one.

"Very good, Doc, very good." The captain laid down his knife and fork. "Daily orders on the bridge in twenty minutes, gentlemen. Enjoy your breakfast."

Sick-bay duty that morning was interrupted by a knock on the door from the ship's most junior officer.

"Come in, Davis. How can I help?"

"I'm wasting your time, sir," John Davis said bluntly. "That is, unless you have something to cure blind panic."

"Tea and sympathy, and not much else. Sorry." But Kershaw looked at him kindly for all that, although Davis didn't see it, being too busy staring at his own feet. "This morning's news, is it?"

"I thought I'd be all right," Davis muttered. "I wasn't expecting to feel this way."

There was another knock. Kershaw said, "Tell you what. After I've seen today's lot, come back here and we'll talk."

"You sure?"

"Yes, or I wouldn't have said so," came the patient reply. And as the sub-lieutenant walked away, "Good morning, PO. What can I do for you?"

After Petty Officer Williams had been supplied with aspirin, and Leading Cook's Mate Marsh been treated for scalds from injudicious handling of a kettle, and one or two minor patches and pills applied to others, the sick-bay office was empty again. Kershaw began to write up his Medical Officer's Journal.

The weather was, if anything, worse even than it had been for the last few days, and the smell of antiseptic and ink did nothing to help. He generally had time to reach the weather deck before sea-sickness got the better of him, but now it came on too fast, and he was thankful to have a basin within reach. He flushed the heads, rinsed and disinfected the basin, and was finishing his journal by the time Davis knocked on the door again.

"Are you sure you don't mind wasting your time on me, sir?"

"It's no waste, Davis, and by all means dispense with the sir and consider us to be temporarily off duty. Do sit down. One moment." He closed the inkwell, and scratched his initials at the foot of the page: A.F.K. for Alan Francis Kershaw. *Francis Allan, I was. Francis Allan and Douglas Murray, two undergraduates on a walking holiday, sharing a room to save money.* He blotted the wet ink, and put the journal away. "Tea?"

"No, thanks, sir."

"Sympathy, then?"

"You know what it's about, after what I said before. What with them sending us to Zeebrugge to support the main force." Davis glanced up and looked down again, as if he could not bear to look him in the eye.

Kershaw nodded. "We shan't be the only ones, of course. Does that make you feel any better?"

"Not much. I – I suppose I always thought I'd be safer in a big tin box. But tin boxes can blow up too. Jutland taught me that if nothing else did – that, and Grant going – *dying*," Davis said fiercely, as if to avoid using a word was to give it power. "Was Grant afraid, do you think? Did he feel sick as soon as he heard there would be a battle, as if his pulse was going to block his windpipe, and –" He stopped abruptly. "I'm sorry. But *I want to see my girl again*. I never slept with a girl yet, do you know? To hear the rest of them talk, they slept in every brothel from Pompey to Portland and back again."

"It's talk," Kershaw said, although he knew that often it wasn't: he had treated enough VD cases in his time. "I know what you mean, but I can't tell you what's going to happen, or that you'll see your girl again, I'm afraid. Not for certain."

"Of course you can't. I don't know why I thought you could, but – you knew Grant."

Oh yes. I knew him all right. Carefully Kershaw said, "I've wondered the same thing myself, before now. What was he thinking, was he afraid? Did it hurt? But – Grant – he would have been too *interested* in what was going on. Too busy. He wouldn't have had time to think about fear. Believe me, when it comes to the point – and I was at Jutland too, I know what it's like –" *his ship sank while I watched, and I couldn't talk about him, not to a single soul –* "you just keep on at the job and, and if you're still alive at the end of it, it's a bloody surprise and you go and drink yourself blotto to celebrate being alive." *Or to forget.* "Ship's duties allowing, of course," Kershaw added.

"I see. Well, thanks, I suppose." Davis got to his feet. "You don't mind?"

"No, of course not. I'm used to being proxy chaplain, since the Slug doesn't bear one." Kershaw sighed. "Remember, though – drink afterwards, if you must, when you're allowed. But not before, or you're no good to the ship, let alone Captain Linscombe tearing you off a strip is *not* something you want to experience."

"Thanks. I'll bear that in mind." Davis saluted, which he shouldn't have done without his cap on, and closed the door behind himself before his senior officer could point this out.

Kershaw stared at the blank grey paint. *After Oxford we had twelve years of snatched weekends, nights, moments. Looking over our shoulders, taking adjacent rooms, hiding our names, hiding our nature, always hiding. Twelve years of love, ended in a moment.* He put his head in his hands and sat, motionless, until six bells of the forenoon watch sounded.

The weather grew worse still, and worse. Kershaw didn't take lunch, but drank tea instead, and ate some dry biscuit. He was flat on his back along a line of wardroom chairs when the First Lieutenant crashed the door open and said, "Rat alert!"

"Oh lord. Where?"

"Right there in the roundhouse – you know the voice pipe runs through it just above eye level? I looked up and there the bastard was, sitting there with his paws held in front of him like a little old lady at the bus stop. Staring at me."

Kershaw grunted. "Haven't the stokers a cat? Ask them if we can borrow it."

"Of course. Tally ho!" Lieutenant Vernon cantered off, and returned in short order, holding a skinny and indignant black-and-white object, rather tattered about the ears, which he deposited in the roundhouse before closing the door. "Now, Whisky, do your damnedest."

News had got round the ship. Slowly the wardroom filled with listening officers, intent on the small compartment across the gangway from them; awaiting the sound of battle. Wind, rain and storm beat on the portholes. Inside, all was silent. Ten minutes passed.

"Open the door, Number One," Captain Linscombe said, and Vernon tugged at the handle. The door jammed at first, then flew back with a crash. Kershaw, still supine, lifted his head to see into the roundhouse.

The rat was slumped motionless on the voice pipe. Kershaw wondered if it really was swaying as the Slug rolled, or whether his imagination was working too hard. The cat Whisky was not working hard at all, but sitting with front paws together and tail curled round them, eyeing the rat as if trying to work out what it was.

"Damn cat's turned conchie," someone remarked.

"It's certainly incompetent," the captain said. "Sling it back in the gangway, Vernon, it can find its own way back to the engine room. Then pick up the rat and chuck it in the ditch."

"I'm not picking it up, sir, if you don't mind," Vernon said. "It doesn't look healthy to me."

"Hmph. What do you think, Doc?"

"Probably isn't," Kershaw said. "Diet of chocolate biscuits, picric acid, paper, card, glue, leather – I wouldn't be feeling too good myself."

"You look exactly as if that's what you *have* been eating," Vernon said. "And that reminds me, as Mess President I'm fining you a bottle of port in advance of Trafalgar Night. Improper use of mess furniture."

Kershaw sat up from the line of chairs, fought down a surge of nausea, and did his best to smile. "You're a hard man, Ver. I'll tell the Mess Treasurer to write it in the book."

"But you are the – oh, never mind." Vernon turned and glared at the rat, which hadn't moved. "I suppose tongs would do. Someone go find an AB and tell him to bring a pair. Sub-Lieutenant Davis?"

"Yes, sir." Davis was grinning as he saluted, and Kershaw thought: *Grant would have been laughing his head off by now ... 'Are you lot too jessie-like to pick up a rat?' he'd have said, and done it himself.*

Davis came back, still grinning. "Permission to admit Able Seaman Harris to the wardroom for Ratbane purposes, Lieutenant Vernon, sir?"

"Permission absolutely granted. Carry on, AB."

Kershaw closed his eyes. Ridiculous as it was, much as he hated that rat, he didn't want to see it carried to its doom. But there was a general drift of the other officers to the gangway and, to judge by the sounds, up the ladder to the weather deck, where they could shelter in the lee of the bridge for as long as it took.

Within a few minutes they were all back.

"You realise," Kershaw said to nobody in particular, "that this means I win the sweep? I was the one who bet it would be a junior rate."

"So you did," replied Vernon, "but you're lying on the wardroom chairs again."

"I'll charge myself two bottles of port, don't worry." Kershaw got to his feet once more. "I'm for my bunk, if you'll excuse me. I'll check on my appendicitis first. PO Uniacke, I should say. Don't expect me for dinner." He turned back at the door. "AB Harris have any trouble with the beast?"

"It never moved a muscle," said Vernon. "Limp as a Christian thrown to the lions. Reckon you're right, and it was ill. Or do rats get sea-sick?"

"Not that I ever heard." Kershaw sighed. "I wish humans didn't, I can tell you that."

Vernon clapped him on the shoulder. "Don't you worry, Doc; nobody thinks the worse of you for it. Nelson was always sea-sick, you know."

"So I have heard. Often. But I'm not Nelson." Kershaw's face lit with a sudden grin. "Thank goodness. I need all the eyes and hands I can muster, on the Slug. See you later, Ver."

They had been sailing south-east since leaving Harwich, but in the afternoon Captain Linscombe, to avoid being ahead of time, directed his Navigating Sub-Lieutenant to change course to northward. The rain had stopped, and the wind lessened somewhat, although the sea was still choppy and heaving. The sun was setting below the cloud-ceiling in a blinding dazzle of gold, so that the look-outs were facing eastward, to starboard, when it happened: *Arion*'s port bow, dropping into a wave-trough, struck a mine.

In his cabin Alan Kershaw crashed awake out of a light doze, woken by the feel of the explosion as much as the sound: a long, shuddering quiver that rattled the ship from end to end. He sat up, pulled on his shoes, and was half through the doorway, still rubbing his eyes, when *Arion* struck a second mine. This time the explosion flung him against the door-jamb.

He managed to stay upright by clinging on with both hands. *First aid posts.* The ship was listing already, and there was a noise of escaping steam, and footsteps running, everywhere, beating like mad pulses through the whole frame of the ship. A smell of smoke, burning, metal hot beyond endurance. Someone barged past him from the starboard quarter: PO Williams, of the headache.

"Anyone back there, PO?"

"No, sir, not now. If you –"

Another explosion, a horrifying roar which never fell silent but was absorbed into the noise of flames and the hiss of steam, knocked them both off their feet.

PO Williams staggered up again, nursing a forehead wound from which blood dripped into his eyes, and hauled Kershaw up too. No time for protocol. "I was going to suggest that we shut off B magazine. Too late now."

Sick-bay. Kershaw started to run forward. "Patient in the sick-bay."

"Jim Uniacke, isn't it? Can I help?"

"No – yes." Kershaw flung open the sick-bay door. *What I said about being busy, being interested, stops you feeling afraid? It's not true.* Glass-fronted cupboards were shattered, chemicals and water and God knows what running down the canted deck, the smell clawing at his throat so that it ached and stung. "First aid packs in that haversack, as many as you can. Ah, SBA Maskell, thank you. Take the picric acid dressings, please, you know where they are. PO Williams – before you go – something on that cut of yours." *Oh, Grant … I hope you weren't as bloody stricken terrified as I am.* Kershaw held a dressing to Williams's forehead, tore at a reel of Elastoplast, and stuck it down. "There you are."

Somewhere above them a bugle sounded, its note piercing the uproar.

Davis. Where in all this is John Davis? Grant would never forgive me if – Grant would never have forgiven him if he had lost sight of his duty for Grant's sake, let alone for Davis's. Kershaw, with Maskell close behind, pushed on to the far side of the sick-bay. "PO Uniacke? All right, man, we'll have you out of here. Still sore, I suppose?"

"Pretty much, sir," Uniacke replied. "But I can walk."

"I hope you won't have to. On my back, and don't strangle me if you can help it. SBA, clear the doors for us, please." The man's weight dragged at Kershaw's shoulders. *Arion* settled into the water a little. The reek of cordite and steam, something burning, like meat, except – *that's not meat* – and he was almost sick again. He staggered, climbed, crawled out onto the terribly slanted deck, the SBA always ahead of him to lend a hand, up – *up, for God's sake, the world's turned upside down* – and over the rail. The hull, curved like a whale, was before them. *I can't do that face down; it'll skin my hands off.* "PO," Kershaw said, "you think you can move? Lie along the front of me like on a stretcher? I'll try to sledge down the hull if I can."

"I can do that, sir. But they've put the nets out." The man was more alert than he was. "We can hand ourselves down if you go forward a little way."

"Good man." In the distance – no, terribly close by, but Kershaw's ears were trying to deceive him – someone was screaming. *Arion* settled again, with a hiss of sea-water on fire, and the noise stopped. Kershaw began to crawl forward.

"Let me off, sir," Uniacke said. "Crawling I can do."

"Stay flat, then. Don't cough if you can help it. Use your arms rather than your legs as much as possible." *Arion*'s sides and hull were the stuff of nightmare: the grey hills he had climbed, Sisyphus-like, in his dreams for weeks after Grant had died, reaching the brow and finding himself at the foot again, reading the notice pinned, absurdly, to a five-barred gate standing closed in the wilderness, with not a fence to be seen. *To conquer Grief you must climb the grey hill.* He had opened the gate to begin the climb again, and again, and again, and had never reached the top.

Kershaw glanced up, which is to say, forward: what had been 'up' on the ship was now to his left. There were the nets, and figures clinging to them. The ship must have keeled over slowly enough to allow the port boats to be launched from the davits. Two were being rowed around *Arion's* bow, and men were being hauled from the water into them. A voice somewhere ahead of him: PO Williams, doling out dressings and rough comfort as he went.

Kershaw kept on until he could hook one hand in the first loop of net. Someone else was there already: the chief stoker, with a black-and-white bundle under one arm, lashing its tail. *Cat leaving a sinking ship,* Kershaw thought. And then: *We should never have ditched the rat.* "Chief McKenzie," he said. "Have you seen Sub-Lieutenant Davis?"

"In this tea-party, sir?" McKenzie said. "No, I've not seen him – last I heard, he was on the bridge with the captain. Are you all right, sir?"

"Yes – hey, PO, here. Let me." He shook his hand free of the nets, hauled PO Uniacke towards him by the collar, and pulled at the netting for the man to get a hold on it. They were still at the very edge of the net, and Kershaw's feet scrabbled without purchase. His hands were cold, he hadn't realised how cold. "I can't –" he said, and lost his grip.

His slide down the hull was a plunge into nightmare: he barely had time for thought, let alone fear. The shock, when it came, was not the deadly cold of North Sea waters that can kill a man in three minutes, but the appalling, bone-crunching force with which the bilge keel broke his fall.

Kershaw's legs folded under him; his right foot slid off the six-inch flange of metal so that it dug hard into the side of his knee. A small, calm, professional voice inside his head murmured: *Fracture of os calcis right, Pott's fracture left.* But what troubled him more was the stinging burn of raw skin, where barnacles had abraded the left elbow of his uniform jacket and shirt clean away as he slid. Beyond the pain, his mind was too blank for either hope or fear; he leaned back against the steel hull, and did nothing. It could not be described as waiting. *I've never been able to grieve for you, not properly. Perhaps it doesn't matter any more. Perhaps I'll be with you soon.*

A voice pulled him from his reverie. "Lieutenant-Commander Kershaw, sir?" and something struck him gently across his face: a rope's end. Slowly, almost sleepily, he lifted his head. "PO Williams."

"Yes, sir," the PO said. "Come on, now. Can you move?"

"Not to stand." Kershaw pushed himself to a sitting position. "One ankle gone. Might be able to take a bit of weight on the other."

"Lift your arms, and I'll fix the loop safely round you. Best you sit and shuffle, I think."

Spray fell on them in a cold, sharp rain. Kershaw started to say something which faded into a mumble. He tried again. "What about you?"

"Roped, sir, well tied on. You'll be all right, sir. Come on. I don't want you falling off here."

Carefully, one arm at a time, they managed to get the rope under Kershaw's armpits and secure it. "Thank you," Kershaw said. After a moment he added, inconsequentially, "It's very kind of you to take so much trouble."

"Lieutenant Vernon's orders, sir," PO Williams said. "He says to tell you, you're not getting away without buying those two bottles of port."

"Tell him … oh, it doesn't matter." Kershaw blinked away salt from his eyelashes. "What now?"

Arion had been vibrating gently with the escape of steam and the last coal in the engines; now she fell silent in the vast noise of the sea.

"The ship's boats are on the way, sir, and HMS *Lydiard* isn't far off, it seems. Sparks got a message to her right after we struck, and they're sending a motor launch. You'll be fine, sir. But I'd feel a bit happier if we can get back to the nets."

"Captain Linscombe? Sub-Lieutenant Davis?"

"They're safe, sir, in one of the boats."

Relief helped to dull the pain a little. With someone at the far distant end of the rope to take his weight, Kershaw, half-lifted by PO Williams, shuffled forward for interminable minutes, until there were ropes and netting under his hands again.

"You got a good hold, sir?" Williams asked.

"I don't know. My fingers are so cold. I can't feel much." Tears ran down his face. The tug of the rope at his armpits was as if another's arms held him; the netting round his wrists like the grip of another's hand.

Without a word spoken, meaning no more than the oldest human solace of warmth, Williams covered Kershaw's hands with his.

It has to come to an end, some time. But for now, I'm back at the gate again. Alan Kershaw laid his face against the cold curve of the ship's side, and thought about Grant Hamilton.

O friend I loved, I raise in thoughts of thee
the heart that beat at one with thine.
There is a sound of guns upon the sea;
now ... thy hand in mine –

E.H. Young
'At the Gate', HMS Vindictive, 1918

Jay Lewis Taylor

Despite having spent most of my life in Surrey and Oxfordshire, I now live in Somerset, within an hour's drive of the villages where two of my great-great-great-grandparents were born. Although I work as a rare-books librarian in an abstruse area of medical history, I am in fact a thwarted medievalist with a strong arts background.

I have been writing fiction for over thirty years, exploring the lives of people who are on the margins in one way or another, and how the power of love and language can break down the walls that we build round ourselves.

twitter.com/jaylewistaylor
jaylewistaylor.livejournal.com

After & Before

September 1918
Wallace House Military Hospital, Cheshire, England

On hearing the knuckle rap against the study door, Robert Wallace buried his head in the stack of buff-coloured folders that had held his attention all morning and pretended to ignore it.

"Doctor?" A muffled voice followed the knock and Robert immediately recognised it as being from the same shy nurse who had been attempting to disturb his peace all morning, and who had at some point slipped in and placed a mug of tea on his desk.

"I'm busy," he mumbled back, whilst cursing to himself. There was no doubt she had been ordered to bring him lunch and whilst, yes, his stomach rumbled lightly, he had already promised himself he could hold out till later.

At his words the knocking stopped and Robert glanced impatiently towards the door. Thankfully now only the sound of footsteps echoing down the corridor could be heard and he let out a small sigh of relief. Sometimes he thought it funny the way the nurses coddled him, tried to feed him, and treat him like the others, whereas other times, like now, it just frustrated the hell out of him.

Looking down the typed notes in front of him he soon became lost in the paragraphs. At some point another mug of tea and a plate of sandwiches appeared, having been placed gingerly on his desk without comment. He'd quickly eaten them, and then returned to his work, lost in the information once more.

"Doctor? Are you there?" a voice asked.

Really? Again? Have they no respect?

"I asked not to be disturbed today. I'm busy," Robert answered rather curtly, waving away the clicking sound from the iron latch of his study door and heeled footsteps that marched their way across the parquet floor. "Nurse Ollrenshaw. I said –"

"I know," she answered, cutting him off. Her tone sharp and firm – there was no doubt in Robert's mind why she had been the one sent to disturb his study. Nurse Rosamund Ollrenshaw was experienced and the perfect matron; even now her starched uniform was blindingly white and he knew she had been up since daybreak.

He really did like her.

"Our new arrivals are here."

Robert lifted his head, partly in frustration and disbelief. "Now? They're early?" *Surely not.* He looked across to the calendar that sat on his desk and the carriage clock just to the right of it. Did he have completely the wrong day? Had he been so engrossed in work he had missed a full twenty-four hours? "Is it Wednesday already?"

Nurse Rosamund shook her head, the wings of her cap vibrating with the motion. Robert watched as the white flaps bounced as she spoke. "The transport was needed elsewhere. They came today."

Robert huffed, pursing his lips together with force. "I ... we ... we're not ready surely?" *Were they? Was he?*

Their last new arrival had only been three days earlier, a man whose burns covered half of his body. *His* arrival had been felt all round, his cries of agony heard throughout the night. But another three gentlemen? So soon?

Robert forced down the tremor that rolled through his chest. One of them would be ... ? *No*. he couldn't let himself think about it. Instead he ran his fingers along the spine of the folder that sat on top of the pile. "Are we able to take them today? Are the beds ready?"

Nurse Rosamund responded with another nod of her head. "Yes. The rooms are as you requested. Two admitted to the wards, and one private."

At her words Robert sighed and straightened the various hospital notes into an easy to manage pile. He eyed the three names on the typed list sent to him days earlier. "I take it it's everyone we expected?"

"Yes."

"Injuries as recorded?" In truth he had no real need to reopen the buff folder or question her. He could recite the field notes verbatim.

"Yes. Two gentlemen in wheelchairs, one able-bodied but ..." She paused. "He is, as they say, mute."

Robert nodded; it was as expected.

"Will there be anything else?"

Robert shook his head. What he needed was time alone to collate his thoughts into an orderly fashion. Maybe even brace himself? Time, however, was something he didn't have.

But Robert made no effort to hurry. Pushing himself back on the desk chair he reached for his cane and lifted himself slowly. The leg braces he had worn for three years still felt alien against his body as he straightened each one out, one frame at a time. The right one as always gave him trouble. A little oil later would sort that, but for now he would suffer.

Walking, though, even now, sapped Robert's energy from him; the four-yard gap from his desk to his door still took him far longer than it would any able-bodied person. Shifting from one leg to another slowly – he'd found at some point that this was the easiest method to get by on; the unusual gait it caused could be ignored.

But if the four yards from the desk to his door felt exhausting, the long corridor to the main wards would be even more so.

Rocking from side to side Robert used the cane and the wall to shuffle along, stubbornly ignoring any offers of help from nurses and orderlies as they went about their day.

The reception room he was headed for had once been his mother's morning room. It was bright and airy, with glass patio doors lining the whole length; a theme which ran throughout the house. After his father's death in 1916 the War Office had made the request to convert the house into a military hospital and subsequently made the decision to transform the small ballroom and the dining room into wards, leaving this one to be, essentially, the 'processing' room, a decision which Robert had been glad of at the time. His aim was for the hospital to be welcoming and comfortable, something different from what the men had been used to.

As he reached the door to the morning room, Robert turned his body and rocked slowly inside. The room as expected was a bustle of activity, with nurses lining up, assisting the new arrivals onto chairs. He watched Nurse Rosamund help one of the admissions fix his dressing gown so it was tied firmly, whilst another nurse covered his legs with a blanket and secured his feet into the foot plates.

Robert smiled softly at their care and took stock of the movement in front of him. "Are we settled?" he finally said, turning fully to the room.

Four years earlier
Wallace House, Cheshire, England

As usual for the time of the year, the external glass-paned door to Robert's bedroom sat slightly ajar, a warm breeze threatening to sneak its way through the small gap. Across the courtyard, low-level sun turned the sky golden, and as the sun set further it cast long, roof-turret-shaped shadows over the immaculate gravel driveway.

From his position Robert could only hear the familiar sounds of a day winding down. The locking of doors, the clanking of keys and the birdsong that signalled dusk was now falling upon the estate. Only through a small pane of distorted glass could he see over the well-manicured lawns that flanked the driveway. On a normal day they would seem filled with staff fussing over each blade of grass. Tonight, however, an unusual calmness had fallen on the estate leaving the lawns to the mercy of the low setting sun and clusters of flies that swarmed over the heads of flowers Robert had no chance of knowing the names of. In the distance the rhythmic beat of steam-powered farm machinery still thumped along as it snapped grain from the husks.

It could be, Robert thought, anywhere.

With a glance to his left he checked the hands on the small wind-up carriage clock that sat proudly above the fireplace of his bedroom and tutted softly to himself as he noted the time. The evening routine of the house was now familiar to him, as it should be – it had been a year since he had returned after his accident, the one that had struck him down in his prime. Nowadays his own internal body clock told him that someone would be in soon to serve tea, maybe bring toast and a sweet jam; then that same person – one of his father's many menservants – would later assist him into his bedclothes and lastly into bed.

Robert also knew he would be lucky if they dared to speak to him.

Or even look at him for that matter … but these days it was hard to get any sort of reaction from Albert Wallace – his father – that wasn't a curtly worded question as to his well-being or his opinions on the situation in Europe, let alone from a member of his staff.

Dismissing his annoyance at thinking about his father, Robert forced his frustration to the back of his mind, and with a slow, smooth action he pushed his way closer to the open door, coming to a halt just where the gentle breeze could be felt on skin. As always, he fixed his damaged leg first. Lifting it gently he crossed one knee securely over the other until the limbs settled together into a position Robert knew he would be comfortable in.

"Damn it!" Robert felt the muscles twinge as he pulled his hand away from supporting his knee and the full weight of the scarred leg settled. "You're a damned fool, Wallace," he said to himself as he felt the full extent of energy he had used just to move his legs. His hands ached. His body was still sore; his legs a mere blot on the landscape. And yet somehow he was expected to be lucky and thankful?

Robert had snorted more than once at his father passing such a comment and refused to dignify it with an answer.

How on earth was he lucky? Was there anything to be thankful for? What good were two arms that left him unable to ride a motorcycle or practise medicine?

Maybe the loss of the use of his arms would have been better all round? he thought macabrely.

Robert pushed the thought to the back of his head. He was healing. He could feel it. He had no right to think as he did.

Not now.

Not when …

Looking down at the withered limb, he shifted it slowly until the dreaded pull of the material from the trousers became uncomfortable and rubbed on the burnt flesh.

Oh pity me. He cursed to himself as his limbs now stretched even tighter. A small amount of burn hitting his nerves as the muscles worked harder.

Robert lifted his head up and looked out across the fields. His view now extended all the way to the small cottage that sat at the edge of the grounds and then further across the boundary to Manchester. Even in pain, he couldn't possibly deny that his father had chosen wisely, securing the place when Robert had been a baby. He also, much to his annoyance, couldn't deny Albert had chosen wisely in his choice of study-cum-bedroom for Robert to 'recuperate' in either, a thought that still left Robert deeply frustrated and thankful in equal amounts.

Robert leant forward and gently placed his forearms on the armrest of the chair, his eyes fixed on the small building with the thatched roof. His hands hung limply over the edge of the wooden chair rests and at first glance he saw nothing. No smoke signal, no signs of life that told Robert a person that he might care to be home, was.

A second swift glance confirmed that fact and yet Robert agreed with himself that it couldn't hurt to look a third time, could it?

A knock at the door startled him from his daydream. "Come," he said at the rather lacklustre second knock that followed the first, and, as expected, one of Albert Wallace's smart menservants pushed a trolley into the room.

"Tea, sir?"

Did he feel like tea? Possibly ... Robert hummed, the hint of annoyance he felt at being disturbed was almost immediately directed at the servant.

But of course it had been assumed that since Robert had returned home from the sanatorium he would follow Albert's routine. Get up at first light, eat a full English breakfast (Robert's was obviously brought to his room), read the papers, eat a light lunch, and take in some air from the garden (separately of course from anyone else's daily constitutional). He would then be expected to play chess or read a classic, eat the evening meal and then take tea and toast.

But did he actually want to?

"Of course," he answered loudly. Robert knew full well that a refusal of any kind would create eruptions below stairs and quickly travel up to Albert's rooms via a series of hand signals and nods from the servants.

With a flick of his wrist he indicated to the servant to set up the small table he used to write on within arm's reach of the wheelchair, and watched the servant pour the strong dark liquid into the china cup with a slight shake of his hand.

Robert stayed staring at the china cup decorated with the violet rose until a sugar cube was dropped hesitantly into it.

"Is there something wrong?" Robert asked, finally taking his eyes off the dense liquid and staring up at the servant's expression that had turned pale and nervous. Did the man have a temperature? Robert's first instincts as a doctor should have kicked in but he bit down on them tightly.

"Haven't you heard?" Jones – Robert thought it was Jones: his memory wasn't as good as it used to be – replied quietly, gingerly adding milk to the mixture, his chin pressing hard down towards his chest. "Word is coming through ... from the Front. Bessie in the kitchen, her brother is a Fusilier."

Robert stilled. Of course he had heard. It was all he seemed to read about at the moment in the newspapers. Albert was obsessed with it. The *Evening News* reported on very little else. "Mons?"

Jones nodded. "Bessie's brother ... he said ... we were overwhelmed. The Germans, they ..." He paused briefly. "They were too strong."

Robert flinched. "But they said in the papers it was a victory? We had retaken the area?" He had read the report a number of times and nothing suggested a defeat when the news had first filtered through. Albert had even come to his chambers and attempted to discuss it with him.

Jones shook his head. "Bessie said Ralph sent a message back saying the French retreated and ... well ..." He paused, unable to finish.

"Oh." *Well.* "Is Ralph safe?" Robert asked quietly. Suddenly the damned thing felt so real and close.

Jones simply nodded a response and retreated out of the room, leaving Robert to ponder the small amount said.

The next three hours passed slowly, with Robert receiving one last visit from Jones, who returned to help him into a nightshirt and then to his bed, before indicating to the open glass door as he tucked in the thick woollen blanket that covered Robert's legs.

"Would you like the door closed, Dr Wallace?" Jones asked, using Robert's full title – and Robert saw a silent curse fall from the man's mouth. *Bugger.*

Nowadays only one person still used his full title and made a large fuss of it when he did so, precisely at the moments Robert couldn't protest.

The issue wasn't that Robert had no right to be called doctor; he just had no desire to be addressed that way. His body was useless. He couldn't walk, so therefore he couldn't *do* medicine any more.

Nobody wanted a cripple in their practice.

He waved Jones off with a flap of his hand. "No, it's fine, leave it open, please."

Jones smiled hesitantly. "I'm sorry about my outburst before, sir," he said whilst smoothing the material of the blanket with a steady hand.

Robert looked up at the taller man. "I would rather know than not, if I were to be honest, Jones. I feel a bit isolated at times. Cut off." *As well as lonely, useless and broken,* but Robert didn't say that.

"Your father ..."

"My father tries to cocoon me. Wrap me in swaddling like a baby."

"Your father worries," Jones continued. "I think he is grateful you will never go to the Front, sir," he added with a nod.

Robert huffed.

"Your father is a very proud man."

Robert would never have described Albert Wallace as proud. Stubborn, argumentative, and controlling, yes. Proud, no. He shook his head at the taller man and spoke. "My father is obsessed with who is pointing guns at whom, and has no desire to let me forget how I won't be part of it. *There is no place in war for a man like you, Robert*," he snapped, feeling his chest heave up and down under the thick blanket.

Jones's chin was pressed to his chest again, his eyes pinched closed. "Good night, sir."

Robert agonisingly forced back an apology. "Good night, Jones."

The door closed with a quiet snick.

The tension took a while to seep out of Robert's body as he fought to control his breathing, but finally he began to settle down and allow his head to sink into the pillow. The blankets, as always, enveloped him, resting heavily on his legs. The coolness of the sheets, not yet warm from his body heat, sent a shiver down his spine.

He cursed himself softly.

Albert was obviously right. He would never go to fight for his country. His damned stupid mangled legs prevented him. Like those people who didn't require a cripple in their practice, the propaganda machine didn't require a cripple on the Front Line either. There was no room for men like him – a fact Robert had still not accepted. He shook his head gently against the pillow.

They required fit, able-bodied men more like … *No.* Robert refused to allow his head to travel to such places. Instead he forced the thoughts away with scrunched eyes and cursing. "Damned pathetic leg," he said out loud. Damn the motorbike, damn the fire that left its scars, and damn himself!

It was a while before Robert heard the footsteps, the familiar sound of a work boot on the gravel of the driveway that wrapped the house. Any normal person lying in such a position as Robert's would no doubt worry at the sound and cower at the intruder. Robert simply snuggled back further into the bedding, allowing the warm familiar feeling spreading over his body to push aside the tension that twisted his guts.

When the breeze increased through the small gap of the open door, Robert's breath hitched slightly. It hitched a second time when the tell-tale sound of clothing caught on the door handle began scratching. When the dull thud of stockinged feet hit the floor Robert let out an almost silent moan.

"Shush," a voice said quietly but firmly. If Robert hadn't had his ears peeled back with intent he would have missed the sound.

Robert replied in a whisper, "You're a bossy bastard."

"You love it, Doctor."

Robert stifled a curse, and a chuckle filled the room at his retort. The familiarity of the conversation, the same that took place most evenings, filled him with warmth.

"He put you in that nightshirt again? You might as well leave it off if you were t' ask me."

Robert didn't answer. Of course he still had it on, that was part of the plan. For Robert, just the mere thought of this big brick of a man tenderly stripping the garment from his body was part of the moment.

"Have you locked the door?" Robert asked, quickly changing the subject instead of answering. He pointed at the key on his bedside cabinet.

Robert could see Wilf shake his head in the dim light. "No Doctor, yes Doctor." Another low chuckle rumbled out as Wilf reached for the key. "I don't know why you trouble yourself. They've never bothered us yet, so why would they tonight?"

Robert sighed nervously. Of course Wilf was right: no one had once ever bothered them. But whether the staff or Albert knew about what went on behind closed doors or not, Robert was always going to err on the side of caution.

Robert relaxed when he heard the key finally turn, and he allowed his body to sink further into the feather mattress as his lover of over fifteen years took three large strides over to the bed and pulled at the uneven hem of the work shirt he wore. The glow from the bedside light allowed Robert to take a long lingering look as the strong lithe body revealed itself, the scene never failing to start a slow burn throughout his body.

These days Robert noted to memory the new ridges as they appeared, where the bruises and cuts from the hard labour Wilf did all day healed, and whereabouts on his hands new callouses sprang, just in case he never saw them again.

"Are you well?" a deep voice rumbled, cutting off Robert's thoughts.

Robert nodded, hoping the action could be seen in the shadows. "I am now."

And he was.

The bed dipped slightly as Wilf's bulk towered over him and he knelt first on the edge, pulling back the sheets and blankets, and then slowly moving over Robert, slipping his left knee in between Robert's own, not flinching once as the scarred flesh met his.

"I missed you," Robert whispered against Wilf's bare chest.

Wilf made no sound. Instead Robert felt light kisses and warm lips trace his neck, along his shoulder bone and then make their way back up along his jaw.

"It's only been three nights," he murmured into Robert's mouth.

It had actually been three long nights and four days but Robert wasn't in any state mentally to argue with the larger man whose body dwarfed his.

Wilf's fingers traced their way up Robert's body until he felt those fingers spread out, slip underneath his shoulder blades and hook themselves around the back of Robert's neck. Robert's body arched up slightly at the touch, his back bowed – and a sharp pain ran up his spine as he fell into the hold. "Oh!" he cried softly, feeling Wilf's body still above his.

"Did I hurt you?" Wilf whispered, gently pulling away.

No.

Yes.

Possibly.

"No. It's good," he finally replied out loud, giving Wilf what he was hoped was a clear sign to carry on.

"Are you sure?"

Robert nodded, finally catching Wilf's lips with his own.

Without warning, Wilf gathered up Robert's nightshirt, pulled it over his head and tossed it aside. Robert heard it land somewhere over the other side of the room.

The kissing stopped for a second then started again where it had finished; only now a fierceness had developed between the men.

"No," Robert said firmly, placing a hand on Wilf's shoulder. He had no intent to stop Wilf, merely slow him down, but at his words he felt Wilf's warm body pull away from his. In fact Wilf was already rocking back on his heels when Robert gripped at the muscles in his arms. By God he was thankful for that upper body strength now. "No. I mean, sorry. Let's take it slower."

At Robert's words a flash of something crossed Wilf's face briefly. "Slowly?" Wilf asked.

Robert nodded, ignoring the troubled look. "There's no hurry. There never is. No one knows. No one can hear us." He repeated to Wilf his own words. The room Albert had put him in *was* at the opposite side to the main living area at the end of a long corridor. Robert had been told when he had returned home it was for the ease of access, but he half suspected it was an out-of-sight, out-of-mind thing.

At the words, Wilf didn't move.

"Please, Wilf," Robert pleaded with his lover.

Very slowly Robert felt Wilf's body shift and work its way down; he planted a hesitant kiss on Robert's chest. The movements were familiar and well-practised but there was still tenderness there as there always had been.

"Oh!" Robert cried out at the sensation. "I don't think that's slowing it down any!" he whispered.

Robert dropped his hand, landing it perfectly on Wilf's hair. He automatically twisted his fingers and then smoothed the wild and dark curly strands out tenderly. Normally Robert had very little control during their encounters, he never had. Wilf was so much bigger and stronger and had been since Robert had first set eyes on him, the day he arrived to work on the estate.

A rumble from Wilf's chest caught his attention and Robert looked down. "Oh bugger!" he exclaimed, ashamed slightly by his language. But he had been taken aback by how focused Wilf had turned. "Are you in a hurry?" Robert gasped at the action.

Wilf shook his head. "No," he said quietly. But Robert saw his gaze drift over towards the carriage clock. "I've just missed you," he added.

Robert palmed Wilf's cheek instinctively. "I missed you too," he replied tenderly, feeling lips graze his skin then return back to the place they had just left.

"Wilf!" This time the shout shot across the bedroom like a protest.

Robert wanted to go slower. "Oh …" His hands were rigid and dug deep, tangling themselves into the coarse sheet and Wilf's hair.

Strong, long, work-hardened fingers worked their way up along his skin and Wilf's gaze finally locked with his. Robert couldn't move even if he wanted to. His scarred legs lay pathetically either side of Wilf's body but that wasn't the reason. His body felt wrung out and suspended in the atmosphere.

"Robert?"

"Mmmm?" Robert didn't hear the words over the sound of his fight for air.

"We need to talk," Wilf said.

Robert ignored the words.

"Doctor." This time Wilf whispered.

Robert's body suddenly went still. He heard a hint of insistence in the tone, and the feeling of floating dissipated and the air pressure changed. This was a different *'Doctor'* that Wilf used.

Suddenly Robert's legs felt tense, less fluid. He coughed lightly to swallow any anxiety now creeping up over him. "We … we do?" he asked.

Their bodies turned instinctively so they now lay parallel against each other, their skin touching, legs entwined. The hair on Wilf's legs rubbed coarsely against Robert's still tender skin. The whole sensation felt better than the woollen trousers, however. Now he could feel the light gentle circles his lover drew on his scarred thigh and an increase in pressure as his fingers pushed into the skin. If it had been anyone else touching him so intimately he would have flinched; instead, he buried his head into Wilf's shoulder for comfort.

"I can't stay all night," Wilf said quietly. "I have to get up and be in Manchester by dawn."

Robert nodded as the calloused fingers traced their way up his hip, and whether it was the time, the moment, or whether he knew what was coming, Robert remembered the first time Wilf had touched him in exactly the same place after the accident. Then it had been just as light and tender, and the touches had pushed away the darkness.

Tonight, though, the touch was different. Robert knew what was coming. He'd known, in fact he had known for weeks, months … ever since …

"They gave us a uniform and a kit bag. I tried it on for Ma today." Wilf's voice cut his thoughts off again and Robert could only nod, the hairs from Wilf's chest tickling him, and he buried his head in tighter so as not to miss a moment.

"I signed up last week."

The words stung and hung in the air. *Last week*. Not today, not tomorrow.

Wilf had already done it.

A silence fell over the room, the sound of ticking from the carriage clock the only thing that disturbed the peace.

Robert felt the need to pull Wilf further towards his body. His pulse jumped; he felt Wilf's body weight sag comfortably down onto his.

Selfishly – and oh God he hated himself for this – Robert thought about what would become of him. His lover was leaving. *Going*. Gone. Who knew when this man, his love, would return?

Words and pictures from newspapers flashed in front of Robert's eyes. Everything that he had read and heard reported twisted in his gut. All those brisk conversations with Albert flooded his brain. *You're probably pleased to be left behind', 'weak willed', 'you should never have bought the machine'*. *No*.

By God, Robert would give a limb to be able to go out there with Wilf.

He finally felt Wilf move against him, as if he had been holding his breath waiting for Robert to be the first to speak. "I might be back for Christmas," he said softly in Robert's ear. "It'll all be over."

Tears pricked the corners of Robert's eyes and he wiped them with the back of his hand. "I knew you'd go." Wilf was able-bodied and young enough to fight.

The man responded with a kiss to Robert's forehead. "I have to," he whispered.

"Do you know where you're being sent?" Robert forced the words out.

"No. Possibly Europe. The fight is over there. The recruiting officer said it wouldn't reach England."

Well, that was one shining hope, Robert thought. But Wilf continued before he could say so.

"I'm off to basic training tomorrow and then I don't know. I've joined one of the Pals battalions – the 4th City – part of the 19th." He paused briefly, pushing a lock of hair from Robert's face. "I'll try t' keep in touch, my love. But it might be hard. I won't be able to say what I want in my letters. I might not be able to write. This between us ... it's not ..."

Robert pulled down Wilf's head with the same hand he had used to wipe away the escaping tear and ran his fingers through the dark unruly locks before he could say any more.

"I don't want you to go," he admitted. This was not the time for them to discuss the right or wrong of their relationship.

At the words, Wilf's body sagged against his. His shoulders shook as he breathed in lungful after lungful of air. "I don't want to go but I have to." Tremors wracked Wilf's body and he shuddered against Robert. Breathing hard, Robert dragged his hand through Wilf's hair and held on tight.

Don't go. Stay. We can hide like we have done for all this time.

They had lasted this long with their forbidden love. Why not till the war was over?

"Then stay."

It seemed such a simple thing to suggest.

Wilf leaned his body in further, if that were possible. "I can't."

"We can go north. Or to the Welsh mountains. No one will know." *Could they actually make that happen?* "Or maybe towards the Pennines; or where the lakes are in the Cumbrian hills?" They were silly thoughts, he knew.

Wilf shook his head against Robert's shoulder. "I can't," he repeated.

In the dim light Robert found Wilf's face and lifted it up so their lips met. "Tonight is our last night then." It wasn't a question.

A kiss brushed his lips. "Yes." The word sounded so final. "Let me love you one more time, Robbie."

Robert paused to take in the words. This love, this unconditional love ... After everything he had been through, the man next to him still loved him. Robert's head dipped as the warmth of Wilf's mouth pressed against his neck, and he arched into the touch. "Yes. Yes, please. Yes."

If this was to be Robert's final night with the man he loved, he was going to take all that he could.

Love me.

Hold me.

Now and for ever.

Their bodies fell into a familiar pattern, but this time each touch burnt an imprint onto Robert's skin. Every move Wilf made, Robert responded to with love and feeling, and soon they fell against one another, lost in the moment.

The next morning Robert woke alone as he knew he would do. The coarse sheets were now cold under his hand and on the bedside table sat the key to his door, the glass patio door now closed.

Robert turned slowly. He reached out to the key, noticing a piece of paper fall to the floor as he lifted it from the glass surface.

Robbie, it read. *I'll be home soon. I promise.*

September 1918
Wallace House Military Hospital

Robert shuffled slowly towards the far end of his mother's morning room and waited as the nurses finished their work.

He started from the right and worked to the left, nodding at the first two gentlemen, shaking a hand where he could, taking a mental inventory of the damage. Finally he came to the third wheelchair where the occupant sat quietly. The injuries matched the extensively detailed field notes Robert had read so many times: burns to the neck and shoulder, loss of the arm and right leg, additional burns to the left-hand side, and suspected hearing loss.

All things he wouldn't wish on his enemy, let alone the man he loved.

"Private Wilfred Cahill?" Nurse Rosamund said as she fussed with the blanket, not seeing the glance that passed between the men. "This is Dr Robert Wallace, your new physician."

Robert shook his head softly and caught the small smile that was forming on Wilf's face. It was the same as he remembered from four years ago, yet different. Now, there was something else there also.

Pain?

Sadness?

Relief?

Robert's eyes searched his lover's for an answer before he finally broke the silence between them. "Welcome home, Wilf," he said quietly, not knowing what else to say. Robert had planned this reunion so clearly in his head; yet now it was here, he was at a complete loss.

Finally, Wilf's smile grew wider as if he had remembered something suddenly, and Robert felt his heart skip a beat at the sight. "I promised you, didn't I, Robbie?" his lover said fondly, not seeing the wide-eyed look of surprise Nurse Rosamund shot in their direction.

Robert smiled at her then nodded at Wilf in return. "You did, Wilf, you did." He bent down to touch his lover's hand. "And I'm so glad you made it."

Sam Evans

I live just outside Manchester in an ex-coal mining town, semi-famous for its Rugby League. I've been writing for what seems like ever but only found the MM genre after discovering a paranormal shifter series. I have published a short story in a Dreamspinner Press anthology – and now this, my first historical piece – and I'm hoping these won't be my last. I'm currently working on a contemporary series set in and around Manchester as well as a couple of other short stories.

samevans1975.wordpress.com
twitter.com/samjevansstuff

Ánh Sáng

Barry Brennessel

1908

They met at twelve years old, a week before the Tết festival on the outskirts of Thái Nguyên city proper. The coming year 1909. The Year of the Rooster.

Bùi Vân Minh, potting chrysanthemums outside the hut he and his mother shared, couldn't quite believe it when he saw the pig race by, followed by a boy in hot pursuit. The boy's pained expression as he glanced at Minh seemed a plea for help.

After a moment's pause – Who was this boy? Was he stealing a pig? – Minh decided it would be a noble thing to offer assistance. He brushed the soil from his hands and hurried down the path.

Were it not for the far-off squeals, Minh might have lost track of the pair. When he rounded a steep bend, he spotted the boy on his knees, his body wedged against the pig, which in turn was trapped against a tree stump and the remnants of a stone foundation from a long-gone structure.

The boy was winded, sweat streaming down his face.

That face!

He has a beautiful face, Minh thought. Oh, these strange feelings he'd been having lately! Here they were again, bubbling up in the presence of this handsome boy. The feelings no one could ever know about.

"Thank you," the boy said, with heavy breath.

Even though this boy had concluded logically that Minh had arrived to help, Minh found it presumptuous.

The pig squirmed. The boy laboured to confine the animal.

"How do we control it?" Minh asked, seeing that there was no rope, and that the animal was too large and feisty to carry, even for two people.

The boy was silent. He stared up at the sky. He looked back down at the pig. He eased his grip, leaned out of the pig's way, and nudged its backside with his right hand. The pig trotted away, its squeals almost in song.

"What are you doing?" Minh protested, watching the pig disappear in a stand of trees farther down the hillside.

The boy stood. "It's obvious. I granted him freedom," he said.

"Was it yours to free?"

"My father's. We sold it to a family nearby, for the festival. I'll try to convince my father it got away too fast for me. I'll be punished, but ... I never wanted him to die. He was my favourite. I gave him a name. I don't care if it's a foolish thing to do."

"A pig is so valuable! You cost your father a lot of money just now." Who was this boy to do such an inane thing on his own like that? To squander his father's hard work and income. "Besides, it might end up in a bad position. A situation more painful than a quick slaughter."

"Do you always think the worst will happen?" the boy asked.

"Are you always so impetuous?"

The boy scowled. "That's a big word."

"I like to study words. It's not exactly a crime."

"And I don't study? Because I spend all my time farming pigs?"

"Did I say that?"

"You didn't have to."

"And I don't even know you. How could I have guessed how you spend your days?"

The boy raised his hands in the direction of the pig's path to freedom. He then motioned to his soiled, torn clothing.

While Minh wasn't exactly dressed in *his* finest, which consisted of one decent set of clothes worn only on three occasions, the trousers and shirt he put on to plant chrysanthemums looked far neater than this boy's.

"I didn't mean anything by it," Minh said, bowing his head.

"I'm sorry," the boy said. "You came to help me. I was rude."

"But I lectured you," Minh said. "I'm sorry."

"I'm sorry that you feel sorry," the boy said.

There was silence. Both boys burst out laughing.

"I'm Bùi Vân Minh, by the way."

"Ngô Công Thao."

They smiled at one another.

"What was your pig's name?" Minh asked.

"Napoléon."

The boys laughed once more.

1910

The second time they encountered one another, they were fourteen.

Minh had ventured to the grocer with the meagre money he and his mother had remaining in the coffer. Three eggs and some cabbage would have to last them for two days. Minh walked along the street, crossing to the opposite side before he reached the *boulangerie*, for the smell of fresh bread would have been far too torturous. When he looked away from the baker's window, he spotted the cart with two gutted pigs tied to it, and a boy standing at the handles, ready at a moment's notice to lift the cart and push.

Minh wasn't entirely certain it was Thao. Yet, there seemed ... *something* ... familiar. The posture. The profile. *Something*.

Minh approached, and pointed to the cart. "I hope one of those isn't Napoléon."

A test. If this boy was Thao, he'd remember. Hopefully. If it was another boy, he'd think Minh a fool or a lunatic and Minh would make a hasty retreat.

The boy turned to face Minh.

It was Thao. Thao with bruises on his cheek. Thao with a black eye. Thao with a gash on his forehead.

In spite of all that, Thao managed a smile at the sight of Minh. "Napoléon lives on an island now," he said, his voice strained.

"What happened?" Minh asked.

Thao shrugged. "I gave another pig his freedom."

1917

That there were still people solvent enough to dine at restaurants surprised him. That the line of men hoping to become waiters at La Fourchette – to replace those who had gone off to fight for France – stretched for blocks did not shock Minh.

He knew his chances were virtually hopeless. He convinced himself to try nevertheless. He had to find something to support both him and his mother. The dynamics of the city, and the entire region, were changing so rapidly. Thousands of his fellow citizens had deployed to Europe to help with the war effort. A large number of men remained behind, ready to fill the vacated jobs.

Minh had been in line for an hour when a man stepped out of the restaurant. He wore a nicely tailored suit, his frame tall and thin, his features sharp, his hair thinning, making him appear older than he probably was.

The man spoke to an Indonesian – a Cambodian, Minh suspected, based on the man's accent. The tall, well-dressed man scanned the line, then retreated back inside. The Cambodian man picked out three men, instructing them to step forward. He then pointed to Minh, and called out for him to join the other three. He repeated the order, voice raised, when Minh – who felt momentarily paralysed – didn't react quickly enough.

"Follow me inside," the Cambodian man said to this group of four. Minh fell in line behind the last man, and all five entered the restaurant, the Cambodian practically marching.

The man in the suit, as Minh was told before entering the office, was Monsieur Laurent Chastain, the son of the proprietor. He stared out the window of the room as Minh was shown in. "Please sit down," he said. The office door closed behind Minh as the Cambodian man retreated to the dining area.

Minh scanned the room. Richly appointed, with fine wood furniture, wallpaper featuring an idyllic forest motif, and a crystal chandelier above the desk. A plush chair of red velvet was positioned opposite the desk. Minh sat.

Monsieur Chastain turned to face Minh. "You'd train with Monsieur Sovann. I'm looking for someone to work primarily at lunchtime. Breakfast, if the need arises, which it will on some special occasions. Do those hours suit you?"

It seemed a dream. This man hadn't asked about any prior experience. Or about Minh's background. How did this man know he wasn't about to hire a murderer? A thief? A pirate?

"Do you speak?" Monsieur Chastain asked. "Fluently in French, I hope, as the advertisement stated."

Minh nodded. "Yes," he answered, in French. "Yes. I ... that is to say, that schedule would be agreeable. Fine. Yes."

"All right then," Monsieur Chastain said. "Be here Monday, at ten o'clock. We'll supply you with the uniform. Just be sure you're as presentable as possible. Clean hands, most importantly."

"Yes, sir. Of course."

172

"And I suppose there's the matter of your name."

"Bùi Vân Minh."

The man closed his eyes. "I'll never get used to this language of yours. So tonal."

Minh repeated his name, a little more slowly.

"Minh then. All right. I'll see you on Monday."

Work at a posh restaurant was so coveted, so out of reach for most, yet here was Minh, able to race home and tell his mother that he'd be donning the black trousers and white jacket that were *de rigueur* for the staff at one of the best establishments in the city.

"But how?" his mother asked. "How, with these food shortages, can a restaurant stay open?"

"The French administrators, and the wealthy, need their meals, I suppose."

"I'm so very proud of you, of course. But how did you win out over those with experience?"

It was a fair question. A question for which Minh had no real answer. "My charm and good looks?"

"At least I know one of those traits well enough," his mother said. "I do imagine the other is true. I have an idea in my mind."

"Based on my father?"

"Partly."

Minh had long ago given up on his mother's eyesight returning. Sometimes as he lay awake at night, he held on to the hope that, come morning, she would exclaim some miracle, even if it were the slightest change.

"To just see light one more time before I die," she said, during her most sombre periods.

"*Ánh sáng,*" Minh would say softly to himself at night, a prayer, a plea. "*Ánh sáng, ánh sáng, ánh sáng …*"

Light, light, light …

In less than a week, after trailing Lok Sovann (or *Monsieur* Sovann, he kept reminding Minh, and seemed to bristle at any hint of his Cambodian heritage), Minh was waiting at tables on his own.

Monsieur Chastain was nowhere to be seen those first few days, but gradually he'd emerge from his office, chat with a few patrons, and give Minh a reassuring nod, sometimes accompanied by a smile.

Minh settled into his routine. He was at the restaurant at ten, began serving at tables at eleven, and was done with his shift between four and four-thirty. Each waiter was allowed to bring any leftover food from patrons' plates back home with him, as long as it was done discreetly, in the kitchen, once the tables had been cleared.

The restaurant was rarely full, but those customers who dined there – exclusively European – ordered expensive items, and often drank no fewer than two bottles of wine, in addition to assorted *apéritifs et digestifs*.

Despite the rationing, and the cycle of shortages, Monsieur Chastain spared little expense when filling the pantry.

To Minh, La Fourchette seemed a place for the Europeans to congregate in order to pretend there was no war consuming their homeland.

On Minh's third Tuesday of work, a delivery of pork was scheduled. The items and names of the delivery person were always posted in a conspicuous spot in the kitchen, so that should the delivery arrive when Sovann was occupied with other tasks, one of the waiters could greet the deliveryman and summon Sovann to inspect the goods for quality.

Minh stared at the current delivery sheet:

Viande	*Jour/Heures*	*Nom*
Porc	*Mardi/Neuf heures*	*Ngô Công Thao*

Almost immediately, Minh glanced out of the service door to see Sovann examining three pigs on Thao's cart.

Likely a breach of protocol, and he had little doubt a rebuke from Sovann would follow, but Minh had to. He had to step out to speak to Thao. It had been seven years, and the last time he'd seen him, Thao had been covered with bruises.

Minh stepped outside. He pointed to a pig. "Napoléon?"

Sovann turned and stared as though Minh had dropped a hundred dishes on the floor.

Thao's face was free of bruises, and ever more handsome. Minh felt a flutter in his chest.

"Still on the island," Thao said. "Happily wallowing in mud."

"Monsieur Minh, I'm sure you have your duties," Sovann said.

Minh held Thao's gaze. But he couldn't risk further angering Sovann. How he longed to speak with Thao! He felt paralysed again.

"Monsieur Minh!"

Minh glanced to the ground. He turned and started for the door. From the corner of his eye he could see Monsieur Chastain at the office window, watching him.

Minh stepped out into the afternoon sun. He loved the feel of the rays on his skin. He squinted, the light so overwhelming at first. He thought of his mother. *Ánh sáng, ánh sáng, ánh sáng …*

"Bùi Vân Minh?" The voice called from behind him.

Minh stopped and turned. "You're pig free!" he said. "I think that's the first time I've ever seen that."

"It was a good day," Thao said.

"So you're still at it then. What's your ratio?"

"My ratio?"

"Sold pigs to those set free."

Thao laughed. "No more freedom," he said, "but I give them a happy life. Happiness leads to tastiness."

They studied one another.

"You look well," Thao said. "How long have you been in the restaurant business?"

"Days, really," Minh said. "You can count the length of my career on two hands."

"The uniform suits you," Thao said.

"And do you … is your father … I mean, does he still have the –"

"He died last year. I own the farm now."

"Oh, Thao. I … I'm so sorry to hear –"

"My days of sorrow over his death can be counted on one hand."

They strolled together until the fork in the road that would take Minh north-west toward home, and Thao east to his farm.

"*La fourchette*," Minh said, gesturing to the road.

Thao smiled. "I think I would enjoy it very much if we could spend more time chatting," he said. "If that doesn't make me impetuous."

"A little impetuous."

"One day soon, come. Come and I'll show you my herd of pigs." Thao paused. "That didn't sound very polite. I hope you understood that I meant it as a –"

"No, I understand. I would enjoy that."

"So will the pigs."

"You need to expand your circle of acquaintances."

They held each other's gaze once more.

"It looks as though I am," Thao said.

"Me?"

Minh made a habit of calling out to his mother just before reaching the hut, though with her keen sense of hearing it was impossible to sneak up on her. Even in sleep she often snapped awake at the slightest sounds.

"Me?"

She appeared in the doorway.

Minh clutched a tightly-wrapped cloth. "*Poulet poché aux aromates* tonight!"

His mother still looked so young. Even with her hair pulled back loosely, and her plain clothes, she possessed an air of elegance. "Don't speak French," she said.

As Minh moved closer, he noticed she was clutching a piece of paper.

"Is something wrong?" Minh asked.

"Two officials came here today. To speak with you. I didn't tell them you were at work. I said I didn't know where you were."

Minh stepped inside the hut. He set their dinner down on the small table in the corner, a table made by his father two months before Minh was born. "What did they want?"

"You must register," she said. "A list for the Ministry. For the war." Her hand shaking, she held out the paper. Minh walked over and took it from her. He studied it.

"Me, don't cry. It doesn't mean I'm going. They're just drawing up a list of citizens."

"Eligible citizens," she said.

Minh wanted to reassure her, but he felt as scared as she did. What did it really mean? Could it be that they planned to send him to France?

176

"I won't let them take you," she said. "They can't. They have no right. This is *their* war, not ours."

"Come, sit down. Let's eat our dinner. Don't worry about this any more tonight. I'll see about it before work tomorrow."

"*Their* war," his mother repeated. "We have no business in it. And France has no business here."

The next morning, Minh awoke three hours early, after a night of fitful sleep. His mother was already up, and had brewed a pot of tea. She sat at the table, her head resting against the wall.

"I can pick out twenty-two now," she whispered. "Twenty-two different insects. All clamouring to be heard."

Minh kissed her on the cheek.

Neither of them spoke about his leaving early.

At the fork in the road he saw a familiar sight.

"You haven't come to visit me," Thao said.

"I thought I was supposed to visit the pigs."

"Do you have time now?"

Minh clutched the paper in his hand.

"It's ten minutes away," Thao said. "I promise I won't keep you long. I won't make you late for work."

Minh shoved the paper into his pocket. "Okay. I accept."

The place was not a farm so much as a small patch of land, with a hut half the size of Minh's and his mother's. Five pigs were fenced in a pen that covered more area than the hut.

"My empire," Thao said.

"The pigs are so plump."

"As I told you. I keep them happy. I want them to enjoy themselves while they're alive."

"Don't you worry about them being stolen?"

Thao pointed to his right. "When I make deliveries, I have very kind and watchful neighbours."

Minh nodded. He glanced at Thao, whose shirt was missing a button, spread open to reveal his chest. He glanced quickly away, but not before Thao had noticed.

"I need to meet someone who can sew."

Minh glanced to the ground. He dragged his foot against the grass. One of the pigs squealed and ran the length of the pen.

"Rimbaud," Thao said.

Minh laughed. "Do they all have names?"

"Not yet. I'll need help. Even more when the sow there, see? – in the corner – has her litter."

"So your business will continue then?"

"With luck."

Minh stared back down at Thao's chest, angry that he did so, but unable to stop himself. Thao noticed again.

"Soon I can buy a new –"

"Please," Minh said. "That's not ... I'm not trying to make you –"

"It's okay. I know that I –"

"Just ... no," Minh said. "It's ... it doesn't matter."

"Would you prefer I take it off?"

Minh looked up. He couldn't read Thao's tone. He tensed.

"Thao ..."

Thao unbuttoned the remaining two buttons and slipped the shirt off. The sunlight fell on his smooth skin. He looked up at Minh. "Please. If ... if I'm wrong about ... something ... just leave and never come back. And if you ... just please, leave me to my life. Don't report me."

"I don't understand," Minh said.

Thao reached down and took hold of Minh's wrist. He drew Minh's hand to him, then guided Minh's fingertips to stroke the length of his chest.

"I watch your eyes," Thao whispered.

Minh's mouth went dry. He parted his lips, to speak, but the words caught in his throat.

"Am I wrong?" Thao asked.

Minh shook his head.

In the confines of the small hut, in the rising heat of the summer morning, when Bùi Vân Minh should have been at the office of the Ministry to see about those foolish papers they'd left for him, he instead made love to Ngô Công Thao.

Twice.

It had become part of their routine. Every day, whether or not Thao had any business in the city, he would walk past La Fourchette, once at 10.45, just before lunchtime, when Minh was sure to be in the kitchen and could see out of the window, and once at 1.15, when Minh would be plating lunch for Monsieur Chastain and once again would be in plain view for Thao to see.

"We must be discreet," Minh cautioned, more than once, mornings before work, evenings before he returned home, when he lay entwined, nude, with Thao, inside the small hut.

"How is it we found each other?" Thao said, many times, a question never answered.

"Do you ever feel ... do you think this is wrong?" Minh would say, his back to Thao, times when he felt overwhelmed by some degree of guilt, a shame he wished would vanish.

"My father used to beat me for being unconventional. I gave up on guilt many years ago."

Minh sat in the waiting area of the Ministry of Colonies. The room was sweltering, stuffy, cramped. A young French soldier, with an attempt at a moustache that looked more like something drawn on, called out to him. Pointed to him. Motioned him to the desk.

"Yes?" the soldier asked.

Minh wasn't sure what to say.

"Don't waste my time!" the soldier shouted. "What's your business here? Do you speak French? I don't speak your goddamned tongue. God, how I wish you people, and that goes for all of you in this room, would get it through your heads how much easier your lives would be if you spoke French instead of monkey."

Minh cleared his throat. He held up the piece of paper.

The soldier grabbed it and unfurled it. "It's blank."

"I ... I don't know what it's for." Minh didn't dare admit that he'd had the form for days and not done anything with it.

The soldier massaged one of his temples. "It needs to be filled out. You need to be on file."

"File for what?" Minh asked.

"To be called up."

"Sir, I don't –"

"There's a war going on. You know that, don't you?"

"Yes, but –"

"And whether or not you people want to accept it, your allegiance is to France, and when France needs you, you answer her call, do you understand?"

Minh nervously, quickly nodded. "Sir. But sir, you see, I … Are there exemptions?"

The soldier scanned him. "If you have all your limbs, and all your senses, there are no exemptions."

"But my mother," Minh said. "She's blind. I'm the only one she has. My father died many years ago. I'm her only relative left."

The soldier shook his head. "That's something you have to take up with a senior officer. In the meantime, you need to fill out that form and submit it. Or you'll be in contempt of the law."

Minh turned. He started back toward the row of chairs against the wall. There was nothing to write with. He wasn't about to ask the soldier for a pen or pencil. He'd be in contempt of the law until he could borrow a pen from the restaurant.

The milk swirling in the cup gave Minh the impression of clouds being born. He offered his vision to Monsieur Chastain, who sat at a desk in the corner of the restaurant office. He was so focused on tallying the day's lunchtime receipts that he jumped when Minh set down the cup and saucer.

"A serving of clouds," Minh said.

Monsieur Chastain stared at him, head tilted, eyes narrowed.

"It's not my French skills waning," Minh was quick to announce before Monsieur Chastain could comment. "It's just my creative way to look at the world." He enjoyed his chats with Monsieur Chastain. Especially today. It took his mind off his visit to the Ministry of Colonies.

Monsieur Chastain smiled. "There must be some Tonkin folklore, some ancient Annam mythology about the formation of clouds that doesn't involve *café au lait*."

"But that wouldn't be my own myth, would it?" Minh asked.

"Well, your French is certainly improving daily," Monsieur Chastain said, "despite your peculiar thoughts."

"Thanks to you."

"Are you thanking me for your French skills? Or your peculiar thoughts?"

Minh shrugged.

"You've mastered the language of gestures, too," Monsieur Chastain said. Minh bowed.

"You've worked out very well here, Minh. I can't begin to tell you how pleased I am. You bring a smile to my face, on occasion, and as anyone will tell you, that's not an easy feat."

Minh bowed once again.

Monsieur Chastain shook his head. He waved Minh away. "All right, you can out-gesture me. I concede. Now go. Bring me my lunch."

Minh went back to the kitchen. He was relieved his workday would soon be done. He felt undeserving, in a sense, that he was able to head home, whereas there were so many working from sunrise well into the night, or so many who had volunteered – or been forced – to journey to France to help with the war. He owed so much to Monsieur Chastain. For reasons he still couldn't fathom, Monsieur Chastain had chosen *him* out a pool of dozens to become part of the staff.

When Minh returned with lunch, Monsieur Chastain was holding a bottle against the bulb of his desk lamp. "Have you ever tried Armagnac?" he asked, the soft glow of the lamp enriching the deep brown colour of the liquid.

Minh shook his head.

"My father always insisted on having it brought here. He said no Frenchman should be deprived of his Armagnac no matter where in the world he is." He set down the bottle. He rose from his chair, walked over to the mahogany cabinet in the corner, and brought down two glasses from the top shelf. "A task impossible to fulfil, of course, with this war going on. I'm sure those stuck on the battlefields of Europe are being deprived of so much more than their Armagnac."

He filled the two glasses. He offered one to Minh, who took it with a hesitant, shaking hand.

"A toast," Monsieur Chastain said. He lifted his glass. "To the best waiter we have on the staff." He clinked his glass with Minh's. "Go ahead, don't be afraid. You'll like it, I promise."

Minh moved the glass closer to his lips. The aroma was strong. Yet oddly pleasant. He brought the glass to his lips. He took a small taste. It burned his throat.

"Well?" Monsieur Chastain said. "Your verdict?"

"Unusual," Minh said.

Monsieur Chastain consumed the contents of his glass with one gulp. "Your descriptive skills will strengthen as your sobriety weakens." He poured another glass for himself. "If my father had any idea what I was doing at this instant, he'd book a passage back from Paris immediately and have me flogged. What difference does it make though? We drink this bottle, we drink another. We've been losing money for months anyway, thanks to this damn skirmish with the Kaiser." Monsieur Chastain consumed the same amount as before. He poured a third glass. "I shouldn't have told you that. There's no reason to panic. At least, not right away. But what do I know? How the hell am I supposed to run a restaurant in my father's absence? He just handed me the manager's hat and expected magic."

Minh had two sips to Monsieur Chastain's four glasses. He didn't dislike the drink, necessarily. He *did* dislike the burning sensation in his throat.

"Do you remember the family you served on your third day with us?" Monsieur Chastain asked. "The Dutch family afraid they'd be for ever stuck in Indochina due to the war?"

"Yes. The ones who asked me where to post mail, because they'd written thirty-three postcards."

Monsieur Chastain nodded. "The younger brother of Meener Abspoel. You must remember him. Seated at the head of the table, opposite his older brother."

There was a pause. Minh waited for Monsieur Chastain to continue. But Monsieur Chastain stared into Minh's eyes.

"What about him?" Minh asked.

Monsieur Chastain swirled his glass. "Handsome man. Striking. You can't help noticing people as beautiful as that." He took a sip of his drink. "Whether they're male or female. Beautiful people are beautiful people."

Minh tensed. What was Monsieur Chastain driving at? Could Monsieur Chastain possibly have noticed what was happening that night? Had he been watching as Minh served the Dutch family? *No!* It was impossible. Minh refused to believe it. He'd been discreet, and professional, while waiting on the Abspoels' table. Hadn't he? Surely it wasn't obvious how appreciative he'd been of the younger Meener Abspoel's beauty.

Monsieur Chastain moved closer to Minh. "I think – in fact I *know* –

that your eyes fell upon young Meener Abspoel in the same manner, and as often, as mine did."

Minh didn't answer.

"Tell me," Monsieur Chastain said, "what is your opinion of me? I know I'm no Meener Abspoel the younger. Nor am I the handsome boy who strolls by here twice a day, to gaze in the window at you. Did you think I didn't notice?"

Minh remained silent.

"Still, I've a nice enough face, don't I? I've heard the natives refer to my high nose. Americans and the British have remarked on it too: the Gallic nose, as they say. Do *you* like my nose?"

Monsieur Chastain swayed, his eyes glassed over. He took a few more steps toward Minh. Minh, in turn, backed away. Monsieur Chastain reached around Minh, resting his hand in the small of Minh's back, and drawing him close so that their faces were mere inches apart.

"Do you know why I hired you, Bùi Vân Minh?"

Minh twisted to his left. Monsieur Chastain countered the force and brought Minh close to him again.

"I hired you because you stood out of the crowd. Out of that sea of dogs. You, Minh, are a delight to the eyes. And I sensed something familiar in you the more I studied you. Something we have in common. Something taboo, something wicked, something delicious."

Monsieur Chastain pressed his lips against Minh's.

Minh placed both his hands on Monsieur Chastain's shoulders and pushed, but Monsieur Chastain was much too tall, much too strong. Minh pushed with increased strength, to no effect. Monsieur Chastain wrapped both his arms around Minh and squeezed him close. He pinned Minh against the wall and pressed his lips against Minh's once again. Minh jerked his right arm repeatedly, at odd, random angles, and as Monsieur Chastain's arm loosened to try to fight the motion, Minh was able to free his hand. He reached up and scratched the side of Monsieur Chastain's face.

Monsieur Chastain grunted, stumbled backward, and fell into the cabinet. Minh turned and raced from the office, through the kitchen, and out of the doors.

For hours Minh wandered the outskirts of the city. He sat beneath trees. He lay on his side on brown grass. He stared up at the sky. Had he lost his job now? He feared the lost wages. The lost food. He feared not being able to provide for his mother.

Should he go back to apologise? After all, what had just happened … it was all the fault of that strange drink. Monsieur Chastain could blame that. Everything could go back to normal. It need never be mentioned again.

Minh squeezed his eyes shut. He fought the urge to cry. Why, *why* did everything have to start falling apart, just when he thought everything was falling into place?

Was it punishment? For what he'd done with Thao?

Minh brushed away the tears. He took a deep breath. He would have to make this right. He couldn't lose his job.

When the restaurant came into view, Minh saw a small crowd gathered outside. His heart stopped. Had something happened to Monsieur Chastain? Had he injured himself? Had Minh made him do something irrational?

Minh sprinted toward the entrance. When he was able to see past the crowd, he spotted Thao, on the front steps, his hands tied behind his back. Sovann noticed Minh before Thao did. Sovann hurried into the restaurant.

"Thao!" Minh called out.

Before Thao could answer, Mssrs Sovann and Chastain stepped outside.

"The police are on their way," Monsieur Chastain said to Thao. He didn't acknowledge Minh.

"Monsieur Chastain?" Minh said, and still there was no acknowledgement. A vengeful bit of theatre.

"You natives think you can get away with stealing, but just remember the value of a Frenchman's word over yours."

"Thao!" Minh shouted.

"I didn't do anything," Thao said.

Monsieur Chastain raised his hand and slapped Thao across the face. There were gasps in the crowd. People began to quickly disperse.

"He wouldn't steal from you," Minh said.

"Are you his counsel?" Monsieur Chastain said.

"Please don't do this," Minh said.

"Just how well do you know this young man?" Monsieur Chastain asked. "Tell me, why are you so passionate about defending a simple pig farmer?"

Two officers rounded the corner. Sovann scurried over to greet them, explaining the charge against Thao.

"Threatened you with a knife?" one of the officers said.

They stood on either side of Thao and yanked him to his feet.

"Please don't do this," Minh said, a strained whisper, knowing his words were useless.

"A lesson," Monsieur Chastain called out. "The law doesn't look favourably on liars." He turned and retreated into the restaurant.

Sovann followed, but stopped short of the door. He turned toward Minh. "Show some dignity," he said, then disappeared inside.

Minh sat at the base of a cedar, in the hot afternoon sun, staring at Thái Nguyên Penitentiary looming in the distance. He wondered – should others even notice him – if he would appear simply to be resting, or if it was all too obvious that he was sick with worry over one of the inmates.

Minh stayed in the shadow of the penitentiary until the sun began to set. It had become his daily ritual. He hoped somehow that Thao would know he was nearby, keeping a vigil.

He stood up. He brushed cedar needles from his trousers. He had nothing from the markets to bring his mother for dinner tonight. Such a drastic change from the days he was able to bring home scraps from the restaurant. Bits and pieces left behind from patrons' plates that to Minh and his mother seemed like a feast.

There were such widespread shortages now. And taxes ever increasing. Worst of all, Minh felt his days of freedom waning. He'd so far managed to avoid military conscription, and to be exempted from being sent off to France to work in the factories or the farms. The administrators had understood that no one else would be able to care for his blind mother. But as reports that the European theatre of battle was growing ever more dire, and with the extra effort of the Ministry of Colonies and the Ministry of War offices to gather all male citizens' personal information, he envisioned himself on a ship bound for France.

Still, he knew Thao had it far worse. There were stories of the brutality that occurred behind the prison walls. Only the unfortunate ones who had served time knew the real truth. Most people listened to second-hand tales – those told by friends or relatives – with a good dose of scepticism. There was no mistaking, however, the bruises, the broken limbs, the scars on those whose sentences had been served, and who found themselves trying to blend back in to the fabric of society.

Minh thought of the bruises. The bruises on Thao's face the second time they encountered one another, at the age of fourteen. How many might he have now?

Minh had gathered enough vegetation on the walk home from the penitentiary grounds to make a simple soup for dinner. Tomorrow he hoped to garner a couple of eggs, if he could find a seller willing to come down in price. Significantly.

He often wondered what it was like years ago, when he was still an infant, before his mother's vision was lost, and his father was still alive. Did his father gather weeds along the path on his way home from the rubber plantations? Did he tell jokes? Was he happy to have a son?

Minh's mother rarely talked about his father. She would only state the facts. "He died at the hands of a plantation overseer." No further information was offered. Did she not know the details? Did she not want Minh to know?

So many times he wanted to walk past Thao's farm. But he couldn't bring himself to do it, for he knew the French had likely confiscated the pigs, and burned down the hut. He didn't have the strength to see it.

Do you always think the worst will happen?

Thao's voice sounded in his head.

Minh filled the cooking pot from a marshy area a hundred feet or so from their hut. The colour of the water was like *café au lait*. The exact colour of the coffee he served Monsieur Chastain, that afternoon, two months ago. How he wished he could stop himself from thinking about it. But the memories wouldn't fade, no matter how hard he tried.

He lifted the cooking pot. He heard his mother shouting. He dropped the pot and sprinted to the hut.

Two soldiers stood outside the door, one French, one Indonesian.

The French soldier approached Minh, who was stooped over to catch his breath. "Bùi Vân Minh?"

Minh nodded.

The soldier handed Minh a piece of paper. "Report to this address, Monday morning, eight o'clock."

Without looking at it, Minh said, "But my mother is –"

"Ready your affairs," the Indonesian soldier barked. "You've been conscripted."

Between his agitated state, and his mother's periods of crying, Minh couldn't sleep. To make matters worse, he heard gunfire sounding off in the distance. He wondered if it were training exercises. It seemed a strange thing to do in the middle of the night, but nothing the French did from a military standpoint seemed to make much sense to him.

He tossed and turned. He tried not to think about Monday being two days away. How would his mother cope? How could he get word to Thao? How could he survive war? He felt his life was ending. He knew in a short time he'd be dead on a battlefield in Europe.

"This can't be happening."

The sound of gunfire increased, as though his wide-awake nightmare were a play.

Then he heard it. A whisper. A voice strained, hoarse. "Minh! Minh!" Desperate. Pleading. "Minh! Are you there?"

"Who is it?" his mother called out. That superior hearing of hers!

Minh scrambled to his feet. "Don't worry," he said to his mother. He pulled the door open slowly, the reeds of the frame pressed against his cheek.

"Minh?"

"Thao!"

Gunfire sounded like firecrackers in the night air.

Thao grabbed Minh's arm. He ran, tugging Minh behind. They headed down a path barely lit by the moon. Thao ran faster, faster, and before Minh knew it, they were on the ground, against the stone wall where they'd first met, where Thao had trapped Napoléon.

"Don't be shocked by my face," Thao whispered.

In what little light they had, Minh could see the swelling. The bruises. The half-closed right eye. "Oh, Thao ..." He reached up and caressed Thao's cheek. Thao winced.

"Listen," Thao said. "Listen carefully. Something big has happened. There's been a revolt, Minh. A rebellion."

"Rebellion?"

"Sh! Sh. Just listen. We were all freed. From the inside. Guards working with the prisoners. They've dispersed weapons. They're going through the city right now, securing the –"

"What are you saying, Thao? Is that what all the gunfire is?"

"Minh, there were two men. Luong Ngoc Quyen, and Trinh Van Can. If you could have heard them speak, watched them. Oh, but you *will* hear them. You *will* see them. They made this all possible."

"What?" Minh said. "Made what possible?"

"They spoke of all three regions united. Tonkin, Annam, and Cochinchina, under one flag."

Sweat glistened on Thao's face. His breathing was rapid, his fists clenched.

"How is it possible?" Minh said. "The French will crush –"

"That's just it," Thao said. "They're preoccupied with their own war. Quyen and Can have managed to bridge the … the … Minh, do you realise, do you? Can you imagine a life without French control?"

"Thao … are you … what did they do to you?"

Thao searched the sky. The stars. Tears welled up in his eyes. "Don't ever ask me that again, do you promise? I won't …" His throat caught. He choked.

Minh wrapped his arms around Thao and pulled him close. He shook along with Thao's violent sobs.

"I won't ever ask again. I promise, Thao. I promise."

It was still Thao, but some … different … version of him.

"The French are brutal bastards," Thao whispered, talking past Minh, addressing the sky, the universe.

The gunfire increased in intensity.

"I have to go back soon," Thao said. "I have to join them. But Minh, stay here, please. Stay safe. Wait for me."

He started to rise, but Minh grabbed his arm. "Join them? To do what? Thao, you'll get hurt. You could get killed."

"We can't stop the momentum! Don't you understand?" He searched Minh's face. He took hold of Minh's hand. He pulled him into an embrace. "I … it's … it's still me inside, Minh. I promise you. Will you stay safe for me? Will you wait?"

Minh didn't know whether or not to mention that he'd been conscripted. Did that matter now? Did all this mean it was delayed? Void?

"Will you wait?" Thao repeated.

"I'll wait. I'll wait. You come for me. We'll meet right here. This will be our spot."

"I don't want to leave you," Thao said, clutching Minh so tight that Minh's ribs hurt. Then suddenly, Thao released him. He stood. He turned and he sprinted up the pathway. "I'll be back," he called out.

Minh lay on the ground, his eyes fixated on a star just above the horizon. He couldn't control the tears.

Days of chaos. No communication. Little food.

Minh and his mother remained largely confined to their hut, subsisting on weed soups. Sporadic gunfire echoed from the city proper. No one had any news as no one dared venture from their homes.

Three days after Minh's promise to Thao that he'd wait, he couldn't take it any more. "I have to go see," he told his mother.

"It's too dangerous," she pleaded. "You don't know who's in charge. You could be arrested. You could be –"

"Just to edge of the city, that's all. Just to get an idea. We can't live on boiled weeds. We can't stay prisoners like this."

He'd never have his mother's blessing. He was sick with worry leaving her alone, vulnerable. What if something did happen to him?

Do you always think the worst will happen?

For his sake, for his mother's sake, for Thao's sake, he had to push forward.

He knew the city well enough. He could cut through alleys, wind his away around on less-travelled streets, in the hope that would keep him far enough removed from the thrust of the conflict.

Smoke grew thick the closer he got to the city centre. People ran past him. People with torn clothes, bloodied skin. He thought it a good idea to head somewhere familiar. La Fourchette. He rounded a corner. He cut through two alleys. He was tempted to stop someone, to ask them for details. But he didn't know whom to trust.

When he rounded another corner, he stopped. He dropped to his knees. A line of French soldiers stood in formation in front of La Fourchette. Six bodies lay prone on the pavement. It didn't take Minh long to figure out that two of them were Mssrs Chastain and Sovann. He wondered what might have become of their heads.

The French couldn't have done this. What would they have to gain? It must have been those from the prison.

Minh stood, weak, his body pressed against the wall. His stomach clenched, and his throat burned. He could taste vomit. It came in force, covering his trousers and shirt.

He turned and headed back down the alley. More bodies, face down in the gutter, an Indonesian mother and her baby. Was this the work of the French soldiers?

He didn't know where to turn.

Where was Thao? Was he still alive?

He wanted to scream out for him. But that could result in a bullet to the head.

A man ran past Minh. A second man, his face bloodied, bumped into Minh, sending them both to the ground.

"The tide has turned," he sobbed, clutching at Minh's leg. "They brought in reinforcements."

"Who?" Minh asked. "Please, tell me what's happened?"

"The French are crushing us." The man curled up into a foetal position. "Again. And for ever."

1918

It had become Thao's duty now to wait for Minh.

He'd never venture very far. Just enough to gather weeds for them to eat. He'd expanded their menu options by a dozen in the last month alone, though one tasting had nearly fatal results. But Minh had recovered more quickly than they'd thought possible.

They were deep in the countryside to the north of Thái Nguyên. They carefully timed their movements. Plotted paths with the least amount of impact to vegetation.

They desperately wanted news. Some idea of what was happening. Was the war in Europe still raging? Had the French thwarted the colonial rebellion in its infancy? Would there ever be a union of the three regions?

Most nights Minh was strong. Sometimes, in the grip of severe exhaustion, he would cry for his mother, wondering whether she was safe, if she was even alive. He cried for Thao, for all the pain he must have endured in that prison. He grew angry at himself, for becoming so despondent, when Thao, who'd endured such brutality, whose face had been permanently disfigured, could still be strong, could still hold out some hope for the both of them.

"We've evaded them for three months. They'll give up soon. They can't possibly have the resources or the energy to hunt down each and every escaped prisoner, every deserter, anyone who dared question their policies."

Tonight, the spot they'd chosen to hide in felt especially secure to Minh. He felt they'd disappeared from Earth, that they'd entered another land, another dimension.

He cuddled next to Thao, who felt warm and strong.

"It's the most dangerous time to be out," Thao said, "but do you know how I miss feeling the sun on my face? Just lying on the ground and feeling its heat. How I craved light when I ..."

He trailed off.

Minh knew he was thinking about his time in prison. How the images wouldn't leave his mind. How it tore him up inside.

"That's what my mother used to pray for. To see the light again."

Thao drew him closer.

"I'd say a chant at night, just for her. *Ánh sáng, ánh sáng, ánh sáng.*"

"You're alive for her," Thao said. "Remember that. You'll see her again." He pointed to the moon. "That's our light, for now."

"Like our food. Rationed. But sustaining us."

Minh reached up and traced the contour of Thao's face. He didn't see the partially closed eye, nor the burn scars, nor the torn ear.

He saw Thao.

"I was so afraid I'd lose you," Minh whispered, his lips trembling.

"Look at us," Thao said, "here, together, alive, in each other's arms." He took a deep, contented breath. "We've already won, haven't we?"

It was hard, still, but Minh had come a long way. He no longer thought the worst.

"We have won," he whispered. And he truly believed it.

❖

Barry Brennessel

Barry Brennessel's novels *Tinseltown* and *The Celestial* were Lambda Literary Award finalists. *The Celestial* won the Gold Medal in the 2012 ForeWord Book of the Year Awards. Several of his screenplays have been finalists and prize winners in various competitions, including Scriptapalooza, The Great Gay Screenplay Contest, the Rhode Island International Film Festival Competition (Flickers), The Chicago Screenplay Competition, and the Writers' Digest annual.

barrybrennessel.com

About the Stories

No Man's Land
Julie Bozza

Drew was born neither boy nor girl, but he was raised as a man, and now he is desperate to enlist to prove himself. His lover, who fought in the Transvaal twelve years before, is just as desperate to dissuade him.

I Remember
Wendy C. Fries

Time goes tick-tock forward, turning boys into men and men into soldiers, but sometimes a man is left behind. Christopher Timlock meant to join the London Regiment with James Gant, but the British Army had other ideas. So Chrissie made a promise: he would wait for Jamie, for as long as it took. And he would remember.

War Life
Z. McAspurren

During the war, people lived their lives in different ways. Even separated by a country, however, a sister and a brother's thoughts circled around similar ideas. One was a worker in a factory, and the other was on the Front Line; both had something important taken from them because of the war, and the thing they'd lost had a way of always entering their minds.

Lena and the Swan
or, The Lesbian Lothario
Julie Bozza

While the men are away, Lena will play … She delivers the mail, and happily takes advantage of some of the women on her route whose husbands are at war. But then a Miss Cawkwell moves into the house at Fields Corner, and Lena's world begins to shift.

Inside
Eleanor Musgrove

Alfred Schuchard is a baker, the English-born son of a German immigrant, and stuck in a civilian internment camp for the duration of the war. The last thing he needs is for life to get any more complicated. But then a new arrival at camp turns what little still made sense in his world on its head …

Break of Day in the Trenches
Jay Lewis Taylor
Escaping from the German lines hasn't gone to plan. Second Lieutenant David Lewry is sheltering from the barrage in a German dug-out, literally thrown together with Captain David Russell-Hansford-Barnes. Although the two seem to have nothing in common beyond their first name, they share two things: a desire to get back to the British lines, and a desire to live. Then, as they talk through the wait for dawn, the realisation comes on them that they share still more.

Per Ardua Ad Astra
Lou Faulkner
Summer, 1916. The survival of the young aviators of the Royal Flying Corps depends, more often than not, on absolute trust and teamwork. On the eve of the Somme, two such young men watch the storm-clouds gathering, and prepare themselves as best they can for what is to come.

The Man Left Behind
Eleanor Musgrove
Henrietta's not happy about the men – her brother included – marching off to war, of course not. But perhaps every cloud, however dark, does have a silver lining?

Hallowed Ground
Charlie Cochrane
A doctor, a padre, a packet of Black Cat cigarettes and a night in a shell hole; an unexpected confession provides a ray of hope in the darkness.

A Rooted Sorrow
Adam Fitzroy
The war has an effect on those at home, too. Mrs Mercer, preoccupied

with thoughts of her son, learns about Simon's love for Alfred – a startling contrast to her own unhappy marriage. But what will the implications of this knowledge be, and how might it possibly influence their future lives?

At the Gate
Jay Lewis Taylor

Aboard HMS *Arion*, ploughing southward in heavy weather to a rendezvous off Zeebrugge, Surgeon Lieutenant-Commander Alan Kershaw has much to contend with: seasickness, anxious messmates, and the depredations of the ship's rat on his medical texts, for a start. Worse than all of these, however, is having to keep his grief secret when anyone else would be allowed to mourn ...

After & Before
Sam Evans

It is 1918 and the Great War is drawing to a close. Life in Britain has changed. Men are returning home injured, traumatised and severely damaged by what they have seen on the Front Line. Dr Robert Wallace was never one of those men. Disabled by a motorbike accident and unable to fight, he now cares for the men who went out there and did their duty – men like Wilfred Cahill, Robert's lover, who left him four years before to go to war.

Ánh Sáng
Barry Brennessel

They met as boys in the Tonkin region of French Indochina. Years later, as war rages in Europe, the relationship between Bùi Vân Minh and Ngô Công Thao is tested in ways they never imagined. France clings desperately to her colony as a growing surge of independence sweeps through Tonkin, Annam, and Cochinchina. The two men are caught up in wildly different circumstances, but the one constant they have is each other.

Made in the USA
Charleston, SC
02 May 2015